Rafael Sabatini, creator of some of the world's best-loved heroes, was born in Italy in 1875 and educated in both Portugal and Switzerland. He eventually settled in England in 1892, by which time he was fluent in a total of five languages. He chose to write in English, claiming that 'all the best stories are written in English'.

His writing career was launched in the 1890s with a collection of short stories, and it was not until 1902 that his first novel was published. His fame, however, came with *Scaramouche*, the much-loved story of the French Revolution, which became an international bestseller. *Captain Blood* followed soon after, which resulted in a renewed enthusiasm for his earlier work.

For many years a prolific writer, he was forced to abandon writing in the 1940s through illness and he eventually died in 1950.

Sabatini is best-remembered for his heroic characters and high-spirited novels, many of which have been adapted into classic films, including *Scaramouche, Captain Blood* and *The Sea Hawk* starring Errol Flynn.

D0925835

TITLES BY THE SAME AUTHOR
ALL PUBLISHED BY HOUSE OF STRATUS

FICTION:
ANTHONY WILDING
THE BANNER OF THE BULL
BARDELYS THE MAGNIFICENT
BELLARION
THE BLACK SWAN
CAPTAIN BLOOD
THE CAROLINIAN
CHIVALRY
THE CHRONICLES OF CAPTAIN BLOOD
COLUMBUS
FORTUNE'S FOOL
THE FORTUNES OF CAPTAIN BLOOD
THE GAMESTER
THE HOUNDS OF GOD
THE JUSTICE OF THE DUKE
THE LION'S SKIN
THE LOST KING
LOVE-AT-ARMS
THE MARQUIS OF CARABAS
THE MINION
THE NUPTIALS OF CORBAL
THE ROMANTIC PRINCE
SCARAMOUCHE
SCARAMOUCHE THE KING-MAKER
THE SEA HAWK
THE SHAME OF MOTLEY
THE SNARE
ST MARTIN'S SUMMER
THE STALKING-HORSE
THE STROLLING SAINT
THE SWORD OF ISLAM
THE TAVERN KNIGHT
THE TRAMPLING OF THE LILIES
TURBULENT TALES
VENETIAN MASQUE

NON-FICTION:
HEROIC LIVES
THE HISTORICAL NIGHTS'
ENTERTAINMENT
KING IN PRUSSIA
THE LIFE OF CESARE BORGIA
TORQUEMADA AND THE SPANISH
INQUISITION

The Gates of Doom

A Romance

Rafael Sabatini

HOUSE OF
STRATUS

This edition published in 2001 by House of Stratus, an imprint of
Stratus Books Ltd., 21 Beeching Park, Kelly Bray,
Cornwall, PL17 8QS, UK.

www.houseofstratus.com

Typeset, printed and bound by House of Stratus.

A catalogue record for this book is available from the British Library
and the Library of Congress.

ISBN 07551-153-6-8

Contents

1	THE PLAYERS	1
2	THE GAME	12
3	MR SECOND SECRETARY	20
4	FATE'S AGENTS	32
5	THE WARNING	48
6	THE ENCHANTED GARDEN	62
7	EVELYN'S CONSCIENCE	74
8	AT "THE WORLD'S END"	82
9	THE ALIBI	98
10	TWO LETTERS	108
11	PAUNCEFORT'S MOVE	119
12	NATURE TRIUMPHANT	126
13	IN THE ROSE-GARDEN	137
14	THE ROAD TO TYBURN	149
15	EXECUTION	162
16	RESURRECTION	172
17	PAUNCEFORT THE SOWER	182

Contents (contd)

18	IN CHECK	195
19	THE CAPTAIN GOES INTO ACTION	206
20	MR TEMPLETON IN RETIREMENT	216
21	LORD CARTERET UNDERSTANDS	225
22	ISRAEL SUAREZ	238
23	THE LAST THROW	248

Chapter 1

THE PLAYERS

The room – somewhat disordered now, at the end of that long night's play – was spacious, lofty and handsomely equipped. On a boldly carved, walnut side table of Dutch origin there was a disarray of glasses, bottles, plates and broken meats. From a mahogany wine cooler beneath this table's arched legs sprouted the corkless necks of a half-score empty bottles. About the card-table in the room's middle stood irregularly some eight or ten chairs, lately occupied by the now departed players. One overturned chair lay neglected where it had fallen. Cards were still strewn upon the table's cover of green baize and some few lay scattered on the scarlet Turkey rug that covered a square of the blocked and polished floor.

Overhead in the heavy chandelier of ormulu and crystal the candles were guttering, caught by the draught from one of the long French windows which his lordship had just opened. In the gap he stood, gazing out into the chill grey dawn and the wraiths of mist that hung above the park.

By the carved overmantel, his shoulders to the shelf and the ormulu timepiece, which marked now the hour of three, stood Lord Pauncefort's only lingering and most important guest. He was a man of rather more than middle height, slender as a rapier is slender, of a steely, supple strength. He was simply yet very elegantly dressed in black, relieved only by the silver embroidery on his stockings, the paste buckles that flashed from his lacquered, red-heeled shoes, and the lace at his throat, among which a great sapphire glowed with sombre fire. Enough remained, however, in his erect carriage, his Steinkirk, the clubbing of his hair and the bronze of his face to advertise the soldier.

His keen blue eyes were upon the figure of his host, and in them was reflected the faint smile that softened the somewhat hard lines of his mouth. Yet the smile was scornful – of his host and of the night that was sped; scornful and something sad.

Was it, he mused, upon such as these that his king and master relied in his dire need? Was it to gain such support as my Lord Pauncefort and his precious friends could offer to that desperate cause that he, himself, had ventured once more into England where a thousand guineas was offered for his head?

The play, he reflected contemptuously, they had urged as a wise measure of precaution: let them do their plotting about a faro-table, had been their plea; thus they should pass for a parcel of idle gamesters, and none could dream that the game was a pretence, a mere mask upon their real business. Thus had they deluded themselves, but not him. He had seen, and soon, that the plotting was the pretence, and play the business. And what play! A gamester all his life, a man who had beggared himself a score of times in twenty different lands, never had he known such stakes as those which had been laid that night, never had he seen such sums change hands across the green baize of a card table.

He checked the contemptuous current of his thoughts to reflect that he himself had plunged as headlong as the most reckless of them into the game that was afoot. Had he not won a fortune 'twixt the commencement and the abandoning of that monstrous play? His winnings amounted to something over ten thousand guineas, and at no one time in his vagrant, adventurous life had he been master of half that sum. Yet it did not follow that he was quite as they. If he had risked that night certain moneys that he scarce dared call his own, so did he hesitate to call his own the vast sum which he had won.

Ten thousand guineas! Ten times the value set by the Government upon his own poor head, he reflected whimsically.

And then Lord Pauncefort turned from the window and the sight of his lordship's livid, distorted countenance drove all other considerations from his guest's mind, brought a sudden cry of concern from his lips.

"My lord, are you ill?"

His lordship made a gesture of denial. "It – it is not that," he said, and his voice was husky with emotion. He was a man of some thirty years of age, of a swarthy male beauty that was almost arresting. His large eyes were dark and liquid, his mouth delicately limned, his nose intrepidly arched, with fine sensitive nostrils. But the brow was alarmingly shallow and there was a cleft in the square – the too square – chin. He stood now, dabbing his moist brow with a flimsy kerchief that was not whiter than the hand that held it.

"Captain Gaynor," he explained abruptly, almost fiercely, "I am a broken man. I have ruined myself this night."

There was scarce one of the departed guests, Captain Gaynor bethought him, who had not left that house a winner, and in all his lordship's losses must amount to almost twice the sum of the Captain's winnings.

None the less, his lordship's outcry jarred upon the Captain's nice sensibilities. Such an admission made to one who was a heavy winner – and that one none so intimately admitted to his lordship's private confidences, when all was said – seemed to Captain Gaynor an outrage on decorum. He held that the man who cannot lose with calm and grace, no matter what the game or what the stakes – even though it should be life itself – has not the right to enter into play. And this was no abstract creed. It was the one by which the Captain lived.

The sight of the stricken man before him moved him to no pity. Rather it inspired in him a contempt that amounted almost to physical ill being, to disgust. His immediate impulse was to take his

3

leave. If, indeed, he had lingered at all after the departure of his fellow-guests, it had been in the hope that my Lord Pauncefort might yet have something for his private ear concerning the real business that had brought him to England and to that house. And perceiving now how idle had been this hope, observing his host's suddenly altered condition, Captain Gaynor's inclination was to depart.

But he reflected that to depart abruptly after that confession might be to offend. On his own account this would have troubled the Captain not at all. But for the Cause's sake, and for the sake of the service it might be Pauncefort's to render to that Cause, he did not wish to give offence to his host if it might be avoided. He was in a quandary, and vexed thereby; for quandaries were not usual in the life of this man who lived by swift decisions and swift action.

He shifted uneasily where he stood, and his face assumed a mask of polite concern. His lordship had sunk into the nearest chair, like a man wearied to exhaustion. There was a wildness in his eyes, and he continued nervously to dab his brow – that brow whose shallowness belied the general nobility of his countenance.

"You think, maybe, that I exaggerate," he resumed presently. "But I tell you, sir, that I have played the knave this night. I have lost four thousand guineas to Martindale, another two to Bagshot, and I have lost my honour too, for I have forfeited all chance of ever being able to pay those losses."

The concern in the Captain's face appeared to deepen.

"They are your friends," he said slowly. "Surely they will be glad to wait upon your convenience." In his own breast pocket rested his lordship's draft upon his bankers for the eight thousand and odd guineas he had lost to the Captain.

"My convenience?" cried Pauncefort, and his white face writhed in a spasm of mocking laughter. "I tell you, man, that in all the world I cannot claim ten guineas for my own. You are a gamester, Captain Gaynor?" he ended between question and assertion.

"So rumour says of me – I confess with justice," the Captain admitted, and the faintest of ironic smiles quivered on his firm lips.

"I am engaged at present in a game wherein I have staked my head. Has your lordship ever played as deep as that?"

"Ay, have I. Do I not tell you, man, that I have staked my honour; and honour, surely, is more than life."

"So I have heard say," answered Captain Gaynor, like a sceptic.

He had little comfort for his host, little encouragement for the confidences that Pauncefort insisted upon thrusting on him. Indeed, it was his deliberate aim to stifle them. He desired them not. Although his acquaintance with Lord Pauncefort was considerable, it was not an acquaintance that had ever ripened, or promised to ripen, into friendship. The link that bound them was their common devotion to the Stuart Cause, whose agent Captain Gaynor was. Beyond that they had no common interest, although, when all is said, that might be accounted interest enough to bind two men at such a time.

But, despite the Captain's chill aloofness, his lordship was not to be repressed. In the nature of this man of so strong and noble-seeming a countenance there was a strain of weakness almost feminine. He was of those who must forever be proclaiming griefs and grievances, finding it impossible to bear in silence and in dignity the burden of their woes. He was of those who in their trouble must forever be confiding in the hope of lessening their oppression. Moreover he had at present another motive for his confidence: a faint hope that it might bear him fruit, as you shall see.

"Listen," he said, and upon the heels of that exhortation swiftly poured out the tale of his condition. "I was broke six months ago, when the South-Sea Bubble was pricked. I gambled heavily in the stock and, like many another, woke one morning to find that a fortune had melted in my hands. This rascally Whig Government – " He was beginning upon a side issue, when he broke off abruptly to return to his main theme. "To buy that stock I raised heavy mortgages. I raised still more to clear myself after that cataclysm, and I mortgaged what was left to recoup my losses. Instead – But there! Tonight I played for my immediate needs. I played to twice the extent of the losses I could meet, and in that I played the knave. But my need was very urgent, Captain. Now – it is over." He dabbed his brow again. His voice grew calmer with the dead calm of despair. "If I have the courage to be alive by noon tomorrow, the spunging-house awaits me." He shivered in his splendid garments, and the jewelled buttons of his salmon-coloured waistcoat twinkled roguishly as if conscious of the irony of their presence in the apparel of a pauper.

Captain Gaynor stood considering a moment, the expression – the mask – of studied concern upon his face, increasing contempt and disgust in his heart.

Was it upon such men as this that his master counted? And he recalled the eulogistic words in which his prince had spoken of this adherent.

"Pauncefort is powerful and loyal," he had said. "He is ours body and soul and to the last penny of his fortunes."

That was the dream of that august man of dreams. Here, confronting Captain Gaynor, was the reality – a broken gamester who whimpered over his losses.

"Surely, surely," said the soldier slowly, "there is one thing you have forgot."

Pauncefort looked up quickly, his black brows contracting. "If it be aught I can raise money upon, in God's name tell it me quickly," said he, with a wry smile.

"I think it is," replied the Captain. "You have forgot Miss Hollinstone."

The contraction of his lordships brows grew heavier still, and the fine countenance assumed a something of haughtiness and of challenge. Undeterred Captain Gaynor proceeded to make plain his meaning.

"Your betrothal to Damaris Hollinstone is known to all the world, just as it is also known that she is the wealthiest heiress in England, mistress of a fortune that is colossal. Surely, sir, with such a prospect before you, your creditors – "

He was interrupted by a sharp laugh.

"You have had no dealings, sir, with the tribe of Judah. That is plain," said his lordship bitterly. "Oh, be very sure that I have

6

attempted it – to be met with veiled derision and open isolence. You do not know the Jew. You do not know the hatred of the Christian that underlies his dealings, the vampire spirit that actuates him. Shakespeare, sir, knew his nature when he limned his Shylock."

"Perhaps," suggested Captain Gaynor, "the Christian has deserved no better at his hands."

It was a point of view so revolutionary, so subversive of all the notions upon which Lord Pauncefort had been bred, that for a moment it drove every other consideration from his mind, leaving his face blank with astonishment. But his own affairs swept back upon him in an instant to turn him from any disputing upon so wild a matter.

"You are a gamester, Captain Gaynor, and all gamesters are prone to come to such a state as mine tonight. Let me give – it is all that remains me to bestow on anyone – a piece of advice upon the subtle art of raising money. See to it ever in such affairs that betimes you raise at least twice as much as you can ever repay out of your own resources. Then your creditors, for their own purses' sakes, will afford you every opportunity; they will handle you tenderly; they will nurse you with care; they will watch over you as never mother watched her babe at its first steps.

"Had I but had such advice given me and acted upon it, I should not be in such case as this in which you find me. Money would have flowed freely to my hands upon the prospect of my marriage, because upon the consummation of that would have depended my creditors' reimbursement. As it is, sir, I have fallen into the error of borrowing no more than my estates can bear.

"The chief of my creditors is a Spanish Jew, one Israel Suarez, an evil rogue of fabulous wealth and destitute of mercy; one who seems to draw a Satanic joy from the torturing and breaking of such men as I. I tell you, Captain Gaynor, that I have abased myself to plead with him. I have besought him in terms I cannot recall without shame that if he will not concede me a loan upon my marriage prospects, at least to postpone his demand for settlement of my present debts until my marriage shall have taken place.

7

"My intercessions have been met with the sneers and insolent jests of this usurious dog. He holds my mortgages for everything that is not in the entail. That almost covers my debt to him. The balance he will recover from the interest on the entailed estates what time I am rotting in a debtors' gaol. Frankly he tells me this – that since he can retrieve his own he will run no risks. And so, tomorrow – " He spread his hands, shrugged, and sank back scowling again into his chair.

Captain Gaynor understood, but he answered nothing. What answer could he make? He looked towards the windows, which were glowing now like moonstones in the increasing light. Again he thought of going, and vaguely he wondered why Lord Pauncefort should have chosen him for these confidences. He conceived that it was fortuitous – the result of his having lingered after the others had departed. But in his lordship's next words he had the correct answer to his unspoken question.

"Had I refrained tonight," his lordship was saying presently in a small unsteady voice, his fingers plucking nervously at a card which he had picked up from the floor, "all might yet have been well. By meeting a bill that is due tomorrow I might temporarily have satisfied the demands of that foul vulture, Suarez. I should have gained time, and with time salvation might have come. I have sunk money in a trading venture which may yet repay me. But for this, time is needed; time and – and the money I have lost tonight. I held it in readiness for this, but the cursed cards – "

He broke off with a bitter oath. But he had said enough. It would have been impossible to have asked more plainly for the help that it was in Gaynor's power to render him.

The Captain understood at last the reason of these confidences. Understanding brought with it some pity and more contempt. I fear me his nature was a little hard. He spoke out plainly, his voice crisp.

"You are inviting me, my lord, to return you this," he said, and from his breast pocket he took Lord Pauncefort's draft upon his bankers.

He was, as I have said, a man of swift decisions, and here he had decided swiftly, but not at all as his host conceived.

Pauncefort threw back his head under the goad of that voice. It seemed to him that it conveyed a deadly insult. For all that the matter was true enough; the manner could not, he thought, have been more outrageous.

"Sir!" said he, with a very frosty dignity, and upon the word he rose, frowning darkly. "Sir, you affront me."

"Forgive me," answered the soldier gently. "Such was not my intent." He replaced the draft in his pocket. "And yet," he sighed, "I conceived that I saw a way to assist you."

The unexpectedness of this withdrawal scattered his lordship's fine dignity to the murmuring winds of dawn. His jaw dropped in sheer astonishment; his eyes stared foolishly; the card he had held fluttered from his nerveless fingers. He leaned against the table, and looked at his guest.

"Perhaps…" he said, faltering on the word, "perhaps my refusal was churlish."

"I understand it," said Gaynor quietly. But behind his imperturbable mask he was laughing at his lordship.

"When all is said," the other resumed, "if you could – if I might so far trespass upon your patience and you would wait until a more convenient season – "

Captain Gaynor took him up at once. "Wait?" he echoed, and he frowned thoughtfully. "Wait?" He laughed, a little laugh that was singularly pleasant despite the tinge of irony that invested it. "Ye have indeed mistook me," he said.

"How?" quoth his lordship, flung back once more upon his dignity.

"Faith," said the Captain, "you'll agree, I think, that I am in little case to wait. If it please me to gamble upon my own life it does not please me that others should do the same – leastways without ever a stake set against so very valuable a property. You forget, my lord" (and instinctively he lowered his voice), "a thousand guineas is the advertised value of this head of mine. At any moment that value may be claimed. In England here I walk amid drawn swords. If I consented to do your pleasure in this matter, at any moment one of these might liquidate the debt." He laughed again. "It is a game in which the odds are much too heavy in your favour, and, moreover, a game in which you adventure nothing."

"I – I had not considered that," his lordship exclaimed with earnestness. " 'Pon honour, I had not."

"I do not do you the injustice to suppose it. But consider it now, I beg."

"I do. I thank you for enlightening me." He stood erect, his handsome face pale but quite composed. "Captain Gaynor, there is no more to be said."

"Nay, now, I think there is," returned the other, smiling quietly.

"I do not understand."

"Pray consider further. I am a gamester, as you have said, as every soldier of fortune is perforce. And being poor in point of worldly goods, my life is a stake for which I am well used to playing. Out of consideration for your straits, I will permit that you too play, as it were, upon it and for this eight thousand guineas that I have won. But you must set a stake against it, my lord – and a heavy one to balance all the odds that are in your favour."

He spoke quietly, his face so calm, his glance so steady that none might have suspected the excitement within. Lord Pauncefort stared and stared. At length – "I have talked in vain, it seems," said he. "Yet I have told you plainly that I cannot claim so much as ten guineas for my own. What, then, have I to stake?"

"Something that is hardly yours," came the gentle answer, "and something which, if I win from you, I shall yet have to win another way and may altogether fail to win." He smiled a wry smile, his steely eyes upon the other's face. "You perceive, my lord, that the odds are all with you. It cannot be said that I lack generosity in the risks I take."

"I do not understand you," said his lordship bluntly. "What stake have you in mind?"

There was a perceptible pause before the soldier answered him. He squared his shoulders; his face became set and stern; his glance flickered a moment to the windows and the dawn, which, from the pallor of the moonstone, was warming now to opalescent fires. Then his eyes returned to Lord Pauncefort's impatient questioning face.

"Damaris Hollinstone," he said quietly.

Chapter 2

THE GAME

Lord Pauncefort fell back a pace, as if before a blow. The reflections of a surge of feelings from astonishment through contempt to positive anger sped across his heavily featured face. He leaned against the card-table and surveyed his guest with eyes that from their first gape of surprise came to blaze with unmistakable malevolence.

Captain Gaynor, cool, erect, with something of defiance in his mien, waited patiently until his lordship should choose to break the brooding silence. At length came a little sneering laugh from the viscount, and on its heels the sneering words: "Blister me! You play strange games, Captain Gaynor."

"It is true," Gaynor admitted, "and," he added, stung a little, "with strange players sometimes. You will admit at least my generosity in the matter of the odds?"

"Fore gad, yes!" the other exploded in a storm of contempt. "I am glad ye have the grace to admit it."

"I have never lacked for grace," said the Captain complacently.

His lordship struck the table with his clenched hand. "Let us understand each other," he demanded savagely.

"'Tis what I most desire."

"In a word then: What is Miss Hollinstone to you?"

"In a word, my lord – nothing."

"Nothing? Nothing? And yet you – "

"Spare me your jealousy, I pray," the soldier interrupted, and ran on undismayed by the other's haughty frown: "There is no need for it here. I have never so much as set eyes upon Miss Hollinstone. You see in me no rival for the lady's affections. I know not whether she be tall or short, fair or dark, fat or lean. I know her as the greatest heiress in these islands – a lady of surpassing wealth. I know her in no other way and in no other way do I desire to know her."

The contempt, the disgust on the nobleman's face was overwhelming.

"By God, Captain Gaynor!" he cried, in a voice thick with passion, "I have welcomed you to my house. I have sat at table with you. I have deemed you a gentleman."

"Ah! And you find me?" quoth the Captain, entirely unruffled, yet with a challenging note in the question.

But the other answered him undeterred. "I find you a – a jackal. You have spoken of yourself as an adventurer, a soldier of fortune. I did not dream what depths of degradation the term could imply. You have put an affront upon me in making me this proposal. 'Twas to consider me your equal in baseness. It is an insult for which you shall give me satisfaction. Fore gad, you shall!"

The soldier of fortune stood a little pale before that onslaught. His lips were set, and in his steely eyes there was a cold glitter before which men of bigger heart than Pauncefort had quailed in their time. He moved at length from his position before the empty fireplace, and sauntered, a graceful, supple figure, to the windows. There he stood a moment gazing out upon the breaking day, what time his host's eyes followed him, angry and impatient.

The Captain was revolving something in his mind, debating something eminently distasteful. It went against his wayward, imperious nature to explain himself to any man. Many had misunderstood his motives aforetime; and he had left them in a misunderstanding, for which they had not infrequently paid dearly.

Yet here was a man whom that night's business had taught him to despise, and he found himself urged to offer explanations of his conduct to such a man. It was repugnant to him; yet it must be done if he were to have his way in this, if he were to carry through this thing upon which, with his characteristic swiftness, he had determined.

He turned at last, and with his back to the window he faced his host.

"If I apprehend you aright, my lord," said he, and the calm and dignity of his voice and mien, the force of his singularly compelling personality, impressed the other into lending him an ear notwithstanding the disgust and impatience that possessed him, "if I apprehend you aright it is not with my proposal so much as with my motives that you quarrel. If I had been able to say to you, 'I love Miss Hollinstone,' you would have viewed my proposal differently?"

His lordship flung out an arm in anger. "Perhaps," he rasped. "What matter?"

"Oh! A deal," replied the other. "Had I been able to say that, then, indeed, would my proposal have been base and ignoble; then, indeed, would you have been right to deem yourself affronted and to demand of me satisfaction. You are surprised at my point of view, my lord? I do not think we are like to see eye to eye in many things; but I would you could see eye to eye with me in this, that you could understand – as you are very far from doing – the true motives out of which I am acting."

Lord Pauncefort bowed, not without irony. "Proceed, sir," he invited his guest. "If anything you can say will mitigate the judgment I have formed – "

"I care nothing for your judgments, my lord," came the sharp, almost passionate interruption. "When men have lived such lives as mine, believe me, they are very far from being touched by the judgments of those whose lives have been smooth and sheltered. In all this world there is but one thing I care for, one Cause in which were I not prepared to lay down my life tomorrow I should not be tonight in England. None knows that better than your lordship. If I have a hope of personal fortune, it is a remote and distant hope, to follow upon, as it is bound up with, the fortune of another. For ten years have I waited, acquiring knowledge in foreign service, steeling and tempering myself for the great service that is to come. I am in the twenty-ninth year of my age; the first flush of my youth is over, spent without regrets, consecrated like a novitiate to fit me for my task. The cup of youth's pleasures is one that my lips have never touched. The love of woman has passed me by. The money that has come to me in the course of services that I have hired to others has gone, most of it, to the Cause on which my heart is set. If it please Almighty God that my hopes bear fruit, that my labours yield return, I shall have my reward and I shall rest me at last. If not," and a shadow crossed the face and dimmed the almost fanatical glow of the blue eyes, "I shall still have my reward within myself – in the glory of the memory of the service rendered to that exiled one in Rome.

"You know of whom I speak, my lord, to what service I refer. Tonight I sat down to play here with money that I scarce dared call my own. Had I lost, it would have been so much lost to the Cause; as I have won, it is but just that I count it still money to be devoted to this sacred enterprise; and under no circumstances, sir, would my honour have permitted me, as for a moment you supposed, to return you the draft and await a convenience that may never come.

"My lord, you know full well that our Cause is most desperately in need of funds. His Majesty lives almost upon charity." There was something akin to a sob in his voice. "Think of it, my lord! You count yourself one of his servants, one of his loyal adherents. You plot and scheme and pray for his return because you believe and are loyal to the rightful king. Can you, then, contemplate his straitened circumstances without feeling yourself humbled and ashamed? Consider how the money you have dissipated here – "

He broke off suddenly. "But let that be! I am speaking of myself, I think. I have said that this money I have won from you I scarce consider mine. Yet will I adventure it again as I adventured that other. I will adventure it to win more – to win the fortune of Miss Hollinstone, that I may turn it to a like sacred purpose.

15

"Now, sir," he ended abruptly, "you are informed of the precise height and depth of my baseness; you have the precise measure of the insult I have offered you." And he turned again to the window swiftly, that the other should not see the scalding tears that welled to his eyes, man of iron though he was.

My lord sank to a chair and took his head in his hands, beaten down by the storm of that man's fervour – that man whom he had dubbed in scorn and disgust a self-seeking fortune hunter.

Something of the soldier's enthusiasm had stirred him, and in its wake had come a burning, searing shame at the reflection of what were Gaynor's motives, what his own. The small voice of his conscience whispered mockingly that it was he was the fortune hunter, he that was vile and base, he that, without faith or loyalty, had lent himself to a cause whose prevailing was his forlorn hope, the last perceptible means by which to mend his shattered fortunes.

"Captain Gaynor," he said at last, in a hushed voice, "I ask your pardon for my misapprehension of you."

The Captain swung round and faced him again – master of himself once more, calm and self-contained.

"Is it your pleasure, then, that we play?" he asked.

But here his lordship's face again grew dark, reflecting thoughts of which the soldier could have no knowledge, else he would not have insisted as he did.

"Consider, my lord," he cried, "that all the odds are on your side. On the one hand you stand to win; on the other, to lose nothing that is not lost already."

My lord threw up his head, something between amazement and anger in his eyes. "How?" he cried with extraordinary vehemence. "What is't you mean?"

To himself Captain Gaynor cursed the fellow's dullness. He proceeded to explain.

"You have said that, unless you have this money tomorrow, a debtors' gaol awaits you. In such a case will not Miss Hollinstone be lost to you? Do you dream that her uncle and guardian, Sir John Kynaston, will permit this betrothal to continue? It is your only chance that I am offering you, my lord. For your own sake, no less than for mine, you should consent."

It was so clear and plain that Pauncefort for a moment turned the notion over in his mind, and something else – a further unsuspected advantage that must lie with him in such a game, an advantage, indeed, which made a mock of it and himself no better than a cheat did he consent. He frowned in doubt and perplexity. The perplexity he voiced at last.

"How do you look to profit by my loss?" he asked.

Captain Gaynor considered a moment. He came forward and leaned upon the table opposite to his lordship.

"The conquest of a woman so wounded in her pride and vanity should not be an insuperable task. Under the urge of pique she may welcome a suitor who at another time might be disdained. That is my opportunity; none so great, as you may judge; so that here again the odds are all with you. Given the opportunity, however, I am not unpersonable; I have seen the world, and I could no doubt, upon occasion, develop the antics which delight a woman." He spoke quite coldly. "For the rest, not only is her uncle on our side, not only does he expect me at Priory Close on Thursday, but he holds me in some affection; so that the way lies open to me."

"You speak of wounds to her pride and vanity."

"Those consequent upon your lordship's withdrawal of your suit," said Captain Gaynor crisply, his steely eyes full upon the other's.

But his lordship was not dominated by the glance. He smote the table with his clenched hand.

"No!" he roared. "Sink me into perdition, no!"

It was a cry of conscience; the repudiation which common honesty demanded. But Captain Gaynor rated it at a still higher value. Slightly he inclined his head. He spread his hands a little. "Be it so," said he. "We will say no more. I think, with your permission, I will take my leave. The sun is rising."

But the alternative gaped before Pauncefort like a yawning chasm upon whose brink he tottered. He clutched the soldier's sleeve.

"Stay!" he cried. "When a man has lost all else, what matters honour?"

"There are some causes to which one may sacrifice honour and remain honourable. You will remember that should I win, and should all speed thereafter as I desire it, you will have done the Cause perhaps the best service that lay within your power."

"Should you win?" said the other. His face was ghastly. "Ah, but should you lose – " He broke off abruptly. "How shall we play?"

"What would you propose?" quoth Captain Gaynor, controlling the exultation that strained within him like a hound upon the leash.

My lord rose, his dark face was almost sinister now. He passed a white, jewelled hand over his long, cleft chin.

"Such a game as this," he said, "should be played, I think, with other tools than dice or cards. Honour is here involved, and with honour should go life as well."

"That," said the Captain composedly, "depends upon the point of view, and you and I, my lord, again do not see eye to eye. I do not count this game dishonouring, else you may be very sure I should not engage in it."

"You do not – true!" His lordship winced as he realised the difference, dependent upon their respective motives. "But you do not think of me."

"If I did not," said Gaynor sweetly, "I should accept the game with the tools you have in mind. But those, my lord, are the tools of my trade, and they should place the advantage too heavily with me."

He uttered it as a commonplace; there was no scintilla of boastfulness in his cold statement of an irrefragable fact. His lordship laughed, short and bitterly.

"In that case," said he, "we had better use the tools of mine." And he gathered up the cards that were spread upon the table. "You are, as you have insisted, the incarnation of generosity, Captain Gaynor."

"I am glad that at last you begin to perceive it," said the soldier amiably. "Shall it hang upon a single cut?" He placed my lord's draft upon the table as he spoke.

His lordship glanced at it, and then at the soldier. "Will you not give your generosity a free rein?" said he. "Will you not add to that the other two thousand that you have won from my guests tonight?"

Gaynor, masking his contempt, drew from his pocket another note of hand and a heavy purse. These, too, he placed upon the table.

"Shall I throw in my head as well?" he asked. "It is valued at a thousand guineas."

Pauncefort looked at him with hostile eyes, resentful of the sneer that underlay his words. "I am content," he said.

Captain Gaynor smiled, took the cards from his lordship, shuffled them with steady fingers and placed the pack upon the table.

"A single cut," he repeated, and by a gesture invited his lordship to go first.

The viscount put forth a shaking hand, cut, and displayed the four of spades. His face turned ashen.

"Sink me!" he raged. "I was a fool to have consented! God knows I have had proof enough that my luck is dead tonight."

The Captain made him no answer, but reaching for the pack cut in his turn.

It was then that he gave his lordship the sorely needed lesson in the art of graceful losing. He smiled and shook his head in deprecation of his lordship's passion.

"You cursed your luck too soon, my lord," said he.

He had cut the three of diamonds.

As he walked along Jermyn Street, flooded now with the radiance of the new-risen sun, he smiled pensively. The gods had given him a wondrous chance and a little fortune of ten thousand pounds. He pondered some of the things that might have been accomplished with that sum. Then he dismissed the matter from his mind without another regret.

He was by temperament, you see, the perfect gamester.

Chapter 3

MR SECOND SECRETARY

However undeniable it may be that Captain Gaynor was a man inured to danger and prepared to accept all risks that came his way, yet it is no less undeniable that he never accepted a risk that was unnecessary. Daring he was, but not reckless. The care and precaution with which he laid his plans, the thought which he devoted to their formulation and the elaborate pains he took in their execution were all calculated to reduce his risk to the lowest fraction. He overlooked nothing, neglected nothing, and rarely moved into a situation from which he had not prepared himself an avenue of retreat in the event of sudden danger.

As a result of all this, although the Government was aware of the existence of a singularly daring Jacobite agent, who spied and plotted, came and went between the Pretender's Court at Rome and his adherents in England, and although the country was sown with proclamations offering a thousand guineas for his apprehension, the identity of this agent remained unknown. No definite description of him existed; indeed, the descriptions forthcoming at various times offered such glaring discrepancies one with another that it almost seemed as if his exploits were not those of an individual, but of a group.

He was generally known as "Captain Jenkyn" though none could say how the sobriquet had arisen. As "Captain Jenkyn" he was referred to in all reports concerning his movements which the Government spies were from time to time enabled to lay before the Secretary of State, and "Captain Jenkyn" was the name in those proclamations which offered a thousand guineas for his head.

But no man who was not of the party – and only one or two who were – had ever consciously come face to face with Captain Jenkyn. On the day when that should happen, on the day when a Government agent or emissary should hail him to his face by that *nom de guerre*, on that day, he was resolved, he would sink his own identity – cast it from him like a garment that has served its turn – for the sake of the many whose connection with Captain Harry Gaynor might be traced and whose lives might in consequence be jeopardised. On that day his career as an agent would be at an end. Even if with the mask plucked from him he should succeed in making good his escape from the perils that would then surround him, another must thereafter take up his work. Such was his resolve against a contingency which the elaborate quality of his plans permitted him to account remote.

It is in the perfection of these plans that towards noon of that day whose dawn saw him departing from Pauncefort House we find the Captain in one of the last places in London where we should look for a man engaged upon such a mission as his own – in the anteroom of Mr Second Secretary Templeton's residence in Old Palace Yard.

Three months ago, in Rome, Captain Gaynor had renewed an old acquaintance with one Sir Richard Tollemache Templeton, who had served with him under Marlborough in the days of the late Queen – days in which Harry Gaynor had been acquiring the rudiments of the art by which he was to live. Since then Tollemache Templeton had succeeded to the baronetcy, left the service, and was now repairing an omission in his education by making the grand tour.

Sir Richard was the Second Secretary's cousin, and Gaynor had been quick to seize upon that circumstance, and upon their old acquaintance, to provide against his forthcoming mission into

England. For a month he had flung in his lot with the lounging Sir Richard. Together they had roamed over Southern Italy, the Captain representing himself as a soldier of fortune out of work just then, to whom time was of no account and upon whom the allurements of Sir Richard's company proved compelling. He had very materially improved the acquaintance between them during that month. It had warmed and quickened into a friendship, very genuine on Sir Richard's part, and only a little less so on the other's.

Most subtly had Captain Gaynor succeeded in conveying to the baronet an entirely wrong conception of his aims. So cleverly, indeed, had he done his work that in the end the suggestion which it was his intention ultimately to make to Sir Richard, Sir Richard actually made to him.

They were lounging together on the cliffs at Capri one breathless, languid morning, when the Captain, by way of leading up to what he had in mind, fell to bewailing the passing of the need for the soldier of fortune in Europe. He deplored his own enforced idleness; states were at peace; employment for such as himself was not easily to be discovered; he had come hopefully to Italy, looking for turbulence in the peninsula to afford him his opportunity; but his hopes were proved vain; his purse was growing lighter and no prospect showed upon the horizon; he spoke gloomily of returning to the East, regretted almost having left it. Subtlest of all was the last touch he added, and for the glaring untruth of it the justification he offered to his conscience was the great cause he served, the ultimate good to be achieved, if necessary, by ignoble means.

"There is the Pretender, now," he said slowly, "and I have thought of him. Indeed, he's all there's left to think of here. But there is little to attract me in thought. I may be a follower of Fortune's banner, a man who makes of fighting as much a trade as others make of tinkering or haberdashery, but, on my soul, Dick, there are limits even to that. The Pretender is the enemy of England" (he prayed heaven to pardon him that necessary blasphemy), "and Harry Gaynor's sword although for hire shall never be hired to any disloyal cause." He sighed and laughed his musical, self-mocking little laugh.

I dare swear you'll count me foolish, Dick, to strain at a gnat who have swallowed camels."

But Sir Richard's face was very grave; approval shone in his frank eyes.

"On my soul I do not, Harry," he cried heartily, like the thorough-paced Whig he was. "I honour you for your feelings. I would not have a friend of mine hold any other. But," he continued, frowning thoughtfully, "since you feel thus, why not let profit and inclination jump together? Why not find employment for your sword in the service that enlists your heart?"

The Captain's pulses throbbed a little faster. For here from Sir Richard came the very proposal to which so warily he was leading. But since Sir Richard had proposed it, Sir Richard should persuade as well, and thus the thing would come to stand upon a still sounder basis than ever Gaynor had hoped.

He laughed contemptuously.

"Why, Dick!" he cried, "what is't you suggest? What hire can England offer for my services? Pshaw, man, 'tis not a land in which the mercenary grows anything but lean."

"But there are the colonies," Sir Richard insisted, "and good appointments are to be obtained there for her adventurous children."

"The colonies?" said the Captain, in a different voice, the voice of one who muses yieldingly. "True!" he murmured. And then, as if brushing the matter aside: "But even there," he concluded, "to obtain such posts as are worth the adventurer's attention, influence, much influence, is needed."

"Some, I agree," answered Sir Richard. "And that I can supply."

Captain Gaynor stared at him. "You, Dick?" he cried, and laughed in mockery of his companion.

"You forget that the Second Secretary is my cousin," Sir Richard reminded him without resentment.

"Why!" exclaimed the Captain, like one upon whom bursts a sudden revelation, one who discovers something hitherto entirely overlooked, "why that is true! And you think, then – "

"I know," Sir Richard cut in, "that what my cousin can he will do for my friend. He shall do. I will write to him this very day, and yourself shall bear the letter, Harry."

Thus it befell that the amiable Sir Richard penned his glowing panegyric of Captain Gaynor. He delivered it to the adventurer, urging him to start at once. But the Captain was not of those who quit the moment they have gained their object, and thereby leave behind them a suspicion of what their object may have been. He lingered on a full fortnight in Sir Richard's company, as if reluctant to be gone, and this in spite of Sir Richard's constant urgings. Indeed, they came near to quarrelling over the matter more than once, the baronet holding that the service he was rendering was being lightly treated, the Captain grumbling daily that his prospects, after all, were none so bright, that the English service was a poor one at the best, that heaven alone knew how long he might be left to cool his heels in British ante-chambers ere aught was found for him; that he detested the English climate and had a horror of ante-chambers, which were always draughty, and that he could not abide draughts, being subject to the rheum ever since a fever which had stricken him in Constantinople three years ago.

But in the end he went, though reluctant even then, and leaving upon Sir Richard's mind the unmistakable impression that he regretted having ever mentioned the matter and that he would not go at all were it not out of dread of offending his dear friend by failing to avail himself of that friend's good offices.

In his soul he was most excellently content. He knew this Second Secretary Templeton, whom he had never met, as he knew every member of the British Government and what each stood for. Templeton was the very man for him: a man of little personal influence, no more than the lackey and tool of my Lord Carteret, the Secretary of State; a pompous, self-sufficient fellow who would promise much and accomplish nothing, keeping the Captain hanging upon his promises and thus affording him an excellent pretext for his sojourn in England should it chance to he questioned.

Thus, then, do we find him amid the various clients in Mr Templeton's ante-chamber on that fair June morning. Of the seven hours that are sped since he departed from my Lord Pauncefort's house he has devoted six to sleep, and he comes alert and fresh into the great man's presence.

If last night there were about him indications of the soldier, today his every line proclaims it. He wears a dark blue coat with narrow silver lace, very full in the skirt, white buckskins and jack-boots that are equipped with silver spurs. The hilt of his sword is of cut steel; under his arm he carries a black hat looped and plumed in military fashion, and the only jewel visible upon his person is the sapphire nestling in the fine lace of his Steinkirk.

His heels together, Captain Gaynor bowed stiffly and formally to the Second Secretary. Mr Templeton did not consider it necessary to rise to receive this visitor. He nodded to him across the littered table at which he sat, nodded with the perfunctory nod of majesty, whilst with an imperious yet languid hand he waved away the usher who had introduced the soldier.

"You bring me, sir, I understand – ah – letters from my cousin, Sir Richard – my cousin, Sir Richard." His voice was full and sonorous, his utterance leisurely; his rhetorical tastes were polysyllabic, and he had a trick, common to third-rate orators, of repeating the closing words of a period.

Captain Gaynor considered the long, sallow, aristocratic face under its imposing, full-bottomed wig. He found it cold, supercilious and somewhat forbidding; for it wore the expression that Mr Templeton reserved for those who had aught to solicit from him. All this, the Captain reflected, was as he would have it.

He produced his letter. Mr Templeton received it languidly.

"I think," said he, "that I am already – ah – acquainted with its contents."

"Dick will no doubt have written to you direct, sir," said Captain Gaynor easily.

Mr Templeton nodded shortly and broke the seal. This he did elaborately, as he did all things, clothing himself like all insignificant folk in a vast importance.

Thus – saving for certain orthographical eccentricities, whose reproduction were unprofitable – had Sir Richard written:

MY DEAR NED, – I send you these by the hand of one of my oldest friends. Captain Harry Gaynor was my brother-in-arms aforetime under Marlborough, and is a soldier of very high and notorious merit. He has seen much service in many lands, and goes now to offer his sword to the King, who has no more loyal devoted subject than himself. His experience, whereupon he will himself entertain you, entitles him, if I may presume to judge, to some honourable post in his Majesty's dominions overseas. If you can help him to his ambitions you will be serving me who matter little, himself who matters more, and his most gracious Majesty who matters most. Further still, you will be serving yourself, for I will answer for it that to whatever post you may consider well to appoint him he will do credit upon you for the appointment. As it is for the most part in consequence of my representations to him that Captain Gaynor is journeying to England to seek you, I hope that you will find it in your power to accommodate him speedily and suitably, and thus earn the gratitude of him who is, while he is, your devoted and obedient cousin,

                    RICHARD TOLLEMACHE TEMPLETON.

The reading done, Mr Templeton levelled a quizzing-glass at the soldier, and looked him over. He cleared his throat ponderously.

"My cousin, sir, gives me here a very good account of you – a very good account."

Captain Gaynor bowed in silence.

"A fuller account is contained in the other letter which I received from him," the statesman added. Then after a slight pause, in an altered tone – a tone that appeared to veil something – "I understand that you met my cousin in Rome – in Rome," he said.

"That is so," replied the Captain.

"May I presume, sir, to inquire what you did there?"

"I perceive no presumption in the question." And Captain Gaynor smiled affably. "I was idling there for some days being newly come overseas from Turkey and still undetermined as to whither I should turn my steps, where seek fresh service."

"You did not – ah – peradventure, consider offering your sword to the Pretender?" And ere the Captain could answer him he had added: "You are a mercenary, Captain Gaynor – so I construe my cousin's letter – and to a mercenary all services are – ah – one."

"Not quite, sir. The mercenary who accepts service against his loyal sovereign is indeed a thing of scorn. A man may be a mercenary, sir, and yet devoted to his king and country. Leastways, such is the code I have ever followed. And that were cause enough why I should not take my sword to the Pretender. But there was yet another." A wry smile appeared upon his clean-cut face. "A mercenary's aim is the trader's aim – profit, sir; and heaven knows that in the Pretender's service there is no immediate and still less future profit to be made. That, sir, should answer you."

It was the right note: the note of confidence in the present Government; the note of contempt as to the prospects of the Stuart cause, and the Captain was glad the opportunity had been given him of striking it.

But the frigid, pompous mask before him did not relax, for all that the great head nodded its solemn acceptance of the statement.

"During your sojourn in the – ah – immortal city," said the Secretary, "you would, I conceive, have gathered something of the Court which the Pretender keeps?" He paused at that. But there was a question in the phrase, a question which Captain Gaynor did not for a moment misunderstand. He was being invited to produce what information he might have gleaned.

He was, I have said, a man of swift decisions, and in the twinkling of an eye he weighed the matter, and set his course. A man of nice sensibilities might have affected to misunderstand the question, unwilling to play a part that might savour, though remotely, of the spy's. But it would suit him better to display no such niceness.

Therefore, he waxed voluble. He poured forth scraps of information which he affected to have gathered here and there about Rome. He plunged into a list of the Englishmen who were about the person of the Stuart with all the air of one who is eager to betray, that by betrayal he may curry favour. As he proceeded, the mask of Mr Templeton's countenance warmed a little into life, reflecting his expectancy; but when the Captain came to an end of his disclosures that sombre countenance was cold once more. For Captain Gaynor had betrayed no man that was not betrayed already, had conveyed no single piece of information that was not already the common property of the British Government and of every lounger in town.

Mr Templeton told him so in blunt terms, whereupon his face fell and he looked the picture of dejection for a moment. Then the Second Secretary, considering him with a level eye, put a question that turned the Captain's stout heart to ice: "Have you ever heard, sir, of Captain Jenkyn?"

Taken unawares, his eyes dilated slightly. But the next instant he was frowning thoughtfully. "Why – yes," said he. "An agent of the Jacobites, is he not?"

"Ay, ay" rapped the other one impatiently. "What did you hear? What did you hear?"

Captain Gaynor's fears were dispelled. Yet he wondered was there some purpose more than general in the question, and he made an answer that should test that point.

"Why, sir, I heard it said – I cannot call to mind by whom or in what circumstances – but I heard it said that Captain Jenkyn was in Rome preparing for a journey into England."

And then Mr Templeton betrayed the Government to Captain Gaynor, unable, after the fashion of pompous men, to conceal any particle of knowledge that was his own.

"Pshaw!" he snapped. "Stale news, like the rest of your fine information. We have known it for a week."

Not a ripple crossed the Captain's face to betray the shock of his surprise. But he frowned, and drew himself very stiffly erect.

"Information, sir?" said he. "Mr Templeton, it occurs to me that you have been using me unworthily." And for the first time in the course of that interview he allowed the force of his personality to envelop the Second Secretary, his blue eyes withering the man with their sudden anger.

Thus a moment. Then he relapsed into the sycophant, the humble suitor who pockets an offence and fawns upon the offender. His wry, almost deprecatory smile reappeared.

"I should have been wary," he said. "I am but a blunt soldier; stout enough at blows, sir, I assure you, but dull enough – egad! – when it comes to a battle of wits with one of your mettle. You should have spared me, sir. Fore gad, you should have spared me!" he lamented.

Mr Templeton smiled at last, consented at last to put off some measure of his frigid importance, melting as it were in this warm flattery.

"Nay, now," said he, " 'twas in your own interest that I questioned you – in your own interest. Had you been furnished with any piece of information that we could account of value, it must have been deemed that his Majesty's Government had received a favour at your hands. You would have placed the Government in your debt, as it were, and it would have smoothed my path with my Lord Carteret in obtaining the – ah – gratification of your ambitions. You understand, I am assured – you understand."

"Sir," cried Captain Gaynor, "I have again betrayed my dullness. But – " And his shrug was eloquent. It said as plainly as if the words were spoken: "How can so ordinary a man as I attempt to fathom the methods of one so extraordinary as you."

"Say no more, sir; say no more!" Mr Templeton thrust back his chair, and rose – a tall figure that carried itself superbly, with head thrown back and rather to one side. "We will do what we can for you. You will leave me your – ah – credentials?"

Captain Gaynor had them ready – a bulky parcel which he now drew from an inner pocket of his coat and laid upon the Secretary's table. Of these credentials some few were genuine; but the greater part were forgeries; in the aggregate they accounted for almost every day of his time during the past ten years.

Adventurous as had been the life of which some of these documents proclaimed the genuine record, these adventures were as naught to that which lay before him ere he should come again to claim that package.

Mr Templeton balanced the bundle of papers in his hands. "If these speak as well for you as speaks my cousin, you may depend upon employment being found for you – employment worthy of your – ah- – attainments. You will wait upon me again, I hope, sir, in a little while. Should I need to communicate with you in the meantime, where shall I find you lodged?"

"I go to Chertsey tomorrow," answered the Captain, "to Priory Close."

"To Sir John Kynaston's?" quoth the minister.

The soldier bowed. "He was my father's friend many years ago, sir, and he has offered me the hospitality of his roof for some little time during my sojourn here."

"Why, that, sir," cried Mr Templeton, whose geniality seemed to increase in a measure as the interview drew to its conclusion, "that is a further recommendation in your favour – a further recommendation. Sir John stands well with the Government. He has the ear of Lord Carteret. Now a word from him – "

The Captain bowed, his hand on his heart. "Like all great men, sir, that I have ever met – and I have travelled more than most – you account mighty the little power of any other and little the mighty power that is your own. Mr Templeton, I am content to leave my petition in your hands. I could desire no better advocate, even as I could not find a greater." He bowed again before the smiling Secretary; for the Secretary was smiling broadly now, the dissolution of his iciness complete. "I have the honour, sir, to take my leave of you. I shall keep you informed of my every movement. Sir" (yet another bow) "your very obedient, grateful servant."

He was in the antechamber at last, coughing into his handkerchief as he went. And behind him he left a beaming Mr Templeton, who rubbed his hands and chuckled and told the Cupids on the ceiling what an infernally astute fellow he was. For had he not turned this soldier inside out? Had he not wrung him dry, as it were; sucked him like an orange, ere the fellow had apprehended his aims and become duly ferocious? But even that ferocity had been overwhelmed by admiration of Mr Templeton's superb penetration.

The Second Secretary resumed his seat at the littered table, and his smile faded. After all, he reflected, this adventurer had told him nothing that was not known already. Still, that was because he possessed no further knowledge, else most assuredly it would have been drawn out of him with the rest.

He took up the package of credentials. These must be looked through. Something must be found for a man who recognised dignity, authority and intellect so readily. The Secretary became conscious of a growing affection for Captain Gaynor, a desire to exert himself to serve the fellow such as was very rare with him.

But matters of State impended. He smote a bell. The usher appeared, and the mask of frigid gravity once more descended upon the lofty features of Mr Second Secretary Templeton.

Chapter 4

FATE'S AGENTS

So excellent an impression did Captain Gaynor leave of himself upon the Second Secretary that there reached him later that day an invitation to dine with Mr Templeton on the morrow, which was Wednesday.

He went, and used the occasion well, not only to advance himself further in the favour of the statesman, but also to make a conquest of Mr Templeton's lady, a plump, frivolous woman who none the less governed the Second Secretary with a tyranny that was absolute. Captain Gaynor departed with the conviction that Mr Templeton's subjection to her rule was the school in which he learnt the art of subjecting others.

There was little in that visit that calls for chronicling, unless it be that having expressed himself like the most thorough-paced Whig, and cursed the turbulence of the Jacobites who would disturb a realm in which there was peace and prosperity, the Captain ventured to congratulate Mr Templeton upon the vigilance of the Government and to marvel at the thoroughness of that same vigilance, as evidenced by the circumstance that not a particle of the information he had, himself, been able to bring straight from Rome – including the fact that the notorious agent, Captain Jenkyn, was on his way to

England – but was already known to the omniscient Second Secretary.

Captain Gaynor's aim was to draw from Mr Templeton some hint which should enable him to place his finger upon the leakage that obviously existed. But it failed, and he dared not insist; nor did he consider it worth while, concluding that it was very possible that Mr Templeton did not possess the information which he craved.

He deemed it well, however, to set Pauncefort upon his guard, and with this intent he called upon him on the following afternoon. His lordship received Captain Gaynor's news with obvious consternation.

"How do you know this?" he cried, and his voice shook with a sudden panic that surprised the Captain.

Captain Gaynor enlightened him. Then: "You see," he said in conclusion, "there is reason to fear a traitor from within. For how else could this knowledge have reached the Government?"

"Are you sure that it had?" questioned the scowling Pauncefort. "May it not have been yourself who supplied the information, and Templeton's assertion that it was already known a mere pretence to give himself importance – to efface his obligation to you?"

Captain Gaynor smiled his amused tolerance of such a suggestion. "I did not begin to be a plotter yesterday, my lord," said he.

But his lordship adhered to his point. "Yet it was a folly on your part to have said what you did to him – rank folly."

"I think not, my lord," was the suave answer. "I aimed at testing the extent of the Government's information, and I hold that I succeeded but too well."

"Have it so, then," said Pauncefort. "For myself, I am content to hold to the other opinion. I' faith, I should not sleep o' nights did I not. Gad! For a moment you turned my stomach with your talk of traitors."

"None the less," said the Captain soberly, "I warn you to be circumspect. We meet, then, at 'The World's End,' at Chelsea, this day se'nnight, when the work to do shall be planned. 'Twill be safer thus than at your house or another's."

"Meanwhile," said his lordship, "you are for Priory Close?"

"I am on my way thither. I but stayed to give you this information. I shall see you there, no doubt?"

My lord checked the answer he was obviously upon the point of making. He flushed and hesitated a moment. Then, recovering from his confusion, and attempting to gloze it over –

"I think not," he answered slowly. "My affairs here require attention. There is much to do if I am to set this tangle to rights."

"I rejoice," said the Captain, "to infer that it is amenable to endeavour."

"Indeed, yes – thanks to the trick that Fortune played you here two nights ago. To that I owe it that a way has been opened for me."

"I am glad," said Gaynor pleasantly. "It would seem, then, that your affairs were scarce as desperate as you feared. I am heartily glad, sir."

His tone was so amiable and sincere that none might have guessed that he, himself, had been the loser in the transaction. Thereupon, he took his leave of Pauncefort. But as he was departing, his lordship stayed him. The nobleman's face was troubled.

"At Priory Close you will meet Miss Hollinstone," said he. "Commend me to her and to Sir John. And – touching the lady, and the game we played here, you will remember that – that – " He fumbled vainly for the expression that might inoffensively convey his meaning.

The soldier stiffened. "That I lost, you would say, my lord, and that you, therefore, continue in the claim which every man has upon his betrothed."

"You put it – bluntly," his lordship deprecated.

"It is a blunt matter. But you may quiet your alarms." The Captain all but sneered. "They do little honour to the lady and still less to myself."

Their farewells, thereafter, were repeated with some restraint, and Captain Gaynor took his departure.

He had engaged himself a valet, a shrewd-faced little fellow named Fisher, recommended to him by the landlord of the "George" as a person of so much fidelity and honesty that the Captain had despatched him ahead by the stage to Chertsey with his baggage. The Captain himself rode forth alone and came, an hour or so after taking leave of Pauncefort, to the dreary spaces of Hownslow Heath.

In the distance ahead of him, a solitary horseman moved slowly along the sky-line. Captain Gaynor would have observed him perhaps more closely could he have known that this horseman was one of Fate's agents to himself. For had not that horseman been present there in that lonely tract of country, the Captain's career would have run a vastly different course from that which gives occasion to this chronicle.

A signpost threw a lengthening shadow athwart the ribbon of road that wound through the parched spaces of the heath. The sun was no more than a glowing disc upon the horizon. A black silhouette against it, the horseman passed and dipped out of sight.

Captain Gaynor rode on, his thoughts anywhere but upon that fateful figure. He gained the summit of the rise and dipped in his turn, steadying his horse, for the road was rough and deeply ploughed with ruts of clay that were baked into stony ridges. There was no sign now of the other horseman, no sign of living thing in all that lonely place. But suddenly from the screen of a clump of cedars that spread funereally a hundred yards ahead, the rider reappeared. His back was towards the Captain. He never so much as turned his head, seeming entirely unconscious of the other's rapid approach. Such indeed was his unconsciousness that Captain Gaynor, as he drew nigh, was moved to scrutinise him. He was a heavy fellow, mounted upon a clumsy piebald horse. From under a round hat wisps of black hair floated raggedly in the breeze. He wore a long black riding-coat and dirty buckskins; and that was all that the Captain could perceive until presently he drew alongside and observed in addition a wolfish, lantern-jawed face above a dirty neck-cloth and a still dirtier green satin waistcoat with ragged and tarnished gold lace.

He was as unprepossessing a ruffian as could be met with in the length and breadth of England, and nowhere could that meeting have been less welcome than on the lonely stretch of Hownslow Heath.

" 'Tis a fine evening, your honour," said he in an accent that proclaimed an Irish origin.

"A fine evening it is," replied the Captain, coldly courteous. He rode steadily amain, and must have sped past the other but that the fellow touched up his piebald and kept level.

" 'Tis a mightily lonesome place, this Heath," said he, as if explaining his action, "and if there's a thing in all the world I hate 'tis lonesomeness."

"It is a distaste which I do not share," said the Captain curtly.

"D'ye not?" cried the other. "Now if there's a living man knows a hint when he hears it, 'tis myself, bedad. So I'll not be troublin' you farther with a company that's unwelcome. But there's a word or two I'd be speakin' to you first. Will ye draw rein awhile? Hold, I say! Hold or I'll be blowin' your head inside out!"

Captain Gaynor reined in sharply. The ruffian had levelled a heavy pistol with a long, polished barrel – the only polished thing about him – on which the last rays of the vanishing sun threw a blood-red gleam.

"What d'ye want with me?" quoth the soldier sharply.

The ruffian grinned. "Why, now, there's a plain question, and here's a plain answer for you – faith, 'tis a trifle I'm wanting: just your purse and that jewel at your throat and your watch if so be ye have one."

Captain Gaynor seemed to be measuring the other with his eyes as one who considers resistance. The wolfish face continued to grin, and there was a confident gleam in the hungry, bloodshot eyes. Here was no bungler; but a practised, self-confident knight of the toby, who would have no more qualms about holding up a soldier than a dowager, and still less about shooting either if expediency advised it.

Gaynor's wry smile appeared at last. "Faith," said he, "ye have the advantage of me, I think."

"I'm thinkin' the same, and I'm glad ye're reasonable; for I'd be mortal sorry to shed the blood of such a broth of a boy over a paltry matter of a handful of guineas and a jewel or two. 'Live and let live' is my motto, your honour."

The Captain produced his purse. It was of black silk and bulky, and through the straining meshes of the knitting there appeared a yellow gleam.

The tobyman brought his nag a pace nearer. With pistol levelled and eyes that never left the Captain's face, he held out his left hand to receive the purse. But it seemed that Gaynor relinquished it too soon; just as the ruffian's fingers touched it, in fact; so that it dropped and fell between them with a resounding chink.

The tobyman's eyes were instinctively lowered to follow its fall – a deplorable error this in one so practised in his trade. An instant later the pistol was dashed from his hand by a blow that almost shattered his knuckles. Before he could attempt to defend himself, before he could properly realise what was befalling him, that blow was followed by a second, this time upon his head, so shrewdly delivered that he reeled in his saddle.

Captain Gaynor was standing in his stirrups, which gave him the advantage of being above the thief. He grasped his heavily mounted riding-crop like a cudgel, and like a cudgel he used it with a dexterity and rapidity such as the other had never encountered in all his adventurous career. Before he had recovered from that dazing blow across the crown a shower of others had fallen upon his body, and lifted a cloud of dust from his coat. Bewildered by the suddenness and thoroughness of the onslaught, he was beyond all thought of defence or retaliation.

As arrant a coward without his pistol as he was valiant with it, he realised that he had grasped a scorpion. He stayed for no more. He gathered up his reins and ploughed the piebald's flanks with his spurs. The maddened horse half reared, then flung forward as from a catapult and broke into a gallop. But Captain Gaynor was not yet content. He started in pursuit, brandishing that formidable crop.

The tobyman, flying with terror in his soul, was rendered desperate. There remained him yet another pistol. He plucked it forth with his half-shattered hand, swung round in the saddle and blazed at his pursuer.

His aim was wild and his pistol-hand in no case to serve him accurately. None the less the shot did all that was necessary to arrest pursuit. The charge, at fairly close range, entered the breast of Captain Gaynor's mare. The poor beast screamed and reared and collapsed in a heap from which the soldier was no more than in time to leap clear.

He stood in the road, cursing the highwayman and his own folly in having given chase. Thus a moment. Then, his wounded horse demanding his attention, he drew one of his pistols from its holster and made an end of the beast's agony. That done, he walked back to the spot where the encounter had taken place, and recovered the purse which in his zeal to punish he had all but forgotten. Then, slowly, he retraced his steps to his fallen horse, and considered his position. He was still a good nine miles from his destination, and dusk must overtake him before long.

He stood pondering there when his ears caught a distant clank and rattle, accompanied by the pounding of hoofs. The sounds drew rapidly nearer along the road by which he had come; soon a chaise appeared upon the ridge behind him, and came down the incline swaying and jolting alarmingly over that execrable road.

The Captain stood now awaiting it, the object of suspicious glances from the coachman, and from the footman who hung by a strap behind the approaching vehicle. As it came up with him, he raised his hand, and the chaise was brought gradually to a standstill, for the fallen horse announced plainly enough that here was a traveller in distress.

From the window, thrusting aside the leather curtain, a wondrously coiffed head protruded. A feminine voice, high pitched and querulous, assailed the Captain's ears.

"What now, Gilbert? Why do we stay?" Then the lady's glance fell upon Captain Gaynor, and with a little scream of fear the wondrous head vanished hurriedly into the carriage.

Smiling, the Captain advanced, hat in hand, to the door of the chaise.

"Pray do not be alarmed," he said. "I am a suppliant not an assailant."

" 'Tis is a gentleman what's 'ad 'is 'oss killed," announced the well-nourished Gilbert from the box.

Another head appeared, and the Captain found himself confronted by a young face that was extremely good to look upon – a delicate little face under an elaborate arrangement of golden curls; the eyes that met his own so frankly were very blue and invested with a look of innocence; the little chin was sharply pointed, and the mouth was very small and delicately arched. It was such a face as Greuze loved to paint, the pretty advertisement of a trivial little soul.

The Captain bowed gravely. "Ma'am," said he, "I have met with a mischance. My horse has been shot under me."

Alarmed concern flickered into the blue eyes. "Shot!" she cried, in a slender treble. "La, sir!"

Over her shoulders reappeared the face of the elder lady.

"Shot, did ye say?" she cried. "Lard a' mercy! Who shot it, sir?"

"A rogue of a tobyman, ma'am."

"A tobyman!" The voice shrilled on the word. "Ye hear! What have I ever said, and ye would never heed me. But 'tis the last time that ever I'll cross the Heath. Lard, now! 'Tis a miracle we are not murdered – a miracle!"

"I have some distance to go, ma'am," said the Captain, "and I should be most profoundly obliged if you would permit me to sit with your coachman as far as the next post-house, where I can repair my loss."

The younger lady was first thrust aside, then entirely eclipsed by the elder, whose presence came once more to fill the window. She surveyed the suppliant with an air of grim suspicion.

"How far d'ye travel, sir?" she questioned him.

"To Chertsey, ma'am," he replied.

Upon that she seemed to eye him more attentively. A voice murmured behind her in the coach. She turned a moment.

"It is possible, Damaris," he heard her say. "He has the air of it."

Damaris! The name hummed through his brain.

"May I ask, sir," came his questioner again, "whom we shall have the honour of assisting?"

"My name, ma'am, is Gaynor – Captain Harry Gaynor, your obedient servant to command."

"Why, 'tis so, then!" she cried, and smiled – a comely, well-featured woman. "La, now! 'Tis the oddest of encounters. You are for Priory Close."

The Captain confessed, and added the assumption which had flashed into his mind. "You will be Lady Kynaston. 'Tis an odd chance, indeed."

"James, you lout," she called to the gaping footman, who had swung himself down from his perch, "the door."

The lackey sprang to let down the steps. Her ladyship alighted, leaning upon his shoulder. She proved now to be of a good height and presence, and to carry herself well. And not only was she comely in herself, as I have said, but most fully appreciative of comeliness in the other sex. She dropped the Captain a half-curtsy, and met him now with the most engaging of smiles.

"We count ourselves fortunate to be of service to you, sir," said she, and proceeded to present him to her companions. This presentation she performed, as she did all things, in a superficial manner. "These," she said, half turning from him and with a wave of the hand towards the occupants of the chaise, "are Miss Hollinstone, my niece, and my daughter, Evelyn. She is my only child, sir, a matter which sorely vexes Sir John, for he would dearly have loved a son. 'Tis a thousand pities that heaven should not have gratified his wishes," she ran on, garrulous and inconsequent. "But then, on the other hand, the rearing of sons in these disordered days is so grave a responsibility that sometimes I think perhaps heaven knows best."

The Captain had scarce heard a word of it. His eyes were upon the two ladies who remained in the coach – the golden-headed child with whom already he had spoken, whom he assumed to be Damaris Hollinstone, and another, who was taller and dark, and of a very different type of beauty. He surveyed them both, it is true, and made his bow to them. But it was upon the supposed Miss Hollinstone that his eyes rested with the more profound interest, and certain odd stirrings, which were entirely consequent upon the strange game he had played three nights ago with my Lord Pauncefort.

Perceiving at last that the girl was growing conscious of his scrutiny, the Captain turned to Lady Kynaston with polite inquiries touching Sir John. She replied at long length with a catalogue of Sir John's real and fancied ailments, the conclusion to be drawn from which seemed to be that her husband was in excellent health and looking forward with pleasure to his visitor's arrival.

"It is growing late, mother," said the dark lady from her corner of the chaise, "and Captain Gaynor, no doubt, will be in haste to arrive."

"Where one may journey so pleasantly," said the Captain, as courtesy dictated, "there can be no haste to arrive anywhere."

"La!" said the fair Damaris, and laughed. "Yet indeed, mother, you are detaining him," she added. And Captain Gaynor, reflecting that the child had indeed been as a daughter to Lady Kynaston, found the mode of address a proper and pretty tribute.

Expressing herself in tritely caustic terms upon the pertness of the age and the deplorable lack of deference to elders, her ladyship none the less acted upon the hints of her daughter and her niece, and permitted the Captain to assist her into the chaise once more. Captain Gaynor followed her, and took his seat beside her. The steps were raised, the door closed, and once more the carriage lurched drunkenly along.

By her whom he had assumed to be Damaris the Captain was invited to relate the details of his adventure. He responded to the invitation, but in doing so it was to Lady Kynaston and her daughter that he chiefly addressed himself.

In this he obeyed the somewhat peremptory dictates of his sense of honour. After what had passed between himself and Pauncefort, he felt that the greatest circumspection was incumbent upon him. In no case could he have looked upon Miss Hollinstone as a conquest to be attempted, knowing her betrothed to another. But since she had been the subject of a game; since he must look upon her as upon a stake for which he had played and which he had lost, it was as if a wall had been set up between them, as if she had become in some still more emphatic manner the property of another, which he should be no better than a thief did he attempt to filch.

Reclining in the chaise when his tale was done, and considering his position, what time the ladies chattered of highwaymen, the perils of the Heath and his own singular address in turning the tables upon one who had held him at such disadvantage, the Captain's thoughts strayed again to the matter of that game. A swift judge of character, he found much in that fair face and in that too perfect rosebud mouth to be deplored. If at some time in his life a man must think of mating, let him then mate with one who will be prepared to give as well as to receive. So held the Captain. And this Damaris, he judged to be of those who cannot give because they possess nothing of their own. Being one who seeks upon the surface some indication of what may lie below, the Captain was not merely left indifferent by the girl's undoubted winsomeness, but he found in it something that actually repelled him. That fair exterior he at first accounted a false lure. But this impression he soon corrected as too harsh; falseness implies at least some activity of personality; and here was one whom he judged to be entirely passive. He likened her, at length, to the camellia – and was well pleased with the image – perfect and graceful in shape and colouring, yet exhaling nothing and wilting to the touch.

These swift deductions and the consequent slight aversion which the child inspired in him, led him naturally enough to wonder what course he would have taken had be won that game which he had played. Would he have claimed the stakes? He thought of his master, waiting patiently in Rome, subsisting almost upon the charity of strangers, and he concluded that had he won he must have sought to pouch his winnings for the sake of that king to whom he owed all sacrifices. But on the whole he was content that this particular sacrifice had not been imposed upon him by the cards. Perhaps he was also relieved because, that game being lost by him, he found the task of abiding by its issue an easy one to discharge.

There was, then, no reluctance on his part. But he opined that, further, there must not even be the semblance of it; and to that end he adopted now the course that must be his during his sojourn at Priory Close. He addressed himself almost entirely to Lady Kynaston and her daughter. As he looked at the latter, he could not refrain from contrasting her with Miss Hollinstone entirely to Miss Hollinstone's disadvantage. He considered this pale, thoughtful face, with its liquid brown eyes that were gentle to the point of wistfulness, he observed the sensitiveness of the lips, the nobility of the brow, and he caught himself thinking that had this been Damaris –

In the fading daylight they rumbled over a great bridge, which spanned the river below the thundering waters of a weir, and soon thereafter the wheel-ploughed roads gave place to cobbles; houses loomed on either hand; they were entering the town of Chertsey.

The Captain had desired to be set down at the "Giant's Head" – the hostelry where his servant awaited him with the baggage, that he might give the fellow his commands. So the chaise came to a standstill before the inn, and stood there some five minutes, what time the Captain went within.

Now it happens that those were five as momentous minutes as any that he had spent that day. They completed for Fate the work which her agent, the highwayman, had begun on Hownslow Heath.

In her corner of the chaise the golden-headed child sat brooding with an ill-humoured droop in the lines of her pretty mouth. If there was in life an influence to which every nerve and thread of her was sensitive, that influence was the interest she excited in the male. The attraction of the other sex seemed to be the very mainspring of her being, and where she failed entirely of this, her natural object, the failure fretted her, leaving her vanity raw and aching, her little spirit bitter. She was accustomed to see her cousin reap the greater harvest of such interest, but she was not inured to it, although she accounted that for this an explanation existed which nowise reflected upon herself. But never yet in all her experience had she failed more signally than on the present occasion; never had she seen a man more entirely absorbed by her demure cousin than this Captain Gaynor, never one who had treated herself with such utter, such almost calculated disregard.

With burning cheeks and quivering lips, like a whipped child, she huddled herself miserably in her corner. Twice she had addressed the Captain, and he had scarce answered her, so intent was he upon her cousin. It was, she vowed, not to be borne. He was an insufferable boor. When he alighted at the inn at Chertsey she exploded – not noisily, but with a quiet, stinging scorn that she knew how to employ upon occasion.

"Heigho!" she sighed. "I do thank heaven, Damaris, that when I am wooed 'twill be for myself and not my money-bags."

And by this speech you learn of the misapprehension under which Captain Gaynor had laboured as to the respective identities of the two girls – a misapprehension buttressed by the circumstance that both girls addressed Lady Kynaston alike as "mother."

The pale face of Damaris showed ghostly almost in the deepening gloom. A shadow crossed it.

"How unkind in you, Evelyn," was her gentle rebuke. "And it is an unkindness of which you never weary. Is it not enough that I know I am wooed and won for what I have?" she inquired, and there was an oddly bitter note in the question, arguing a conviction acquired in suffering. "Do you consider that to be so enviable an estate that you must for ever be reminding me of it?"

"My dear!" purred Lady Kynaston to soothe her, "Evelyn is heedless, no more."

"It were kinder to be less," said Damaris. But Evelyn's little laugh was sharp and unpleasant.

"La!" said she. "You will for ever be misapprehending me. 'Twas not to Lord Pauncefort that I referred, but to this Captain Gaynor, who is an ensample of all the others."

"What have I done?" cried Damaris.

" 'Tis not what you have done, my dear; 'tis what your fortune does for you. That is why I am thankful to be as I am."

"I have always said," put in the inconsequent Lady Kynaston, "that we all have a deal more to be thankful for than we are aware." The good, dull woman scented no quarrel here. 'Twas not by hints that facts were to be brought to the notice of her ladyship.

"Evelyn, I do not understand you," said Damaris. Miss Kynaston moved petulantly. She sat forward, so that a shaft of light coming from one of the windows of the inn threw the golden head and winsome face into sharp relief against the gloom of that interior, and revealed the bitter lines in which the perfect – the all too perfect – mouth was set.

"The man had no eyes save for you," she sneered. You see, she was not subtle.

"Should that be my fault even were it true?" quoth Damaris, and she put out a hand to take her cousin's, in her sweet desire to conciliate. But Evelyn was quick to avoid the contact.

"Nay," she answered, "not your fault. 'Tis what I am saying. 'Tis the fault of other things; the penalty of being so great an heiress."

"I have always said that there is no station in life but has its penalties, my dears," murmured Lady Kynaston, still all unconscious of the duel that was being fought there under her very nose.

And now Damaris answered as she would not have answered – for her nature was all compounded of gentleness – but that she was stung to it by this persistent gibe, and yet more by Evelyn's avoidance of her hand. More, that gibe had wounded her as only truth can wound; for she had more than cause to perceive the truth of it, and her gentle soul was all raw from a cruel humiliation lately suffered, as presently you shall learn.

"Why, as for Captain Gaynor," said she, "I do not believe that he knew which was Damaris Hollinstone, which Evelyn Kynaston."

A laugh was her cousin's only answer – very eloquent of incredulity of so preposterous a statement.

"I can tell you, at least," said Damaris, "that twice he addressed me as Miss Kynaston."

"Did he so?" cried her ladyship. "'Twas an odd mistake!"

"Odd, indeed!" sneered Evelyn. If she had been hurt before, she was in torment now, until vanity came to reassure her, and confidently to assert that this was a deliberate untruth. She estimated herself highly, and she accounted preposterous and fatuous any assumption that in equality of circumstances she could fail to carry an easy victory over her cousin. This and her resentment drove her now to her outrageous proposal.

"If that be so, if he is, indeed, not clear which of us is Damaris Hollinstone, the lady of fortune, shall we" – she paused, and her voice assumed a note of slyness – "shall we convey to him the impression that I am she? – that you are just penniless Evelyn Kynaston?"

"My child, what are you saying?" broke in her mother. "You are very far from penniless; you are – "

"I speak comparatively, mother dear – as compared with Damaris here. Come, Damaris, what do you say?"

"Say?" echoed Damaris, amazement ringing in her voice. "I say that you are out of your senses, Evelyn."

Evelyn hummed a moment through closed lips; then her scornful little laugh trilled forth again. "Heigho! I fear me you are a boaster, Damaris."

"Evelyn!" interjected her shocked mother.

"A boaster – I?" quoth Damaris warmly.

"What else – since you dare not put your assertion to the test?"

"Dare not?" Damaris was moved to something almost approaching anger. Gentle she was; but she was also conscious of what was due to herself; and here it seemed was one who craved a lesson on that subject.

"Dare not," Evelyn insisted, snapping.

"But, my dears, it would be so vastly confusing!" protested Lady Kynaston.

Damaris took her resolve. " 'Twill be only for a day or so," she said. "And you must induce Sir John to countenance this pretence. 'Tis for your daughter's good, I assure you," she added, something grimly.

"You – you consent, then?" cried Evelyn, a little breathlessly, gripped now that the matter was to be tested, by a sudden fear of failure.

"You leave me no alternative. Be Damaris Hollinstone, then, and should you fail in the unworthy task you have in mind, never let me hear again this taunt with which you have so often wounded me." She sank back into her corner.

Evelyn's answer was a laugh. Her momentary fear had passed. If in addition to the beauty heaven had bestowed upon her, she had the embellishment of a fortune, there was little cause to fear that she would fail.

But at this point her mother intervened, grasping at last the drift of what was afoot and whither it might lead.

"But, my dears," she cried, "I do not desire Captain Gaynor's wooing of my daughter. I will not have it, Evelyn; leastways not until I know more of this gentleman. I am not sure that he is a desirable husband. He is a very gallant, handsome gentleman, to be sure, and that is something almost unusual in these days; but I understand that he is a soldier of fortune."

"A soldier of fortune!" breathed Evelyn. "He is a soldier of fortune, and yet you would have me believe that he – But here he comes! Chut! Henceforth I am Damaris Hollinstone, mother – please remember."

The footman opened the door of the chaise for the Captain, who ascended briskly, breathing apologies for the delay.

Chapter 5

THE WARNING

It would really seem as if Fate were determined to leave the Captain no way of escape from the situation into which she had thrust him. Her agents had been first the highwayman and then Miss Kynaston. What the acquisitiveness of the one had begun, the vanity of the other had continued. Even so, however, circumstances had not yet gone so far astray from the proper road but that a word from Sir John Kynaston must presently have set all to rights once more. But here again Fate was at hand to round off her ironic work. When the chaise bearing the Captain and the ladies arrived at Priory Close, they found Sir John, spurred and booted, on the very point of departure, summoned an hour since by a courier to the bedside of his brother who lay ill at Bath. The baronet had but waited to welcome Captain Gaynor ere he set out.

It was twenty years since the Captain last had visited Priory Close. He had retained, however, a very vivid recollection of the house to which, as a little lad of nine, he had been taken by his father. Between his father and Sir John the very deepest friendship had existed, and Harry Gaynor himself was conscious of an inheritance in this respect, for Sir John had ever treated him with almost parental affection. Nevertheless, on no single one of the occasions of his visit to England during the last seven years (his father had followed James II to France and Harry had gone with him, his mother being dead) had Captain Gaynor set foot at Priory Close or made the acquaintance of the baronet's lady and daughter. This had been by his own desire, and lest in the event of his apprehension and the discovery of his business Sir John should come to be implicated with him. And when Sir John had formerly pressed him to make of Priory Close his headquarters during his sojourn in England, pointing out that he would receive additional shelter from the circumstance that the baronet himself stood high above all suspicion, was a Justice of the Peace and universally accounted the most solid of Whigs, Captain Gaynor had ever made answer that these were but additional reasons why a person so very valuable to his master should not jeopardise the position which he held.

On the present occasion, however, the Captain had considered that in view of the more than ordinarily elaborate precautions he had taken and the excellent pretext upon which he was in England – a pretext which, if the worst befell, might clearly be urged to have imposed upon Sir John as much as upon any other – he was justified in accepting the hospitality which the baronet was so affectionately eager to extend to him.

Sir John received him now with a welcome of quite extraordinary warmth.

Vigour of constitution, tranquillity of conscience, clean living and abundance of exercise had marvellously preserved Sir John against the undermining work of time. In this, his sixtieth year, he had the air of a man of little more than forty. True, he inclined to portliness, but not unduly so; and being tall of body and erect of carriage this portliness seemed in him but an attribute of vigour. His blue eyes were clear, keen and unusually mirthful; it was, indeed, his eyes that were chiefly responsible for his youthful air. His skin was healthily tanned, and under the grizzled periwig which he invariably wore, his countenance was noble and genially handsome.

Esteeming Captain Gaynor highly as he did, for qualities of whose existence in him none was better aware than Sir John Kynaston, and having no son of his own to succeed him, he had for some time nourished the secret hope that his daughter and the Captain might come to make a match between them. To the fact that upon his own merit there was no man whom Sir John would more cordially have welcomed for his son-in-law was to be added that old-time friendship between the baronet and the elder Gaynor, and the thought that such a union would for that friendship's sake have delighted Harry Gaynor's father had he lived.

Sir John would have built confidently upon this hope, but for one thing – his daughter herself. The one cloud in the singularly cloudless sky of his life was Evelyn. He cherished no delusions concerning her. He knew the dangerous extent of her inherent vanity, frivolity and irresponsibility. Yet he loved her perhaps the more because of these very failings, with an affection that was blent with pity for infirmities.

Just so had he always loved her mother, with a love that was largely compounded of compassion for shortcomings that matrimony had revealed to him in the woman of his hasty, youthful choice. There was something almost noble in the care with which he had ever concealed from his wife the disillusion she had occasioned him. He had thrust from his sight her shortcomings. He magnified to himself her virtues of docility and simple good-nature, and sturdily he took consolation in them. To his councils, however, she was not admitted. She knew no more of the inward workings of his mind than she knew of any other man's; she had, for instance, the same notion of his politics as had Mr Templeton and the other gentlemen into whose eyes he flung dust with the hand of calculation.

Where another might have inveighed against his wife and attached to her the blame for the shortcomings which her daughter had inherited, Sir John, with a rare fortitude and breadth of outlook, inveighed against himself alone, and neither upon wife nor daughter did he visit a fault that proceeded from his own error. Sir John, you will have gathered, was something of a philosopher.

There remained Evelyn's future to concern him. Being as she was, he foresaw an ocean of trouble in her married life unless he could contrive for her a husband at once tender and dominant, a tried man whose patience and strength would mould her perhaps as he, himself, had failed to do so, and at the same time cherish and shelter her and steer her clear of those shoals of life upon which, without strong guidance, she seemed foredoomed to suffer shipwreck.

In Harry Gaynor he believed that he had found the very man for his purpose, and if at times he deemed it impossible that Harry Gaynor, being as he was, should bestow so much as a thought upon Evelyn, yet at others – being a philosopher, as I have said – he would reflect that in Nature's inscrutably admirable way it was often ordained that precisely such men should be attracted by just such women. Upon this slender foundation, then, he would build his hope what time he waited.

When so much is understood some notion is formed of the affectionate quality of the welcome which Sir John extended to his guest and of the concern for his guest's welfare which inspired him. Being, as he was, in some haste to depart, and as some days might elapse ere he returned, he was yet anxious to know how fared with Captain Gaynor the dangerous matters which had occasioned his visit to England.

So with little more than a word of explanation and apology, he at once carried off his guest to the seclusion of the library. There, having again expressed his regrets at this urgent need for departure in the very hour of his guest's arrival, and having satisfied himself, as indeed any might do at a glance, of Harry's physical well-being, he questioned him solicitously on the score of his mission. For however urgent the unfortunate circumstance that called Sir John away, he esteemed scarcely less urgent the thing he had to say to Captain Gaynor.

In the golden candle-light from a silver cluster that stood upon the library table, the Captain's bronzed face showed overcast. He confessed that so far he had no reason to be satisfied with the progress of his master's Cause in England.

Sir John nodded slowly, his own face thoughtful. "There," he said, "you do not surprise me. There are moments when – " He paused, and looked at the young man with eyes of the very kindliest concern. "Has no doubt ever crossed your mind, Harry?" he inquired gently. "Have you never asked yourself whether you may not have wedded your young life, your energies and enthusiasms to a dream – to the fruitless service of a company of dreamers?"

"Sir John!" exclaimed the other sharply, the faintest flush stirring under the tan of his cheeks. Then, almost sadly, he asked: "Are you, too, failing him?"

Sir John smiled; his blue eyes were steadfast. "I was speaking of you, Harry; not of myself. You are young, full of enthusiasm, ability and energy. Life lies before you. The world's your very oyster. I am an old hulk, who matter nothing – or very little. Being this, I am content to abide where I am, and to continue to hold by what I have held. But were I you – had I my youth and all my life before me – I am not sure that my loyalty would stand the strain of its fruitless sacrifice."

"Fruitless?" cried the young man hotly. "Have you lost faith in us? Do you think that we shall not prevail?"

Sir John sighed. Slowly and thoughtfully he shook his head. "I hope it, I pray for it, as every decent man must hope and pray for right and justice. But what you have just perceived has been under my eyes for some time. It fills me with despondency. It might well cause me to turn aside if I were younger and mattered more."

"It is that you see this and nothing else," the Captain argued. "If I saw no more than this I might share your fears. As it is, I confess, that gathering at Pauncefort's house three nights ago was a saddening spectacle. There we assembled most of those upon whom his Majesty depends – a round dozen of the men he believes to be his most stalwart and energetic supporters. I was his accredited agent, coming amongst them for the first time, adventuring my neck to bring them news and receive theirs. Yet they had naught for me. The night was spent in gaming, and I saw such sums staked and won and lost, that when I considered the plight of our gracious king, his urgent need of funds, I could have broken that table into slivers under their eyes as some small protest against their foul supineness."

"Ah?" said Sir John. He was profoundly interested. "And the play ran high?"

"Myself I won and lost again upwards of ten thousand guineas," said the Captain coldly.

The baronet gasped. He raised his hands – in one of which he held his hat and riding-crop – to let them fall again to his sides. He laughed softly, sadly contemptuous. "Ay!" he said. "Ay! And yet, Harry, when such is the attitude of those whose very interest it should be to support and encompass the return of our exiled king, what hope can remain that the Cause will ultimately prevail?"

"None if we could not look farther than this. But we can." His eyes glowed, and his voice rang with a sudden confidence. "Scotland will rise again."

"Scotland!" said the baronet. "Build not overmuch on Scotland. It rose before. You were in the rising yourself. It is not so very long since. You were there; you saw, and yet – " He smiled. "Oh, to be young and have youth's eternal faith in the fulfilment of its desires!"

"Things shall be better planned another time," was the Captain's confident assurance. "And, after all, perhaps we despond too soon concerning the conditions of things here. London is not England when all is said."

"It is the heart, at least; and from the movements of the heart you may gauge the liveliness of the body."

But Captain Gaynor disregarded this. "I must to Rochester and talk with Atterbury one of these days. I have messages for him from his Majesty. And on this night week I am to confer with a party of our friends again in London. Pauncefort is sending word to them."

Sir John's brows came thoughtfully together. He turned aside, and with hands clasped behind him he paced the room to the window and back until again he was standing before his guest. Then he placed hat and whip upon the table and set his hands upon the young man's shoulders.

"I speak to you as a child of my own," he said. "Consider well ere you go further. You owe it to yourself. Did I see any reasonable hope

I were indeed the very last to dissuade you. But here I see you wasting yourself upon a dream."

"Have not you done the same, Sir John?"

"It is out of that very experience that I warn you. I have been fortunate and come scatheless through so far. But were it all to do again – who knows? I am old, I say," the baronet repeated, smiling – "too old to change, and of too little consequence."

"And of what consequence am I?" cried Gaynor. "I am a soldier of fortune without kith or kin in all the world."

"If you had these?" quoth the baronet quickly, a sudden gleam in those clear, youthful eyes of his – "if you had these?"

"It were different, perhaps. But I have them not, nor want them – which is as well, for I have no right to them while this duty stands before me. You speak to me as a father, Sir John – "

"I do, my dear boy."

"And yet you know that my father would not have spoken so." It was said in a sad tone of remonstrance, of argument, that contained no offence.

The answer startled Harry Gaynor.

"I am not sure." Sir John's voice was calm and steady. "I try to speak to you as I believe your father would speak were he alive today. You see, I knew him very well, Harry; better far than ever you knew him. But there! We will talk no more tonight. I have far to ride." He took up hat and whip once more. "Use this house as your own home till I return, and – and go warily, lad." He patted the Captain's shoulder affectionately. "Go warily."

"I shall go warily, never fear," was the easy answer; "the more so since the Government is already acquainted with my presence in England."

Sir John threw up his head in alarm, the habitual joviality fading from his countenance.

"Oh, not in my own name," the Captain reassured him. "They dream of no connection between 'Captain Jenkyn' and Captain Gaynor, and Mr Templeton is seeking to find for Captain Gaynor a post in the Colonies. But he knows that Captain Jenkyn is in

England, and his spies are searching for that Jacobite agent very diligently."

"You are sure – you are quite sure that Mr Templeton does not connect you with – "

"Nay," laughed the Captain. "I should be laid by the heels already were that the case." And, further to reassure his host, he related the friendly entertainment he had received from the Second Secretary. "It is not fear that concerns me," he ended. " 'What concerns me is to discover this traitor who is so singularly well informed."

"Well, well!" sighed the baronet, and upon that he seemed to dismiss the subject. He held out his hand in farewell.

"I devoutly hope," said the Captain, "that you will find your brother's condition improved when you arrive at Bath."

"I trust so, indeed, Harry. I shall return as soon as may be."

He had reached the door when he paused again. He turned once more, and his face was very grave, his clear eyes oddly troubled. He came slowly back.

"A last word, Harry my boy," he said, in a low voice. "Be wary how far you trust my Lord Pauncefort. I do not."

The Captain's surprise stared from his eyes. "How? he cried. "What is't you imply?"

"Ah, don't ask me," returned the other, shaking his head. "I have no clear cause, perhaps, for saying so much. Yet I say it urgently – beware of Pauncefort. Good night."

But the Captain would not let him go on that. He caught the baronet's sleeve. "Sir John!" he cried. "You cannot leave it there."

Gaynor's every instinct was to brush the warning aside. But he was never a man to obey his instincts. He required reasons ere he judged, and for reasons he now pressed Sir John. He put it that his life might be hanging in the balance, which rendered him irresistible.

Sir John sighed and frowned. He flicked his boots abstractedly with his whip, and looked the very picture of reluctance.

"God knows," he said at last, "it is against my nature to heap up molehills into mountains that will entomb a man's honour, and it is what you are asking of me, Harry."

"Nay. What I ask you is to produce your reasons that I may combat them. If there are but molehills I shall recognise them and kick them over, never fear. I cannot credit what you imply; but neither can I credit that you would imply it without good grounds – or grounds that you consider good. I beg you to let me have a sight of these that I may judge them for myself."

"Why, then," said Sir John, though still with obvious reluctance, "to be quite frank, first and foremost – indeed, first and last – Pauncefort is a desperate gamester, a gamester rendered desperate by disastrous speculation. There are excellent reasons why I should have informed myself of his affairs, and I know that he totters upon the very brink of ruin, that he is in the clutches of a moneylender named Israel Suarez, who never yet spared any man, and who certainly will not spare his lordship. Now add to this that I dislike him by instinct and by reason – and you should understand why I mistrust him."

"Not quite," said Captain Gaynor slowly.

"You are determined not to spare me, Harry," said the baronet with a sad smile. "My knowledge of human nature has taught me that a broken gamester is never a man to be trusted. When in addition the man is one in whose character I have found the gravest shortcomings, you will understand that I would have you be as wary of my Lord Pauncefort as I am myself."

"As you are yourself?" cried the Captain in amazement. "But, then, how come you to have consented that he shall marry your niece?"

"I have not consented that he shall marry her," answered Sir John. "Had I done so they would have been married months ago."

"But their betrothal? Surely it has your sanction?"

"Their betrothal, yes. I have not the power to withstand it. But as far as goes the power conferred upon me by my brother-in-law, the late Geoffrey Hollinstone, I have exerted it and I shall continue to exert it to oppose this union. Let me explain, Harry.

"Damaris Hollinstone, as all the world knows, is heiress to as stout a fortune as any in England. But by the terms of her father's will she does not enter into the enjoyment and control of it until she shall have reached the age of one and twenty, or until" – he added, with slow emphasis – "she shall marry, provided that she does so with my consent and approval of her choice. Should she marry against my wishes before she attains that age, she receives under her father's will rather less than a tenth of his estate – a modest fortune still, but negligible when compared with the colossal total. The rest of it is to be divided amongst a parcel of cousins.

"It is now six months since Pauncefort first wooed her. She was a child of little more than nineteen, with no worldly knowledge, dazzled by so imposing a personality, and so she fell an easy conquest. But when the question of her marriage arose I deemed it my duty to oppose it, knowing his lordship's ways of life, as all the world knows them. I told them, however, that the matter was not one that need drive them to despair. If my Lord Pauncefort and the lady were of the same mind in a year and a half's time from then – a year from now – I should have no power to oppose their union.

"Damaris was content to wait. Pauncefort, however, attempted to hector me in private, and thus betrayed something of his real aims – aims concerning which I had never entertained a delusion. In the end, however, he was forced to take me strictly at my word. He asked me did I, meanwhile, consent to their betrothal. I answered that I had not the power to oppose it.

"I was content, you see, to leave it to time to reveal his lordship's true character to Damaris, and," he added slowly, "I think at that last she has discovered it.

"Something happened a week ago," the baronet continued, smiling rather grimly, "to open her eyes, and also to open mine. It is this more than aught else that has led me to utter my warning to you.

"His lordship sought me here. He was a little wild and not quite master of himself, and being informed as I was of the state of his affairs, I did not marvel at his condition or his visit or the object of it. He desired me to consent that the marriage should take place at once. Oh he was very vehement, and even very plausible in all that he urged. I answered him that I did not account it my duty to Damaris and to her late father, in whose place I stand, to modify the determination taken six months ago. Thereupon he demanded haughtily and angrily to know upon what grounds I opposed a marriage that all the world accounted eminently suitable. I begged him not to press me, but I was not sorry that he insisted. Knowing what I knew of his affairs, I knew also that I could hold him in a cleft stick did I so choose.

" 'Be it so, then,' I answered him. 'I will tell you, but in the presence of Damaris.'

"I summoned her; and when she came I told her upon what manner of errand his lordship had visited me. In answer she assured me that it had her entire concurrence, and she all but taxed me with abusing the power which her father's will conferred upon me.

" 'Wait, Damaris,' I said. 'My Lord Pauncefort has desired me to state my reasons for opposing this wedding, and I have desired your presence that you may hear my answer.'

"He was standing by that window, yonder, and as if to mark her indifference to any arguments of mine, she crossed to his side, whilst he put his arm about her as if to guard her from me. Oh, it was vastly touching, I assure you; but there was something more to follow.

" 'Of the reasons that move me,' said I, 'I need to state but two – the two most tangible and irrefutable ones. The first is the unsuitability of my Lord Pauncefort on the score of his age. He is, by almost fifteen years, your elder, Damaris. The other is that I am persuaded that the main object of your suit, my lord, is not my niece herself, but my niece's fortune.'

"They cried out upon me together at that denunciation.

" 'It is a foul untruth,' thundered my lord in a great passion.

" 'I shall rejoice to be convinced of that,' said I. 'I am to understand, then, that my niece's fortune weighs for nothing in your calculations?'

" 'No single jot – I swear it,' he answers me, mighty hot.

" 'That your love for Damaris is entirely disinterested? That you would make her your viscountess were she penniless?' I pursued.

" 'Yes,' he answered me fiercely, ''pon honour.'

" 'You swear it glibly enough,' said I. 'But will you prove it?'

" 'Prove it?' quoth he, and I saw a change creep over his face. He was quick enough to discern the trap into which I had lured him.

" 'It is within your power to do so,' I assured him. 'You know the terms of her father's will. I have no power to withstand the marriage if you are both set on't. All that I have power to do is to withhold and disperse the inheritance. But since that counts for nothing with you, since it is Damaris you want and nothing more, since your love for her knows naught of interest, why, take and marry her in spite of me, and God give you joy of each other.' "

Sir John paused a moment, and shook his head in melancholy retrospection.

"Poor Damaris!" he sighed. "You should have seen her at that moment, Harry – her eyes aglow with confidence in herself and her lover, with gladness at the prospect upon which I had opened that crafty window. What cared she for her fortune, poor child? Gladly would she forfeit it to prove her love. I was turned almost sick with pity at the sight of that joyous transfiguration, what time she waited for that swift, ardent answer upon which so confidently she counted from her lover.

"Alas! It never came. He stood stricken there, a little pale, staring at me in anger and dismay, until at last she raised her eyes in inquiry to his face, wondering why the answer was delayed. Before what she saw written on that countenance she blenched, and with a little cry of pain she drew away from his arm, which had grown as limp as all the rest of him.

"He turned to her. 'Damaris!' he cried. 'Hear me! Wait! You do not understand.'

" 'I think that I understand at last,' she answered, and her voice was like a knife. I could have wept for the poor child.

"And Pauncefort still sought to reason with her, to explain that which was clear already beyond all words. 'Don't you see, Damaris,' was his plea, 'that if we do this, we give Sir John the victory – that it is the very thing he desires since 'twill be to his benefit.'

"It was true enough, though I had not given the matter a thought. And yet he could not have employed an argument that must more surely have completed his damnation.

" 'To his benefit?' she questioned, snatching at a straw of hope. 'How to his benefit?'

" 'Why, of the inheritance that is to be dispersed under such circumstances, ten thousand pounds will go into his own coffers.'

" 'It shall go instead,' said I, 'to Chelsea Hospital.'

"But not even so much defence was needed to such an imputation. She looked at him, and never have I seen a deadlier smile on living face.

" 'You are marvellous well acquainted with the terms of this will,' said she, and struck him breathless by the unexpectedness of that overwhelming blow. 'You must have given it some hours of study.' With that and a little laugh, she turned again, and left us here together."

Once more Sir John paused. He looked at his companion with a wan smile. Captain Gaynor met the look with eyes that were gleaming oddly; his lips were very tightly pressed. He had listened intently to every word, and he was reflecting that the questionable game he had played at Pauncefort's had been still more questionable than he had deemed it since; for Pauncefort, it seemed, had staked something that could not be called his own. And what faith can be reposed in a man who stoops to a practice so dishonourable? But Sir John's story had not yet reached the end.

"It was after she had gone that he revealed himself," he resumed. "He stormed and raged, and finally he threatened me."

"Threatened?" echoed the Captain, haled suddenly out of his musings by that word.

"Ay, threatened – covertly. He swore that I should bitterly repent me of that day's work. I ask you, Harry: To what could his threats have reference? What could be in his mind?"

The Captain expressed his disgust and amazement in an oath. "You think he would prove such a dastard?"

"At least he considered it – that is quite plain. Between considering a villainy and performing it there is but a step. But there is little occasion for alarm on my behalf. I have been too cautious; there is not a scrap of evidence against me in existence. I am well viewed by the Government; any story of my defection must be discredited, and any man that bears it must place his own neck in a noose. So do not give it thought. But give thought, I beg of you, to a man who stoops to consider such means of vengeance, and ask yourself whether, being dishonourable, as this proves him, and desperate – more desperate than ever now – he would hesitate to use such means for profit, to extricate himself from his difficulties, to save him from the spunging-house."

Aghast, the Captain looked at Sir John. Then his expression changed; he frowned in perplexity. He was considering something – considering Lord Pauncefort's assertion that his difficulties were less desperate than he had feared. Could this mean, wondered the Captain, that to resolve them he had already taken some such measure as the baronet was suggesting?

"I have made a long tale of it," said Sir John, "that you may judge for yourself whether my warning was well-advised or not."

"I thank you, Sir John," replied the Captain. "Indeed, indeed, I fear me the grounds for your suspicions are most just." Then his face cleared, and he smiled. "Be assured that I shall move with caution – with more than caution, where his lordship is concerned."

And upon that they parted at last, and Sir John rode away, attended by a couple of grooms, to seek his brother who lay ill at Bath.

Chapter 6

THE ENCHANTED GARDEN

Through the grounds of Priory Close a brook winds its course on its way to the Abbey River. It flows in a little ravine, which, moat-like, almost completely encircles a wonderful old garden. You approach it by a path that runs through a plantation of firs on the south side of the mansion.

By this path, through the green shade that was shot here and there by golden sunlight, Captain Gaynor took his idle way on the following morning. It brought him to a rustic bridge, some twenty paces long, spanning the gap at a height of fifteen feet or more above the stream. Over this he sauntered leisurely. He paused midway, and leaning upon the rail, he admired the dense tunnel of foliage formed by the intertwining of the trees that stood on either side of the ravine.

It was a cool, sequestered spot, fragrant with the perfume the sun was drawing from the pines. Somewhere near him throbbed the full-throated song of a thrush; below him was the murmur and babble of the brook as it glided swiftly over the mossy boulders of its bed. Never had the Captain lingered in a spot more peaceful. To his senses it seemed invested with an air almost of enchantment. He could understand that to one dwelling there the world and the affairs of men must shrink to infinitesimal proportions, must seem puny and unworthy, and ambition the emptiest of human bubbles.

He could understand, he thought, Sir John's own lukewarmness towards the Cause. The baronet, no doubt, would judge the country's peace from the ineffable peace of these surroundings, and would tremble at the thought of its being disturbed, at the thought of all the bloodshed and misery that must come ere the upheaval was complete and the erstwhile tranquillity restored.

Captain Gaynor sighed thoughtfully, and went on across that enchanted bridge into the enchanted garden beyond. Through another, lesser plantation on the farther side, over a carpet of pine-needles, he came into the blazing sunlight and a riot of colour, backed by colossal boxwood hedges. These hedges were the garden's pride. It was divided by them into a series of quadrangular courts on his right, and they stood at a height of some ten feet, each with an entrance in the form of an arched gap so narrow that but one person could enter at a time.

On the left of the pathway which he followed, and which ran the garden's full length to the distant redbrown wall, was spread an orchard, all pink and white with blossom, and through the trees in the distance he espied his host's niece and daughter.

They stood near the brook, in a conversation that the Captain might have accounted earnest had not the high, trilling note of Evelyn's laughter reached him across the distance. Thereupon he took his way towards them, never dreaming that he came to interrupt an argument whereof he was himself the subject.

It had sprung from Damaris' desire to make an end of the deceit which had been practised yesterday upon their visitor. She had come to Evelyn that morning with expressions of regret for her own share in it, for having consented to it; she had urged the unworthiness of the thing, the loss of dignity that must attend its ultimate dissipation, especially if this were now delayed.

"Let us tell Captain Gaynor," she ended, "that in jest we permitted him to persist in the error into which of his own accord he fell."

"We can tell him tomorrow or the next day," answered Evelyn airily. "Besides, I do not admit that the error was originally his own. That is the incense you offer to your vanity." And thereupon had trilled out that flute-noted laugh which had caught the sauntering Captain's ears.

A little colour showed in Damaris' cheeks.

"Confess," Evelyn mocked her, "confess now that your concern is reluctance to show yourself without your gilding."

"You are vastly, cruelly unkind, Evelyn," answered Damaris in gentle rebuke, and this answer took her cousin by surprise. For neither Evelyn nor her mother knew of that happening in the library a week ago, knew or guessed of the wound, the deep, cruel wound that Damaris had sustained in her affection and her pride. Damaris was not of those who wring their hands and cry out their wrongs in public or in private. She had kept her chamber for two days upon the pretext of a passing ailment, and in that time she had schooled herself to the dissimulation of her feelings. Contempt had come to her rescue, the coldly fierce contempt that is the offspring of disillusion. She was conscious even of a certain thankfulness that circumstances had vouchsafed her a glimpse of the real man into whose keeping she would so trustingly have delivered up her life, a thankfulness for the timeliness of that revelation. In time, no doubt, this thankfulness would come to be the only abiding feeling so far as my Lord Pauncefort was concerned. But for the present it had not yet come to dominance over her pain and her sense of utter loss.

Desolation and listlessness were her present portion. But of this the unpercipient Evelyn had no suspicion, for Evelyn studied no countenance searchingly save her own.

"Unkind?" quoth Evelyn. "La! In what now am I unkind?"

"In your estimate of me. If Captain – "

A rustle behind her caused her to turn her head, and thus they became aware of the Captain's approach.

Last night he had come to table in a dove-coloured suit and with heavily powdered hair, looking – save for his bronzed face – the very perfect courtier. This morning he had resumed his military exterior.

He wore his laced blue coat, uncompromisingly buttoned from chin to waistband, disdaining the pigeon-breasted mode which left the upper part to gape and reveal a bulging mass of lace and linen. White buckskins and spurred jack-boots encased his legs. He even wore his sword.

Coming up with them he doffed his feathered hat and made a leg with a certain distinct stiffness, craving their leave to bear them company.

It was granted him by Evelyn, with a flutter of eyelids and the demure air of challenge that most men knew in her. And then, with mischievous intent to perpetuate the confusion of identities –

"Then," said the Captain, "pride is well placed for once. I have seen many gardens 'twixt here and far Cathay, but never one in which there dwelt a peace so joyous. Madam," he addressed himself to Damaris, and the serious sincerity of his speech robbed it of any construable impertinence, "your garden repays your pride, for I think that it does justice to its mistress."

The brown eyes of Damaris met his own a moment, as if she were appraising the full value of his words; then they passed on; a faint smile crossed her face, which was of the warm, lustreless pallor of old ivory, and slightly she bowed her head as if in courteous acknowledgment.

Now although her eyes had met his own for but a moment, yet in that fleeting glimpse Captain Gaynor had caught the wistfulness that inhabited them, and something within him had leapt in response to something that was near akin to an appeal. This appeal, he knew, was not to himself; it was to nature, to the world, to heal her of a sorrow or to satisfy a longing, he knew not which. But it touched him and in touching seared him and branded him her servant, to heal or satisfy as her need might be when he should come to understand it, and if so be that she would accept the service that should be hers.

Evelyn had looked on with slightly parted lips, a straining anxiety in her glance, born of fear lest Damaris should there and then repudiate the identity once more thrust upon her. With her cousin's silence and its tacit acknowledgment her anxiety passed, and her rippling, ever-ready laugh expressed her pleasure and relief. Also it served to dissemble her vexation that the first compliment to fall from this somewhat chill and distant soldier's lips should, in spite of all, have been addressed to her cousin.

A more sweet and fragrant picture of maidenhood than Evelyn presented this morning it were not easy to discover. She was arrayed in palest lilac, and her waist, amazingly slender in its firm encasement, sprang from a white furbelow that hung about her lightly as a cloud of vapour. The flimsiest of lace tuckers discreetly veiled the white beauties of neck and bosom, which the low cut bodice must otherwise reveal. Her hair, very carefully massed and curled, was of the colour of ripe corn; her eyes, questing, unrestful and provoking, reflected the flawless sky of June; her cheeks put to shame the apple blossom under which they stood. She was soft and silky and very insistently feminine; the very maid, you would suppose, to compel response in a man so very masculine as the Captain. Yet it was to Damaris that he chiefly addressed himself, upon Damaris that his eyes would linger. She stood a full half-head taller than her cousin, who was small and of an exquisite roundness. She was dressed now for riding, in a brown, high-necked habit laced with gold, than which no raiment could have done more justice to her graceful height, and she wore a looped hat of black beaver, from which a golden feather trailed over, to mingle with her dark brown hair. There was in every line of her something cool, determined and well-knit, as Captain Gaynor noted, for all that it was not his way to note the points of any woman.

Their talk was still of that garden and of other gardens which the Captain in his travels had beheld, to all of which Damaris contributed but little, and that little only when she was, herself, directly addressed.

"I knew," he said, "when I stepped upon that bridge that I was coming at last into the enchanted garden that we have all heard of in our early youth, and of whose real existence the bitter, all-desecrating knowledge of later years has made us sceptical."

"And you have discovered its enchantment?" murmured Evelyn, scenting here the prologue to a speech of gallantry.

"I think I have," he answered, with an amazing seriousness, looking straight ahead. He sighed. "The spell of it is already upon me, I think. Did I unwisely linger I fear that it must overwhelm me utterly."

He was so sober, so solemn, that Damaris glanced at him, her keen ears informing her that behind these words of his lay prepared no such trifling speech as her cousin still expected.

"What is it?" she asked. It was the first time she had spontaneously addressed him, and his glance met hers again, held it a moment, and then, still meeting it, seemed to look beyond and away. Thus may the poet or the fanatic look.

"It is," he said, and his voice sank reverently, "it is that God's peace – God's disregarded, priceless gift to man – is here. Somewhere here, too, is the tree of true knowledge, for its essences hang heavily upon the air. To inhale them is to achieve perception of the true meanness of worldly things, the horror of strife and bloodshed, the contempt of ambition, which is but a euphemism for striving selfishness and vainglory. Who that could dwell here would dwell elsewhere? Who that once has breathed deep of this fragrance would ever again suffer the world's stews to offend his nostrils?"

Evelyn – disappointed Evelyn – laughed on her high note, a little mockingly. "I vow, sir," she minced, "that you are vastly poetical!"

His eye, cold and inscrutable, rested upon her for a moment. He bowed.

"I thank you, Miss Hollinstone," said he, "for having broke the spell. Had it persisted it might well have proved the undoing of a poor soldier."

"What is your regiment, sir?" she asked him. She had something of her mother's inconsequence.

"I have had many; but I have none now," was his reply. "My last commission was in the Sultan's army."

"The Sultan?" cried both girls together, so taken aback were they.

"The Grand Turk," he explained easily. "His cavalry was all disjointed, and I undertook the office of instructing it. Also I saw some service against Venice."

Damaris looked at him with incredulous eyes. "You fought against Christians in the service of the Infidel!" she cried.

"I fought against rogues in the service of rogues, ma'am. That is the pure truth of it. For the rest, it is not the mercenary's to do more than choose the service that offers the best pay."

He saw the scorn gathering in her glance. But he did not know upon what bitter pastures it had been nourished. He did not know that in his own case, it was the sharper because she accounted that she had been mistaken in him a moment ago when he had talked of the garden.

"And do you always," she asked him, "fight for the side that pays you best?"

"By your leave, ma'am, I should account myself a fool to fight for the other."

He had not winced before her cool, appraising eye, nor the half-veiled contempt of her question. He had his part to play – for the sake of that master to whose service was to be yielded up the fruit of all other services. It wounded him – unreasonably, he held – to appear before her in this light. But the necessities demanded it.

"I have made arms my trade," he explained. "I am a soldier of fortune, and in all my seeming inconsistencies of service I have been consistent at least in that I have served Fortune always – more stoutly," he added ruefully, "than Fortune has served me."

"How odd!" sighed Damaris; for his bold frankness had beaten down much of her nascent scorn, yet not quite all. "How very strange!"

"In what is't strange?" quoth Evelyn, as if defending him.

"Strange that men should sacrifice their best for gold, imperil their lives and pawn their very honour for the sake of profit."

"Not all men," said the Captain, with his wry smile. "There is no lack of those who sacrifice all this to dreams and moonshine – the gratitude of princes, the favour of the people, the love of country, immortal renown and other such intangibilities."

"Do you scorn them?" she challenged him.

"As soldiers, yes," he quibbled. "Their ardour detracts from their value, robs them of the proper calm, and I have found that they make but poor opponents to the trained mercenary, who in battle is all calculation and no heat."

"I speak not of that," said Damaris, "but of their aims, of the mainspring of their actions – in short, their loyalty and devotion to the ideal. Do you scorn that, sir?"

He met her glance quite calmly. "No, ma'am, I do not," said he.

"Then," she cried, warmed a little by the argument upon which she was embarked – and the subject was one very near to her poor, wounded heart these days – "then, surely, you must scorn the others, these mere helots."

"Such as myself?" said he, no shadow of offence in tone or voice. "Believe me, did I do so I should change my ways. I think that it is possible to respect both."

Again she measured him with those cool, appraising eyes. She judged him to be good and clean; honest he had already proved himself by the very frankness of his admissions in the face of a scorn that she had scarce attempted to dissemble. She considered his firm mouth and steely eyes, the very poise of his head and uprightness of his carriage, and from it all she gathered intuitively a sense that he was true metal – a man to be relied upon, a man to whom the weak and the oppressed would turn by very instinct, a man who would never hurt the honour of a fellow-man, a man in whom a woman might place her trust.

Because her intuitions showed her all this in him, she desired to understand a point of view that seemed to contradict it all; perhaps she even thought to combat his views, to reveal to him the unworthiness in his aims which was all so clear to her.

"I cannot think," answered she, "I cannot think that respect is due to one who makes a trade of that which should be the expression of profound convictions. Life is surely as sacred a gift as honour, and to

69

adventure it for gold cannot be other than unworthy. If war must be, if men must fight, surely it should be in defence of liberty, of right, of high ideals. Surely there is naught else can justify the risk of life; and to risk life from any other mainspring must be at least a little – base."

She would have added more, but meeting his glance again, seeing him so calm and so entirely unruffled, the ghost of a smile hovering upon his tight lips, she checked. A wave of colour swept across her face. "Forgive me," she begged, "if I have said more than I should. After all, I think I am not so much reproving – to which, indeed, I have no shadow of right – as seeking information."

He laughed gently, on that deep musical note of his. "Indeed, I am relieved," said he. "For I began to fear you lacked for charity in your judgment."

"Indeed, yes," put in Evelyn, who perceived at last a chance of intervention. "And particularly now that you are come to offer your sword to your own country."

"Nay, but that is worse," he exclaimed. "It is to say that I see the error of my ways, and am come to mend them?"

"And is't not so?" she asked.

"Why, no," said he. But it was to Damaris that he seemed to speak. "It is that I lack employment elsewhere."

He found her troubled eyes regarding him with less of scorn than pity now, and it was that glance he answered when he said: "And yet I do not say that if I found a cause that were worth serving for its own sake I should be slow to serve it, perhaps even to my loss."

"I think you would," said Evelyn, those questing, provoking eyes of hers enveloping him in their regard.

He bowed somewhat formally in acknowledgment. "Meanwhile," said he, "I must beware the seduction of this enchanted garden ere its magic prove the undoing of a wandering mercenary."

A liveried groom approached them through the trees, and Evelyn, who was the first to see him, announced his coming, and its object.

"Here is Gibbs, sweet cousin," said she, "to inquire if you will ride the nag you bade him saddle."

She conceived that at last she would be rid of Damaris and would have the Captain entirely to herself. From this you are not to gather that the captain, per se, was of any account to her. He was of account in that he was a male, and so, thought she, a proper person to burn incense on the altar of her little vanity; further he was of account that she might make good upon him her challenge to her cousin – a challenge which at the moment was proving a source of considerable alarm to her.

But it so chanced that the Captain had not come forth in jack-boots and spurs to saunter all the morning in a garden. He too was minded to ride, as he now announced.

"And so, Miss Kynaston," he ended, addressing Damaris, "if you will suffer me to be your escort, you may repay me by acting as my guide over a countryside with which I am unacquainted. You see that in all things I am true to my mercenary's character."

She hesitated a moment, whereupon he bowed submissively, as to a refusal.

"It was presumptuous in me to proffer even for payment a service which I had not first ascertained to be desired," he said. "Ladies, I am your obedient, grateful servant."

He swept them both a bow, and was turning to depart, when Damaris stayed him.

"You are very quick, sir, to suppose me churlish."

Evelyn's eyes were sparkling angrily, and Damaris observed it, but was not deterred. It were a gross discourtesy to a guest to allow him to depart thus. "I shall be glad to ride with you, sir," she smiled, "upon the terms you name."

What time the furious and humiliated Evelyn – for humiliated she felt herself by the turn events were taking – was inveighing to her sympathetic mother against the shameless wiles of Damaris and her brazen conduct towards the other sex, Damaris and the Captain rode through the green lanes of Surrey attended by the groom Gibbs, who followed at a respectful distance.

It proved a fruitful ride for both of them, and for Damaris even more than for him. She drew him into talk of himself, of his travels, the countries he had seen and the many services in which his mercenary's sword had been engaged. And he talked frankly and entertainingly. The absence of that boastfulness of exploits so usual in his kind went far to impress her favourably, confirming much of the judgment of him which already she had formed.

That ride did much to heal the bruises that her gentle heart had taken a week ago. In the Captain's company she seemed to be regaining something of that buoyancy which but yesterday she fancied had left her for all time.

The image of Pauncefort faded in her mind to a proper insignificance. She drew a parallel between him and this man beside her, and she seemed to discover that if once she had set his lordship upon a pedestal and gone near to worshipping him, it was because in the seclusion in which her youth had been passed it had been hers never to meet a real man.

But at the root of all was that foolish compact she had made with Evelyn, which she had so keenly regretted and to which that very morning she had sought to set an end. Had she but done so, how differently must she now be feeling, with what suspicions, with what convictions of unworthy motives in him must she now be regarding the frank and pleasant comradeship of this soldier of fortune; how the regard he had been quick to show her must have but served to increase the bitterness she had been carrying in her heart – a bitterness of which, all being as it was, he was gradually and surely effacing all trace.

She rejoiced now in that compact – rejoiced as only one who had been through her torment of disillusion could rejoice. What matter that its ultimate disclosure must be attended by some loss of dignity? Here was one who was a self-proclaimed mercenary, a man whose life was dedicated to Fortune's service. In such a one the pursuit of the wealthy heiress Damaris Hollinstone was the thing to be expected. How potent then must have been the magnet that had drawn him as completely from her whom he believed to be that person as though she had never been in existence.

The fact is that Captain Gaynor had come into the life of Damaris Hollinstone in an hour of crisis. Coming then, the flattery of his obvious preference and regard, which in another season – whether he believed her to be Damaris or Evelyn – would have been to her a very trifling matter, was now a flattery most sweet and healing.

By the time they reached Priory Close again, Damaris was actually grateful in her heart to Evelyn for the deception that earlier had vexed her. And she was as reluctant now as earlier she had been eager, to set a term to it.

Chapter 7

EVELYN'S CONSCIENCE

It is to be feared that in the week that ensued the real aims of Captain Gaynor's visit to England engaged his attention but indifferently. The spell of the garden was upon him, or else the spell of one of its most constant inhabitants. The brook that wandered through it became to him symbolical of the Lethean waters. Oblivious of past and future, he lived but in the present like any lotus-eater, and if there was a thing to vex him in those brief, happy summer days it was the consideration of the character – truthful in much and in much else untruthful, as we know – in which necessity had demanded that he should appear to Damaris. Yet, when all is said, it did not seem that he must suffer for it at her hands; notwithstanding her betrayal of scorn when he had first divulged it to her, yet he observed that she did not on that account avoid him. But he was not to know that it was on that very account that his society was welcome and that she admitted him to her confidence.

Meanwhile the deception on the score of identities continued to be practised upon him, though more than once it had gone very near to shipwreck at the hands of servants and in other almost inevitable ways. But it was Evelyn who steered it clear in every shallow, compelled to it for all the reluctance and vexation that had now come upon her. For she found the tables most ludicrously turned.

Supported by her mother, she had taxed Damaris with unmaidenliness of conduct when on the second morning of the Captain's visit her cousin had made her appearance dressed again for riding.

Quite calmly had Damaris stood to listen to Evelyn's denunciation. She had wasted upon it no shadow of indignation. Conscious in her own mind that her conduct was above criticism, conscious no less of the true mainsprings of the criticism that was offered, she received it with the contempt it merited, met it with a bantering defiance that revealed how swiftly now she was recovering her habitual spirit.

"Why, Evelyn," she protested, "I am doing no more than you have forced upon me."

"Forced upon you? I?" cried Evelyn, round eyes staring.

"Did you not insist that you would be Damaris Hollinstone and that I should be Evelyn Kynaston? As the supposed daughter of his host, the Captain has a right to look for certain attentions from me in my father's absence. To withhold them were to be neglectful of the common duties of hospitality, and I would not be that for Sir John's sake."

"Why, that is true now," purred Lady Kynaston. "Yes, that is very true. I have always said that hospitality is the duty of an English lady."

Evelyn almost choked with anger. "I think," said she, "that the sooner we resume our proper identities the better will it be."

Alarm leapt in the soul of Damaris – this Damaris who had been so reluctant to lend herself to the duplicity, who had considered it unworthy and undignified. But her face remained calm, her eyes even smiled.

" 'Tis what I have always held, and I am glad that at last you agree with me. I shall leave you, then, to enlighten the Captain."

"Why not enlighten him yourself?"

"Because I am sure it will become you better. Let us consider now what you shall say. You will tell him that misliking such admiration as you have observed bestowed upon your cousin Damaris, but being persuaded that this was a tribute entirely to her fortune, you induced her to – "

"Am I mad, d'ye think?" cried Evelyn, with an angry stamp of her satin-clad foot.

"Well, then, say what you please; but be very sure that such is the construction which he must place upon anything that you tell him. There is not room for any other."

"I think you wish the deception to continue," Evelyn announced.

"I am indifferent," answered Damaris. "You have forced me into a part, and I must play it until you relieve me of it again. Throughout I have been entirely passive. Never so much as once have I addressed you as 'Damaris' to aid the deception."

"What deceit!" exclaimed the scandalised Evelyn. "What unworthy quibbles! You have aided it by your silence."

"So much I admit, and by your leave, Evelyn, my dear, I will continue in silence."

"From the first I disapproved of it," sighed Lady Kynaston. "You see in what a difficulty it has placed you."

"I understand," said Evelyn slowly. Her cheeks were burning, as were her eyes. "Oh, I understand you!"

"I gravely doubt it," answered Damaris.

But Evelyn laughed her confidence and her scorn. Judging all women's natures by her own, conceiving that the admiration shown by the other sex must be the mainspring of every woman's being as it was of hers, she fancied that she held the explanation of her cousin's indifference on the score of the revelation to be made. Damaris, having won the Captain's regard in the character of Evelyn Kynaston, was confident of holding it still more securely as Miss Hollinstone the heiress. Thus Evelyn judged, and judging thus her anger increased. It increased further at the reflection that there was no way out of the situation she had herself created save that which Damaris indicated. She even exaggerated the matter, for she was not true-sighted. In no way, she thought, could the explanation, when it came, be hurtful or humiliating to Damaris; but it might, it must be humiliating to herself. Finding that the weapons she had hitherto employed were shivered in her hands, she turned to snatch fresh and more formidable ones.

"You are forgetting Lord Pauncefort," she said tartly.

"I am endeavouring to do so," Damaris admitted, though in a fuller sense.

Evelyn stared. "You confess it!" she exclaimed. "Mother, you hear her! Oh, never could I have believed you so shameless, Damaris, so lost to all sense of what you owe yourself. Never!"

"I am glad you should have held me in such high esteem," was the smiling answer. And then, suddenly realising the pettiness of this battle, the unworthiness of it, her manner changed and she advanced towards Evelyn with hands outheld. "Come, Evelyn dear, let us call a truce," she besought her cousin.

"A truce?" echoed Evelyn. "A truce to what, pray?"

"To foolish, bitter words and unfriendly glances."

"Cease, then, to deserve them," was the ungracious answer.

A wan little smile crept into Damaris' face, her patience inexhaustible. She turned to her aunt.

"Mother dear," she besought her, "can you not move her to a gentler mood?"

"She means you well, dear Damaris," was Lady Kynaston's answer. "Hence her concern for you. I must confess that I do not think you show a proper regard for your betrothal to Lord Pauncefort. He would not be pleased did he know how you receive Captain Gaynor's assiduous attentions."

"How she receives them!" Evelyn apostrophised the ceiling. "O la!"

"My betrothal to Lord Pauncefort – " Damaris began, and there she checked. She could not submit herself to all the examination which her announcement must provoke; she could not suffer to parade before Evelyn's eyes the shame that in secret she had endured, the humiliation she had borne. Since yesterday that shame had been diminished, the humiliation fading. But these feelings were strong again within her now that she came to the point of alluding to them. Therefore she paused. "Heigho!" she sighed, with a rueful smile. And upon that she moved leisurely towards the door.

"Do you intend to ride daily with Captain Gaynor?" her cousin flung after her.

"You mistake, Evelyn," came the soft answer. "It is not a question of what I intend, nor have I any intentions in the matter. But should Captain Gaynor desire to ride daily, as the daughter of his host I am under the necessity of showing him some attention in my father's absence. Blame none but yourself for this if you do not find it meet with your approval." And upon that she took her departure, leaving Evelyn in a mood of which her poor mother was to appreciate the bitterness.

Saving for similar daily scenes, that week to Damaris was as happy a season as it was to Harry Gaynor. Ere it was sped, the desolation left in her soul by Lord Pauncefort's self-revelation was changed to a glad thankfulness.

From Sir John in Bath came letters to announce that his brother's condition, although still critical, was hopeful, and that soon he trusted to be able to return. For Captain Gaynor came a brief special note, in which the baronet gracefully regretted his continued absence at such a season and closed with a veiled reminder of his warning touching Pauncefort – a warning which roused the soldier from the dream in which he had been living to a consciousness of the perils that surrounded him, for the morrow was the day appointed for that fateful meeting at "The World's End."

So when the morrow came – it was a Thursday, completing the little cycle of a week since his advent at Priory Close – he announced to the ladies that he must ride to town that afternoon; that he desired to see the Second Secretary and spur his memory on the matter that lay between them.

"Your idleness, no doubt, is fretting you, sir," said Evelyn.

"And you must find life very dull in this quiet corner of the world," her mother added as a corollary.

"Not dull, ma'am, but too happy," he replied. "I dare not forget that sooner or later other things – of a vastly different quality – await me."

Damaris said nothing. As she sipped her chocolate her mind lost itself in the mazes of a dream. She was wondering whether it was the mercenary's nature to rest contentedly, to abandon the adventurous life for one of peace. If it were not – Ah, if it were not – That was a thought she dared not pursue. She feared; her soul faltered when she had got thus far, and there she halted, content to wait.

That morning she rode forth alone – save for her groom – for the first time since the Captain's coming. An appalling loneliness – a loneliness that was full of amazing and disquieting self-revelation – kept her company.

She thought of Pauncefort that morning, and she thought of him with kindness. She owed him a debt, she discovered. For without the lesson that she had received at his lordship's hands she would never have come by so swift a knowledge of the sterling qualities of her Captain – this mercenary who moved adventurously without ideals and whom she had begun by despising for his avowed pursuit of fortune.

She saw Captain Gaynor again at dinner – they dined at three o'clock at Priory Close, too early by at least an hour to satisfy the mode. And from her window, discreetly hidden, she watched him ride out on his great black horse, watched his blue-coated figure along the white ribbon of road until it vanished, and so left her lonely again.

And whilst she sat alone in her chamber there, below stairs Evelyn was spurring her mother to perform what Evelyn conceived to be her mother's duty in the absence of Sir John.

"You must write to his lordship, mother," she was saying, "and inform him of what is taking place."

"Nay, now, but what is taking place?" quoth her mother querulously. She had a distaste for being drawn into situations that might afterwards require to be eased by explanation.

Evelyn shrugged impatiently. Those hungry, questing eyes of hers were very angry. "Do you need to ask me, mother?"

"Let us await your father's return, child," the mother pleaded. "He will know best. And meanwhile the Captain has gone."

"But he will return tomorrow."

"How do you know that? He may be given this appointment he is seeking, and so may return no more."

Evelyn smiled, contemptuous in her assurance that there existed at Priory Close a magnet to draw him back in spite of anything that might betide.

"Then I will write myself."

"Evelyn, I forbid you."

"My father is absent, and my mother will not use her eyes. What help have I? I hope I have a conscience. It is for Damaris' sake. What, after all, do we know of this adventurer?"

"Nay, now, you must not speak so of him," her ladyship remonstrated. "His father was your father's dearest friend. Your father loves the Captain as a son."

Evelyn looked at her mother a moment. Then she turned away and went without another word to write the following letter:

MY LORD, – My great regard for your lordship bids me delay no longer in writing to tell you that if you would not see that which you most value lost to you, you had best make haste to come to Priory Close. There is one here who is very like to steal away from you that which you cherish most in all the world. I send you this timely warning,

EVELYN KYNASTON.

Having written, Evelyn paused. Within her a voice – a little mocking voice – was proclaiming that what she performed was an act of purest spite. She crimsoned and took up the sheet to tear it across. Then she paused.

"I am too sensitive," she assured herself. "Clearly it is my duty, since my mother will not. Damaris' future happiness depends on't." Which, after all, was very true.

But it was not until next morning that the letter sped to London by her messenger.

Chapter 8

AT "THE WORLD'S END"

Standing on the outskirts of the pleasant village of Chelsea, as one of London's western outposts, "The World's End" was a house of great comings and goings, of much bustle and consequence. Hence had it been preferred by Captain Gaynor to any quieter hostelry for the business which he desired to transact. In the constant ebb and flow of travellers to and from the Metropolis there was but little chance that any particular man or group of men would attract more than passing notice. Moreover, Maclean, its Scottish landlord, was a circumspect but ardent Jacobite, and the house had yet the additional advantage of being – both on the score of its remoteness and of its traffic – a most unlikely place for such a meeting.

It stood a little way back from the King's Road – which runs from St James's to Hampton Court – fronted by a patch of turf on which were planted a couple of trestle-tables flanked by plain wooden forms, and it looked out over a stretch of meadowland that sloped gently to the river.

Before its doors on this June evening the wonted bustle was toward. A great black and yellow stagecoach on its way to London was drawn up on the very edge of the patch of turf, and the hoarse-voiced driver passed the time of the day with the ostler in terms which knew little of decorum and less of dainty ears. A nobleman's travelling chaise, a sombre mass of wood and leather drawn by six horses and with bold escutcheons on its panels, stood cheek by jowl with the stage, but facing westward.

About these was a huddle of lesser craft, a post-chaise, a couple of hackney coaches, a carrier's cart, and lastly, stretching adown the road in line like the tail of a kite, some half-dozen waggons on their way to market for the following day. To increase the general bustle and to swell the throng there were men on horseback and men on foot, watermen from the moored barges and wherries, grooms, ostlers, drivers and waggoners, whilst a motley company derived from all of these sat about the trestle-tables over their ale, a noisy, babbling, quarrelling, laughing assembly.

Into this scene of activity rode Captain Gaynor at a little after eight o'clock of that summer evening – the hour appointed for the meeting of those six confederates who were to receive from him and in their turn disseminate those messages of which he was the bearer and of which he carried upon him a note in cipher. The substance of those messages has not survived, and there are no means today of ascertaining the details of the precise plot that was the object of this particular mission of Captain Gaynor. Whilst regrettable from the point of view of historical research, from our own it is a matter of little moment, since we are here concerned with the personal history of Captain Gaynor and not with that of any of the perennially budding Jacobite conspiracies.

We gather from stray records that have come down to us – and more particularly from the bulky memoirs which were penned by Mr Second Secretary Templeton to while the tedium of his subsequent retirement from office – that this was one of the earlier of those conspiracies which ultimately were to prove the undoing of that ambitious, plotting cleric, Atterbury; for we are able very plainly to trace that this mission of the notorious Jacobite agent, "Captain Jenkyn" – who was hanged at Tyburn under the extraordinary circumstances with which we are directly concerned – was undertaken at the Bishop's urgent instances.

To receive Captain Gaynor, as he drew rein on the outskirts of that throng, came a shock-headed, sweating, surpliced ostler, who was thrust aside almost immediately by a younger man. That the ostler submitted without demur showed that the youth who usurped his functions on this occasion was a person of some authority, as did indeed the latter's garments which, though of plain homespun, indicated a station superior to a groom's. He was, in fact, Maclean's son, set by the vintner to watch for the Captain's coming.

Harry Gaynor tossed his reins to the youngster, and swung himself lightly from the saddle.

"I stay but a little while," he said, "so keep my nag saddled for me."

With that he pushed forward through the throng about the door, a throng which before his brisk, authoritative manner opened a way for him readily enough. He strode into a narrow, flagged passage upon which the taproom door stood open. From this issued sounds of voices and a reek of tobacco. Under the lintel leaned a tall, loose-limbed man in his shirt-sleeves with an apron girt about him. He turned at the sound of the Captain's steps, and disclosed the mellow, jovial face of Maclean.

His eyes welcomed the guest, and the Captain's returned that welcome. It was as if they had clasped hands. With the other Jacobites who were assembled above stairs there had been question and answer on the score of wants to veil the giving of password and countersign. But Captain Gaynor was known to the vintner.

"Ha, landlord!" quoth the soldier, after that real greeting of the eyes. "A pint of claret laced with Nantes!"

"At once, your Honour," replied Maclean, in formal landlord's tones.

The Captain stood halting upon the threshold of the taproom.

"Ye're somewhat crowded here," he said, and coughed as if the smoke had jarred his windpipe.

"There is another room above," Maclean replied, approving the Captain's easy acting. "Will you be pleased to go up, sir?"

The soldier turned and made for the stairs. "The first door to the right, your Honour," Maclean called after him. "I'll bring the claret." He coughed significantly, and Captain Gaynor, turning as he went up, caught from the host's quick, expressive gestures that the door he was to take was on the left instead. He nodded his understanding, and went on. He knew the chamber from another visit some two years ago. It was peculiarly well fitted for a secret meeting in such a place, access being gained to it across another room, through a door that looked for all the world like that of a cupboard in the wall.

But as he went he was puzzled by the almost excessive caution which the landlord had shown, by the loud announcement that the door was on the right followed by a correcting gesture. Maclean, the Captain reflected, must have some good reason for this, some notion that there was a spy at hand.

Such a notion Maclean had, indeed, and his suspicions on that score were almost immediately changed to certainty. For as he turned he found himself confronted in the doorway of the taproom by the very object of his suspicions – a burly fellow in snuff-coloured clothes, in whom he had sniffed a Bow Street messenger. This man had sat apart, unobtrusive, in a corner of the taproom whence he could command the passage, and for all his unobtrusiveness – or, perhaps, because of it – Maclean had furtively watched him with increasing mistrust. He had taken care when Captain Gaynor entered so to place himself before the soldier as to screen him from the prying eyes of that suspected spy. And it was the intention of misleading that same watcher that he had uttered aloud his misdirection.

Confronted now by the man, and his every suspicion thus confirmed, Maclean, affecting to await the fellow's commands, effectively barred his way until it should be too late for him to perceive the real direction taken by the Captain.

"What d'ye lack, sir?" was his formal question, smiling his anxiety to supply the needs of this guest – and in that smile dissembling the greater anxiety which this guest occasioned him.

The fellow coughed affectedly. "This reek of tobacco smoke," said he, "is more than I can suffer. I'll go upstairs to this other room of yours."

Maclean made way with a bow and a readiness that were entirely disarming.

"Pray do so," said he, and waved a hand towards the stairs. "The room is on the right. You'll find some company there. I'll send a drawer to wait on you."

The burly spy – for a spy he was, and moreover had a warrant in his pocket and six men at his orders outside at the trestle-tables – felt himself checked by the landlord's ease and the readiness with which the way was opened for him. Maclean was a born conspirator, a man who knew how a plot should be laid if it were to baffle discovery. To mask that meeting above stairs against precisely such a contingency as the present one, he had placed a room above at the disposal of such of his guests as appeared to be persons of quality, and it was into this room that the spy now thrust himself, notwithstanding the loss of confidence occasioned him by the landlord's imperturbability.

He found himself in the company of some dozen gentlemen who eyed him somewhat askance, a circumstance which reawakened fading suspicions. The assembly was, it is true, rather more numerous than he had been led to look for, and he observed that it was broken into detached groups of twos and threes. These, surely, could not be his quarry. Yet, being a man so suspicious of ruses that he saw ruses where none existed, considered innocence itself the most damning mark of guilt, the messenger sat down in a corner, and, when presently approached by a drawer, ordered himself a nipperkin of ale. But the scrutiny to which he furtively submitted each separate group and each member of it gradually convinced him that either he had been deliberately led or else was fallen into error. This conviction was complete when anon the door opened to admit a couple of fresh arrivals, the first of whom was a portly, pompous man in a full-bottomed wig, in whom the messenger recognised Sir Henry Thresh, one of the Middlesex justices.

Meanwhile Captain Gaynor had crossed the empty room on the left of the passage, and through that deceptive narrow double-door had entered the farther apartment, where his friends awaited him.

This was a small chamber facing westward and flooded now with the roseate glow of sunset. It was very plainly furnished, and about a polished, oblong walnut table in mid-apartment sat four gentlemen over their wine. A crystal bowl of water – inevitable appendage to every Jacobite gathering – occupied the middle of the board and shed upon it a wedge of prismatic light. Near this pipes had been placed, a tinder-box and a leaden jar of cut tobacco; but only one member of the company – an extremely tall and slender young man, very fine in a green riding-suit with white satin linings – was smoking. This gentleman had dark, vivacious eyes and a pleasant face under an extremely modish and ample periwig; his name was Partridge, and he was said to be a person of considerable importance in Wiltshire.

Of the other three, two were men of forty or thereabouts. One was Viscount Harewood, a gentleman with whom allegiance to the Stuarts was a family matter, since he claimed the patriarchal second Charles for his grandsire. Indeed, some resemblance to that too-merry monarch was to be discerned in his lordship's swarthy tint and saturnine cast of countenance; the other was Mr Stephen Dyke, a pale, hawk-faced man in a brown bag-wig. The last member of that quartette was the staunch and almost brazen Jacobite, Sir Thomas Leigh. He was much older than his companions, very tall and straight nevertheless, with something military in his air and carriage, and something military, too, in the vigorous oaths with which his speech was peppered, for he had seen service in the late queen's days. In countenance he was fresh-complexioned, frank and jovial.

They rose to welcome Captain Gaynor, who came a full quarter of an hour behind the time appointed for the meeting; yet, as he perceived, he was not the last to arrive. Lord Pauncefort and an Irish man named O'Neill were still awaited. He made his excuses and sat down to await with them their missing confederates, giving them meanwhile such news as they sought, until they were interrupted by the entrance of Maclean with the Captain's claret.

Having set down the jug and glass, the vintner leaned a hand upon the table, and addressing himself more particularly to Captain

Gaynor, he gravely announced the presence in the house of one whom he suspected of being a spy.

They listened in consternation and in silence, with the exception of old Sir Thomas, who let fly a volley of sulphuric oaths which no one heeded.

"What do you counsel us to do, Maclean?" was Captain Gaynor's quiet question.

"Why, do the business upon which you are come, gentlemen. The rogue is safe bestowed for the present, watching the guests in another room across the passage. I had disposed against any such surprise as this. And, after all," he ended, "it is not impossible that he is after other quarry than yourselves. Still, I thought it well to set you on your guard."

He withdrew upon that, leaving relief behind him; for all but one accepted as certain the supposition that the Bow Street messenger might be on the spoor of other game.

"It must be so, egad!" cried Harewood. "Else were we betrayed, and that is not possible."

"Not possible, indeed," agreed Sir Thomas. "The fellow will be some thief-taker on the trail of a tobyman belike. Maclean starts at shadows."

But Captain Gaynor did not share their confidence. Pauncefort's absence fretted him. The mistrust implanted in his breast by Sir John Kynaston and what he had learnt from him was stirring uneasily now.

"I wonder where the plague these others tarry," he muttered, and then almost immediately to answer him the door opened and O'Neill reeled into the room.

There is no other way in which to describe his entrance. He was a red-headed youngster, whose face was usually florid and mischievously good-humoured. It was of a deathly pallor now, and clammy; his blue eyes were a thought wild. His boots were white with dust, and all about him there was an air of haste, disorder and alarm.

His advent brought the others to their feet. Questions rained upon him on the score of his condition.

He sank to a chair, snatched up a glass of Nantes that belonged to Sir Thomas, and unceremoniously drained it. Then he explained himself quite tersely.

"The game is up, gentlemen." He rolled his eyes about the company that stood above him. " 'Tis betrayed we are; undone entirely."

There fell a pause, all eyes upon this bearer of ill tidings. Then Lord Harewood fired a question.

"By whom?" quoth he, so fiercely that had the betrayer heard him he must have looked to his skin.

"I don't know," was the answer, "and faith 'tis the only thing I don't know. We've been sold – devil a doubt of that, and 'tis a miracle I am here to tell you of it. Clinton, Brownrigg, Holmdale, Spencer Gamlin and Sir Vernon Bewick have been arrested today upon warrants. Other arrests are to follow – yours, Harewood, and yours, Sir Thomas."

"Let them arrest me and be damned to them," said the stalwart veteran. "What else?"

"There's a warrant for myself too, bedad, and you may be thankful for't, as otherwise I should never have had any warning at all."

Came a fresh volley of questions, quelled at last by Captain Gaynor. He spoke for the first time since O'Neill's arrival.

"Shall we discuss this matter calmly, gentlemen," said he. "Thus shall we make the better speed, and time may be of more consequence than we deem. Will you be seated?"

He spoke in a crisp voice of authority. Outwardly he was the calmest – indeed, the only calm – man in that room. He was instantly obeyed. They realised that in this extremity a leader was needed, and the natural leader, as much by the position which his mission gave him as by his natural endowments, was Captain Gaynor. They sat down at once, and the Captain sat down with them.

He was familiar with desperate situations, and he had been too long an actor to permit himself now to be surprised into a betrayal of his true feelings. And so he remained outwardly as unmoved as if the thing before them were but of trifling import. Inwardly his soul sickened. Years of planning were overthrown thus at a blow. All was to do again, it seemed; and heaven alone knew whether he would live to be in at the ultimate victory which he was assured God must accord the right. Yet nothing of this showed in his countenance. If it was stern and singularly hard, it had all the calm that goes with hardness.

He took up one of the long-stemmed pipes, and began deliberately to fill it from the leaden jar.

"Firstly," he said, his voice very quiet and even, "will you tell us, Mr O'Neill, how you come by your knowledge?"

"I have it," answered O'Neill at once, leaning forward across the table, "from my cousin, Jocelyn Butler, who is my Lord Carteret's private secretary. 'Twas his own hand prepared the warrants by my lord's directions, and had not my own been among the names we should never have had this warning. As it was, Jocelyn came to me soon after six this evening, as I was on the point of setting out – in fact, 'tis what delayed me. At first he told me no more than there was a warrant out for my arrest on a charge of conspiring against the peace of the realm, and urged me to take horse and begone at once. But I swore I wouldn't stir a foot until he had told me all there was to't.

"He demurred awhile, but bethinking him that 'twill be the talk of the town by morning, and that as most of the arrests were made already 'twas little he'ld be betrayin', he spoke out, and told me all he knew, or leastways all that I asked him, and I asked him all that mattered. Thereupon I rode hither as fast as horse could bring me, for amongst other things my cousin told me that the messengers from Bow Street were on their way hither to surprise a meeting of plotters."

There was a stir about the table.

"Ah!" said Captain Gaynor. "That, too, was known, then, eh?" He reached for the tinder-box as he spoke.

"Faith, yes. But glory be to heaven, I've arrived ahead of them."

" 'Sblud! But ye've not," roared Sir Thomas Leigh, and hubbub broke out afresh, through which O'Neill listened in increasing alarm to the announcement that one of the messengers was here already.

"And what's to be done, then?" he cried.

"That we will now consider," said the Captain, and by the very tone of his voice restored order about the table. He struck steel against flint, and having kindled a flame applied it to his pipe. Then "You did not learn," he inquired, "whether Lord Pauncefort had been arrested?"

"I learnt that he had not."

"But a warrant will have been issued for him, of course?"

"Not so. I asked that, too, and I was relieved to learn that he, at least, has been overlooked."

"Overlooked? How very fortunate," said Captain Gaynor, with the faintest note of irony. Sir John Kynaston's warning was humming now in his mind. "This being so, can any here suggest why my Lord Pauncefort is not with us?"

A hush followed that significant question, broken at last by Harewood, who was Pauncefort's friend.

"Now, sink me, Captain Gaynor, what is't you mean by that?" And his swarthy face was flushed by sudden anger.

"Before I answer you, my lord," said the soldier, maintaining his outward calm, "let me ask you all a question. Has any one of you mentioned to a living soul that we were to assemble here tonight? If any has, I entreat him to speak frankly now in the interests of us all."

Followed a little spell of silence; then from one and another broke firm and sturdy denials.

"I will remind you, then," said the Captain, "that no living man knew of this meeting save those who were to assemble – ourselves present, and one other who is absent."

"There is yet one other – Maclean," Mr Partridge reminded the Captain.

"Ay!" roared Harewood. "What of Maclean?"

Gaynor's smile and a little gesture with the fingers that held his pipe brushed aside the question as frivolous.

"Maclean did not know the names of those who were to assemble, and you will bear in mind that Mr O'Neill has told us that the warrants are out with those names set forth. Maclean could not have possessed such knowledge. Nor yet, had he possessed it, could he have betrayed it without running his own neck into a noose, and there is still the further trifling matter in his favour that 'twas he, himself, brought us word of the presence of the messenger.

"You must see, sirs, that there is but one person could have betrayed us to this extent; his absence more than confirms the suspicion – a suspicion which amounts to certainty with me. And I am not a man to form hasty judgments. I will further remind you that my Lord Pauncefort is a gamester, broken and desperate, and – I do not suggest, I state, and I will maintain my statement wherever and whenever opportunity is afforded me – he has taken this dastardly course to mend his shattered fortunes. In a word, gentlemen, he has sold us; and I make no doubt that he has obtained a handsome price from the Secretary of State for his Judas services."

Harewood got angrily to his feet. "By God!" he swore. "I'll not hear a man thus abused in his absence!"

"You shall not find me slow to accuse him to his face," said the Captain. "The opportunity of that, I think, is all that I can now ask of Fortune."

Harewood looked round with glaring eyes, in appeal to the others to repudiate this hideous charge against his friend; but on every face he saw conviction written. The thing was all too plain. The viscount felt that conviction being borne in upon his very self, yet loyally he sought to hold it off.

"I'll not believe it! Sink me, I'll not believe it!" he exclaimed, although his voice almost broke on the words.

"The decision," said the Captain, "does your heart more credit than your judgment. Yet, my lord, lest you or any here should think that I judge rashly, let me add something that is known to me – something that I confess has spurred me on to this conclusion." And briefly he informed the company of the threat which Pauncefort had uttered to Sir John Kynaston. "Now," he concluded, "I hold that in such a matter there is no ground for thinking that the man who is so lost to honour as to threaten will hesitate to perform."

Convinced, Harewood sat down and took his head in his hands. "He was my friend," he said in a dull voice.

Smoking quietly, Captain Gaynor turned again to O'Neill. "You have not said that there is a warrant out for me."

"I was coming to't," was the answer, and the Irishman's face quickened with excitement. "There is and there is not."

"How?" Gaynor looked at him with knitting brows.

"There is a warrant issued for Captain Jenkyn," was the explanation, "and it is expected that he will be taken here with the rest of us."

The soldier stiffened visibly. Here was the last ounce of proof against Pauncefort. For but two men in England knew of his identity with the bearer of that sobriquet – his lordship and Sir John Kynaston. Not even these gentlemen gathered here together had hitherto suspected it. At the announcement now there was an outcry, dominated by Leigh's outflung hand and thundered monosyllable –

"You!"

The Captain smiled at them, and slowly, deprecatingly, shook his head.

"Sirs," he said, "you cannot really think that Captain Jenkyn is any particular individual. Rather, I think, is it a title conferred by the Government to fit any Jacobite agent who visits England. On this occasion, from what O'Neill tells us, it would seem they thrust the honour upon me. But," and he turned again to the Irishman, "I am not specified by name in the warrant?"

"By no other name – no."

"That is very odd."

"Ay," returned O'Neill, "until we have the explanation, which is still more odd, bedad. You were specifically accused to the Secretary of State. But when he desired Mr Templeton to issue a warrant in due form, Mr Templeton urged that there was some mistake – that his lordship's informer was perforce in error; that Captain Harry Gaynor was no Jacobite but a soldier of fortune whose entire record and whose credentials were in his hands, a man who had no sympathy with the Stuart Cause and who had been recommended to him by his own cousin, Tollemache Templeton, an old friend of your own.

"Lord Carteret, it seems, sought to combat Mr Templeton's confidence; but the Second Secretary is an obstinate man who claims that he is never at fault. He laid Captain Gaynor's credentials before Lord Carteret, and when his lordship suggested that such documents could be forged, Mr Templeton took coach and visited the embassies of two of the governments from which certain of those credentials proceeded."

"What embassies?" quoth the Captain, his eyes preternaturally bright.

"The Austrian and the Turkish."

The Captain sighed his instant relief from that sudden tension. He even smiled as the Irishman continued: "Mr Templeton was assured at both that the documents presented were entirely genuine. The Turkish ambassador, indeed, claimed a personal acquaintance with Captain Gaynor made in Constantinople four years ago, and spoke, I am informed, in terms of high praise of you to the Second Secretary. With this information Mr Templeton returned to Lord Carteret, and boldly informed his lordship that he would resign his office ere he made himself the laughing-stock of the town by issuing a warrant against a gentleman so unimpeachable and accredited. This, sir, in my cousin's own presence. My Lord Carteret was swayed by that assurance; he bowed before it to the extent of consenting that the warrant should be made out for 'Captain Jenkyn' – whose identity, he was informed, was one with your own. To this Mr Templeton made no objection, confident that the result must prove the correctness of his own and the error of his lordship's information."

"It is a confidence," said the Captain, smiling, "in which we must see to't that Mr Templeton is encouraged." It gratified him to observe the good fruit borne by the thoroughness of his dispositions, and he was thankful for it in this extremity.

"And how is that to be accomplished now?" quoth Mr Dyke from the other end of the table.

The Captain smoked in silence an instant. Then he removed the pipe from his lips, and spoke.

"Let us for a moment consider our position. I do not think that it is one that need cause us any undue alarm."

"Do you not, by God!" growled old Sir Thomas. "Then, you're monstrous slow at taking alarm, sir."

"When you have heard me perhaps you will abate your own," the soldier answered him, and with that proceeded: "If, gentlemen, you have been properly cautious, you should not now stand in any grave peril." He was thinking swiftly, speaking almost as he thought. "These arrests are premature. In a month's time they might have occasioned concern. As it is, what can be proved against any man of you?

"Return then quietly to your homes, and pursue your avocations. Should you be arrested, suffer it in patience, and in the conviction that your liberty must very speedily be restored to you. It would not surprise me," he continued, "if this prematureness were deliberate. It is Lord Carteret's policy to stifle our work at its very source, and to strike terror into our leaders by a display of the Government's omniscience rather than allow any treason to spread to punishable lengths. It is devilish shrewd of him, for he knows that martyrs to a cause beget sympathy for that cause, and ten emulators for every one that falls. Therefore, he does not desire martyrs. Should you be arrested the matter will probably end in a private admonition from Lord Carteret to each of you ere you are restored to liberty. That, sirs, I think, is the position."

His calm, so admirably dissembling his own inward despair – fell like a balm upon those five disordered minds.

But Sir Thomas Leigh found an objection to his reasoning.

"You do not overlook, I trust, that our betrayal proceeds from within?"

"I do not, Sir Thomas. But it would be unreasonable to suppose that our ranks have yielded more than one traitor, and the word of one man alone – actuated, no doubt, from motives of self-interest – whilst serving the ends of Lord Carteret to damp us with terror of his omniscience, as I have said, is very far from sufficing to produce the conviction of any who does not betray himself.

"You are further to remember that it is in the last degree unlikely that our betrayer will come forward to accuse us. That, indeed, would be a foolish procedure on every count. Pauncefort must have made it a condition of his bargain with the Government that he shall remain in the background, and the Government itself must have desired this, for once the informer were proclaimed his value would be at an end – and a man in Pauncefort's position is of very great value, so great that the Government may well desire to retain his services for the future – that is, assuming that Pauncefort is to live. But I think we owe it to ourselves in this case to make assurance doubly sure."

His voice rang with so sinister a note that all eyes were turned to search his countenance. It was hard now to the point of cruelty.

"It should, I think, be a point of expediency and honour with any who is so fortunate as to escape the trap laid for us here tonight to seek out my Lord Pauncefort, and – " A swift, trenchant gesture with the pipe-stem completed his meaning.

There was a gasp from Mr Partridge; dismay was written, too, upon the face of Harewood.

"We are not children, sirs," said the Captain in a rasping voice, "and our game is not a child's game. When a man betrays us we have a duty to discharge to ourselves, to one another and to the Cause we serve. For a traitor there is but one punishment all the world over. That punishment Lord Pauncefort has incurred, and I, for one, pray heaven that I may be spared long enough from the clutches of the law to administer it myself. So would I have each of you think."

The white hawk-face of Mr Dyke looked singularly vicious as he swore what he would do, given the opportunity, and he was followed instantly by O'Neill and old Sir Thomas.

"One risk, however, we do run, sirs, in spite of what I have said," the Captain resumed, "and it is somewhat serious – the risk of my being taken in your company. If I am so taken the identity of Captain Jenkyn is established and attached to Harry Gaynor, and Mr Templeton is proven wrong in his assurance. Whatever happen to the rest, for Captain Jenkyn there will be no mercy; he will receive the very shortest shrift.

"If, then, I am taken in your company, I am destroyed by being found with you, as was promised by our betrayer; and similarly you may suffer grievously for being found with me. Our chief danger, then, lies there. If you are taken without me, your danger is reduced to insignificant proportions, as I have said. If I am taken anywhere but here, my own risk also is lessened to vanishing-point."

Their agreement with this reasoning was immediate and unanimous.

"And therefore," added Mr Dyke, "it is of the first importance that we should be rid of you and you of us."

"Precisely," the Captain agreed. "All that remains to be determined is how we shall achieve that most desirable consummation; and the means, I confess, do not seem quite ready to our hands. Can any of you propose a course?"

"Where the devil is that rascal Maclean?" roared Sir Thomas.

" 'Tis what I've been wonderin' myself," said O'Neill, "for savin' the brandy I've filched from you, Sir Thomas, 'tis devil a thought has been bestowed upon my thirst."

"Is there no safe way of calling him?" quoth Partridge.

"No way that is not fraught with danger in a house that is watched," said the thoughtful Mr Dyke. "If he has left us alone 'tis a sign he is convinced we are besieged and fears to come to us lest he should show the way to others."

And then, at last, the door opened, and Maclean himself came in. He was rather breathless, and his broad face had lost much of its habitual florid tint.

Chapter 9

THE ALIBI

Twice before had Maclean attempted to repair to the conspirators, but each time prudence had compelled him to abandon the attempt. On the first occasion he was crossing the outer room when he heard the door open softly behind him, and, looking over his shoulder, found himself observed by the spy.

He betrayed no uneasiness, but affecting to continue on his way, reached the overmantel and took thence a couple of candle branches, with which he returned.

The face of the Bow Street messenger betrayed the extent to which he was intrigued. He had been on the watch, and observing Maclean's cautious approach he had inferred from it that at last he was to be put upon the trail of his quarry. Instead he found the landlord seeking a pair of candle branches in an empty room. The spy felt naturally aggrieved.

"D'ye lack aught, sir?" Maclean had asked him, between landlordly solicitude and challenge.

"I do," replied the spy, practically at bay. "I am seeking some friends o' mine who are expecting me here. One is Sir Thomas Leigh; belike you'll be acquainted with him?"

Maclean's expression was that of one who innocently searches in his memory. He shook his head. "Not by name," said he slowly. "Have ye looked in the room yonder?" And he indicated the room across the passage to which he had earlier directed the spy.

"I have. And he's not there."

"Perhaps he'll be below stairs, then."

"Neither is he below stairs." The messenger's tone was grim; his eyes intently watched the landlord's baffling face.

"Then, sir, I'm afraid he'll not be here."

"Ah!" said the spy. "Very odd! Ve-ry odd!"

But the face of the dour Scot remained politely blank. Clearly, the spy considered, there was naught to be made of this fellow, and to push insistence further just then might be to give an alarm that must result in the flight of his game.

"I'll wait," he added shortly, and, turning, made his way back to the room which he had lately quitted. But he did not enter it. Maclean had bowed and passed on down the stairs. The spy stood watching him with a certain hope. This, however, was frustrated. He was completely baffled by the circumstance that never once did Maclean so much as turn his head. Such indifference argued a quiet conscience. Was it possible, he wondered, that Maclean might be in ignorance of the meeting that was taking placed under his roof? The fellow's obvious unconcern scarcely admitted of any other conclusion.

He wandered down the passage, listening outside doors as he went, but gaining no useful information until he came to the end, where he found a door ajar. He gently pushed it, and made the discovery that it opened upon a narrow staircase. He peered down and ascertained that this led to the kitchen and to the garden at the back of the inn. He realised to his dismay that this back staircase formed an emergency exit of whose existence he had been in ignorance. Was it possible that while he had been wasting his time in that room on the right, the landlord, smoking his business, had got the plotters away?

99

He turned and came thoughtfully back. And now he perceived the host coming upstairs again. Straight towards him came Maclean.

"Is your friend a tall, elderly gentleman with a red face?" he asked.

"Ay," said the spy. "He answers that description."

"Then he is in the taproom below there."

The spy thanked him, and descended, leaving the host upon the landing. But it is not to be supposed that the fellow was imposed upon. He simply availed himself of this petard of Maclean's to hoist Maclean himself. He turned into the taproom. But the next instant he had thrust out his head to see what course Maclean was taking, and he was just in time to see the landlord again vanish into that room on the left where earlier he had surprised him.

The messenger flung out of the house at once to his men who sat sipping their ale at one of the trestle tables. He was a shrewd, calculating fellow, and he made not the slightest doubt about what must follow. He took his six bullies round to the pleasant garden at the back, and bestowed them and himself very carefully behind a hedge of laurel, the gathering dusk assisting his manoeuvre.

Meanwhile Maclean had, at last, penetrated to the inner chamber where the conspirators were gathered, and had announced to them that beyond all doubt the Bow Street messenger was seeking themselves, having gone the length of asking for Sir Thomas Leigh by name.

"There's a pack of ruffianly fellows outside, and it's not a doubt but they will be his followers. Ye must take t'other way – by the back; and now is your opportunity, whilst the spy is gone on a fool's errand for me."

They were on their feet at once, ready and anxious to be gone.

"Your horses are ready for you in the stables, and my lad awaits you there. Come, sirs."

They moved at once, but Captain Gaynor detained them yet a moment.

"We part here," he said. "I will wait until you are safely away. If I succeed afterwards in making my own escape, I shall be found at 'White's' at noon tomorrow."

"Will you not go first, Captain?" suggested Mr Partridge.

"No, no," he answered. "I have something yet to do ere I can run the risk of capture. Away with you, then, and good luck go with you."

When they had departed, Captain Gaynor took a taper from the overmantel, lighted it and reduced to ashes certain papers which he carried between the leathers of his sword-belt. He sighed over the act, for it marked the end of the business upon which he was come. Since that was discovered there was an end for the present to the need of such papers, and since his own arrest perhaps impended, their destruction was imperative.

Leaving a little heap of ashes in the grate, he quitted the chamber in his turn, went swiftly across the outer room, and, having assured himself with due precaution that the coast was clear, he stepped out into the corridor, and made his way to the door at the head of the back staircase.

He reached it without encountering anyone, and having pushed it open he was on the point of descending when a sudden uproar below brought him sharply to a halt. Above the din of voices rang the call: "In the King's name! Surrender! In the King's name!" Lastly came a cry of: "Hold there, or I fire!"

Gaynor rapped out an oath. His friends, it was plain, had walked into a trap. The house, he concluded, was surrounded, or, at least, both back and front were being watched. He was thankful for the others' sake as much as for his own that he had not accompanied them. He caught the sound of a scuffle; a pistol-shot cracked suddenly and was followed by a cry. Then the din gradually receded.

But there was now commotion within doors, for the inmates of the house had been disturbed by these sounds of battle. He heard steps and voices in the corridor behind him, and he was grateful to the gloom that gave him cover. He must not be found there; that was of the first importance now, and it would be more than probable that there were other tipstaves in the approaching company.

There was a door on the captain's right. Unhesitatingly he turned the handle. It yielded. He slipped in, closed the door softly and turned the key, which he was thankful to find on the inside. Then he faced about to make the discovery that he was in a bedroom. It was untenanted at the moment but there was no lack of evidence that it possessed a tenant.

A cloak was thrown over the back of a chair, and under it stood a pair of feminine shoes with high French heels. On the bed lay a petticoat and a wrap. A valise gaped on the floor, its contents bulging, and among these the Captain noted a prodigious display of laces and ribbons.

Through the window, facing eastwards towards London, he had a glimpse of trees and fields and hedgerows, backed by the fine grey pile of Beaufort House, all very soft and mellow in the evening light.

And then, from a curtained alcove hitherto unperceived by him, came a clear, young voice to freeze him where he stood by its unexpectedness.

"Is that you at last, Henry?"

His recovery was instantaneous. Reflecting that Henry was indeed his name, he had no hesitation in answering the question with the shortest affirmative in the language.

"Yes."

"Where have you tarried so long?" came the voice again, and it contained a note of petulance. "You knew that I stayed for you. And I am hungry, and – "

Quite suddenly she appeared between the parted curtains, her speech cropped short at sight of him. It had been his dread lest she should be in an incomplete condition of toilet, in which case he thought that outraged modesty combined with alarm would most surely set her screaming. To his relief, however, she appeared before him fully dressed, save for a slight and very charming disorder of her hair and the absence of tucker from her alabaster neck.

She was a handsome, regal woman, and she made a very engaging picture standing there between the parted curtains of red velvet. But it was a picture which, however delightful in itself, delighted Captain Gaynor not at all. Before she could give expression to the alarm that stared in her eyes and blenching face, the Captain bowed low and most reassuringly.

"Most profoundly do I crave your indulgence for my error, ma'am," said he.

His voice was so serene and courteous, his air and manner so much that of the fine gentleman that her fears sank down a little; but not quite.

"Who are you?" she demanded, her voice vibrating. "What do you here?"

"I am just a blunderer who has strayed into the wrong room," he explained.

"You have locked the door," she accused him, and her alarm appeared to rise once more.

" 'Twas that I desired to be alone," he answered.

"You" – her voice was growing shrill – "you answered to the name of Henry," she remembered.

"My name is Henry, ma'am," he assured her.

There fell a pause. She stood with knitted brows and quickened bosom, waiting. At last – "Why do you stay, then?" she challenged him, and as she spoke she came forward towards where the bell-rope hung.

"I but await your leave to go," he answered her.

"My leave?" said she, pausing in her amazement. "Depart at once, sir."

"At once, ma'am," said he submissively. But on the words, greatly to her alarm, he advanced resolutely into the room. "By your leave," said he quite coolly, "I should prefer to go by the window."

"By the window?" she echoed, and began to wonder was he mad.

Along the passage outside the door sped hurrying feet; a murmur of voices reached them through the panels.

"You hear, madam," he said, waving a hand in that direction. "I hope I am not so utterly lost to consideration for the fair name of a lady as to permit myself to he seen issuing from her chamber. You will agree, I am sure, that the window is most opportune."

She eyed him narrowly, barring now his way. And he admired her spirit as much as the ripe beauty of her.

"Do you know who I am, sir?" she asked. "I am Lady Tresh. My husband is Sir Henry Tresh, one of the Middlesex justices."

"Sir Henry is a man to be envied, ma'am," said he, no whit abashed. Indeed, the situation was becoming humorous. He made her a leg, his hat upon his heart. "I should have preferred, ma'am, that we had met under circumstances more auspicious to myself. But even so, I am honoured – profoundly honoured." And he bowed again. He was in no haste to depart either by door or window. Indeed, the longer he delayed, the better would it suit him. Already, he observed, the sounds in the corridor were receding.

"Unlock that door, sir," she commanded, standing before him like a queen of tragedy, with one arm out-flung to emphasise her stern command.

"It were so unwise," he deprecated. "And the window is so very opportune. It cannot be more than a dozen feet above the ground."

Her queenly bosom heaved in agitation. "Will you tell me who you are?" she demanded once more.

He shrugged, his eyes smiling ruefully. He was on the point of answering truthfully, accounting that perhaps the best course might be to cast himself upon her mercy, when suddenly he saw a fresh alarm leap into her eyes and one hand fly to her bosom.

Down the corridor came a heavy, lumbering step – a step to which she was listening and which was known to her. It paused at the door, and the handle turned with a rattle. Then a double knock rapped on the panel and a gruff voice called: "Kate!"

"My husband!" She no more than breathed the words.

The Captain spread his hands, and his face showed concern for her. "You see," he whispered back, "that the window becomes more opportune than ever."

She wrung her hands. Her eyes were upon him in a look that was between distress and anger.

"I am undone!" she moaned.

"Nay, nay!" He tiptoed past her to the window, and flung it open.

Raps more numerous, louder and more insistent came again upon the panel. Again the handle of the door was rattled. "Kate!" that gruff voice was yelling now.

"It is you, Henry?" she called back. The intruder was already astride of the sill.

"Whom else were you expecting?" growled the voice. "Damme! Why must women for ever be locking themselves in?"

She crossed the room leisurely, and fumbled an instant at the key. Captain Gaynor had vanished.

He dropped from the window – a good fourteen feet to the ground – and landed somewhat shaken. But he did not stay to consider it. He found himself in the stable-yard, and he sped across it like a hare, to find cover in the stable itself. He gained it before Sir Henry had crossed the threshold of the room above. He found there young Maclean in a state of considerable perturbation.

The young Scot muttered a short thanksgiving at sight of the Captain.

"Your horse is ready," was his greeting. "Come, sir."

From him now Captain Gaynor learnt that his five friends had all been taken. They were gone in hackney carriages to London with the tipstaves. Sir Thomas Leigh had drawn his sword, and had been shot through the arm in consequence. Mr Dyke, too, had attempted to resist the messengers, and had received a broken crown. Maclean the elder, his son assured the fugitive, need occasion the Captain no concern; he would know how to answer any awkward questions he might he asked.

Having heard all that the young man could tell him, the Captain took his decision. He would leave his horse where it was until he called for it again. In its place he desired to be supplied with a post-horse.

The bitterness which had assailed Captain Gaynor when first he had learnt of the shrewd blow with which the Government had demolished for the present any Jacobite development was now dispelled. It would return, no doubt, anon, and be the sharper perhaps for this respite. But for the moment he rode in a spirit of elation born of the adventure upon which he was now set.

He reached Charing Cross some time after nightfall, and having surrendered his horse at the post-house, he disappeared to execute the project in his mind.

A half-hour later he was leaning in the shadow of a tree near Whitehall steps, observing with interest a watchman who, with lanthorn and staff, was pacing the river-front not far from his hutch. Captain Gaynor produced from his breast-pocket a flask containing close upon half-a-pint of brandy, which he had procured at parting from young Maclean. He drank rather less than half, poured the remainder into his waistcoat, and flung the flask into the river. Then he reeled forth until he was level with the watchman's box. Into this he hurtled, sat down and – apparently fell fast asleep. At least he was discovered to be breathing stertorously a minute later.

The watchman swore at him, prodded him with his staff, shook him and bellowed in his ear, to all of which the Captain remained as insensible as a stone image.

From these signs and from the overpowering fumes of brandy which the fellow exhaled, the watchman came to the conclusion that he was very drunk. Now there was an Act promulgated under the late queen which accounted all drunkards to be disturbers of the peace, and enjoined upon watchmen their apprehension and consignment to gaol. If you were not drunk beyond all speech, you might for a shilling or two obtain instead that the watchman should abandon his post to escort you to your residence. But in such a case as the Captain's there was but one course to pursue, and that course this member of the law pursued.

He very carefully picked the Captain's pockets as a preliminary, a proceeding which yielded him a profit so disproportionate with the Captain's dress and appearance – the Captain having previously bestowed his valuables beyond the reach of prying fingers – that the old rascal was forced to conclude that those pockets had been picked already. Then he whirled his rattle and brought up the constable and a posse of other watchmen, besides a small crowd of watermen from the riverside and several loiterers. Into the hands of his brethren he delivered the inanimate body of the Captain, informing the constable in a whisper of the state of the gentleman's pockets, so as to save the constable the trouble of going through them on his own account.

Thus Captain Gaynor was carried off to the Gatehouse at Westminster, which was the nearest prison. There he was flung into a dank, noisome chamber, tenanted already by some dozen of the very foulest scourings of the streets. These would have gone over the Captain's person for the sake of any pickings that the constable and watchman might have left, but that the Captain, growing partly sobered as the first filthy fingers touched him, roused himself sufficiently to crash his fist into the face of their owner. The fellow sank down with a howl that turned into an agonising cough. His few remaining teeth had been loosened by the blow.

Thereafter the Captain was left in peace. For a man who could smite such blows when too drunk to stand must be terrible indeed when sober, and they might so have to reckon with him did they abuse his present condition.

He reclined, then, against the wall with his legs stretched straight before him; and thus he spent one of the most horrible nights of his existence. But to comfort him he had the knowledge that all had fallen out precisely as he had planned, and that there remained but little doubt that its sequel in the morning would fully compensate him for his present discomforts.

Chapter 10

TWO LETTERS

Mr Second Secretary Templeton sat at breakfast in the dining-room of his stately mansion in Old Palace Yard. It was a spacious, sunny chamber, panelled in white with an abundance of gilding, and its long French windows stood open to the terrace, over whose grey stone balustrade surged a riot of roses and geraniums.

The statesman was at his ease in a bed-gown of blue brocade, his cropped head swathed in a silk kerchief, whose rich colouring exaggerated the shallowness of his long, aristocratic face. Facing him across the round table sat Mrs Templeton, short, long-waisted and inclining to stoutness. Like her husband, she was dark-complexioned, and age had rendered masterful and rather too aquiline a face that in youth had been accounted beautiful. Between them sat the Second Secretary's cousin, Sir Richard Tollemache Templeton, returned but yesterday from his foreign travels.

Although the baronet was quite ten years the statesman's junior – Sir Richard cannot have been more than thirty at the time – Mr Templeton, whose manner was patronising with all the world, treated him with the deference due to the head of a family into which he accounted it his greatest honour to have been born. Family was a religion with Mr Templeton, and before the head of his own he unbent to a most extraordinary degree; upon occasion he went even the length of courting his approval and sympathy. He was courting them this morning. He made philosophy for the purpose.

"In this world, my dear Tollemache," he was saying – he considered "Richard" a form of address much too familiar to be used towards one who occupied his cousin's exalted position – "in this world the truly great but too seldom receive the recognition that is their due. The vulgar – ah – undiscerning crowd will ever believe what it is told. It has no judgment, no – ah – percipience of its own. It considers great those who proclaim themselves great, without reflecting that to true greatness such – ah – such a proclamation must be in the last degree repugnant – in the last degree repugnant."

"It is a repugnance undiscernible in your own case, Edward," said his lady, with a gleam almost of malice in her pale eyes.

"My dear – my love!" His mellow, sonorous voice quivered with emphatic protest at such an implication. "Here in the – ah – sacrosanct intimacy of my own domestic hearth, it may be permitted me to – ah – denude myself."

"It will nevertheless be more becoming in you to retain your gown," she snapped, in reproof of his too florid rhetoric, and Sir Richard could not repress a smile.

"I do not speak of the body, madam, but of the soul – the mind," her husband boomed. "Surely, I say, at his own table, to his own wife and to the head of his own family, in the presence of his Lares and Penates, a man may speak with complete freedom, and without the – ah – encumbrance of excessive modesty. Modesty is a garment that every decent man must wear in public. But the public, knowing naught of decency, account him truly great who goes without it."

Thus he swung back to the subject from which his wife's interruption had all but diverted him. "Now here is my Lord Carteret, and here, Tollemache, am I. To Lord Carteret the rich emoluments, the fawning sycophancy, the smile of majesty, the great honours of his office as Secretary of State: to me – in comparative obscurity – the labour that preserves him a fame which he himself does naught to merit – naught to merit." And angrily he fell to stirring his chocolate.

"But your own turn will come, Ned," said the amiable Sir Richard.

Mr Templeton paused in the stirring that he might level a denunciatory spoon at his cousin. "And who will warrant me that?" quoth he. He laughed almost angrily. "You do not apprehend, I see, with what buttresses my lord props up his greatness. Let me explain, Tollemache, let me explain.

"In affairs of State my Lord Carteret stands in the same relation to me as the – ah – figure at the prow of a ship stands to the – ah – navigator. No, no!" he reproved himself. "My metaphor is too broad. Were it so, indeed, all would be well – all would be well. But I have drawn you a false image."

"You would be more intelligible," said his wife, "if you dispensed with images. What you mean is that it is you who steer the ship of State, whilst my Lord Carteret takes the credit."

He nodded thoughtfully. He was impervious to the veiled sneer in her words.

"You put it – ah – crudely, but truthfully – truthfully. But it should be made clear to Tollemache that his lordship takes the credit when there is credit to take. One of these fine days – mark me! – one of these fine days, as a result of his unceasing interferences with the – ah – navigator, the ship of State will run aground. Do you think his lordship will take the blame of that as he takes the credit of all smooth sailing? Do you think so?"

His eye roamed from Tollemache to his wife, and told them plainly the opinion he should hold of their wit if they did think so.

"No!" he boomed, having reached his climax.

"You are spilling your chocolate," said his wife.

"No!" he repeated, ignoring the frivolous interruption. "On that day, at last, my lord will point out that he has a helmsman to steer for him; he will protest that the shoal upon which we founder was one of whose presence his helmsman should have been aware. Will any blame him? Will majesty cease to smile upon him or sycophants to fawn? No! The obloquy will fall where never fell the credit – where never fell the credit. In short, upon myself." He sat back in his chair, and stroked his massive chin. "That, Tollemache, is the way reputations are made and reputations blasted."

He was almost in a towering passion.

"But," said Sir Richard soothingly, "so long as you are at the helm, you can guard against any such disaster."

"Ah! There's the rub, Tollemache – there's the rub. I could, were I left – ah – untrammelled; were I left to follow my own judgment; did his lordship not perpetually interfere with me, and suggest courses that are undesirable and sometimes perilous. Now take this Jacobite business. You are a man of the world, Tollemache – head of a great family, a soldier and a scholar." (Sir Richard dropped his eyes before Mrs Templeton's stony stare.) "I ask you, Tollemache, were you Secretary of State, would you, could you commit a blunder so – ah – ineffable?"

"I think," said Sir Richard, not without some hesitation, "that I can perceive the drift of Lord Carteret's policy."

Mr Templeton frowned; then his features relaxed into a smile.

"Drift!" he cried, and again, "drift! My dear Tollemache, I thank you for teaching me that word. It is most excellent, most apposite. It precisely describes his lordship's policy. It suggests that – ah – driving before the gale of circumstance that is so characteristic of his statesmanship. 'Drift' expresses it completely – completely."

"Fiddlesticks!" said his wife. "Y'are a clever man, no doubt, Edward, but you fall into the grave error of considering all other men fools."

The statesman spread his hands. He apologised for her to his cousin.

"Woman's logic, Tollemache!" quoth he, and cast an upward glance at the ceiling. Then, to his wife: "My dear," he said, "do you not perceive that the two propositions may not be reconciled. If I am a clever man such an error is not possible to me."

"Then perhaps you are not a clever man," said she.

"That, my dear, represents a retraction inadmissible in intelligent argument. You – ah – you merely interrupt, my love." He was unusually bold.

"But is it not possible," suggested Sir Richard, his frank young eyes upon his cousin, "that in stifling these Jacobite smoulderings, in stamping them out before they can show a flame, his lordship is discharging an easier task than that of quenching a later possible conflagration?"

"You think so?" Mr Templeton was as sardonic as he dare be with so august a person as the head of his family.

"I merely ask," said the baronet. "I am not a statesman."

"A loss to England, my dear Tollemache – a loss to England. But you ask, and you shall be answered." He cleared his throat that he might deliver himself without physical hindrance. "The contention you make is his lordship's own. It is – ah – specious, but delusive. If – if what you suggest were possible, the course would be an excellent one; but it is not possible. The thing has no legal sanction – it is almost illegal, for it is premature. And this is shown by the consequences. We arrest these men, but do we put them upon their trial? Aha! We dare not. We have not the means. The – ah – accusation emanates generally from a single informer. We keep our captives in prison for a week or so, and then his lordship has them severally brought before him, reads them a homily upon the heinousness of disloyalty, the folly of Jacobitism, dwells upon the narrowness of their escape, which he attributes to his Majesty's clemency instead of to his own lack of elements for preparing an impeachment. Is that a dignified course for a government to pursue? I ask you, Tollemache."

"Perhaps not," ventured Tollemache. "But it serves its purpose. It instils fear into these plotters, and turns them from their plotting. Thus, as I perceive it, the peace of the realm is preserved."

Mr Templeton sipped his chocolate, swallowing with it some of his rising indignation and chagrin at the obtuseness of the head of the family.

"You are not a statesman, my dear Tollemache, and there are, therefore, excuses for your short-sightedness which cannot possibly be urged for my Lord Carteret," he said presently. "So long as fortune favours these – ah – operations; so long as – to use your own most excellent image – we drift before a favourable breeze of chance, all goes well. But one of these fine days, my lord will put his hand upon an innocent man, and there will then be a blazing scandal, indemnities will be claimed, heaven alone knows what may follow; but I know that, whatever it is, 'twill be upon my own head. Now, take this case of your friend Captain Gaynor – "

"That, of course, was a most foolish misapprehension," Tollemache admitted.

"You see – you see!" cried the Second Secretary, rubbing his long hands. "Yet had it not been for me – had I not bethought me of your own introduction, of your knowledge of this man's life; had I not seen the – ah – preposterousness of such a charge; had I not been in possession of his unimpeachable credentials and had I not exercised the prudence of seeking their confirmation at two of the embassies (*ab uno disce omnes*) Captain Gaynor had been under arrest by now as a Jacobite agent."

"Preposterous!" said Sir Richard. "The man is a soldier of fortune, first and last. I have it on his own word that he had thought of taking service with the Pretender, but that the service could not yield him enough to live upon, whilst as for future guerdon he had no faith in the ultimate success of the Pretender's cause."

"And yet," cried Templeton, "in spite of all that I could say, his lordship persists in his assurance that the information he has received is not to be doubted, and that Captain Gaynor and the agent Captain Jenkyn are one and the same man. It is only as a consequence of my insistence and as a result of the information obtained from the Austrian and Turkish embassies that his lordship consents that the warrant shall be made out for Captain Jenkyn only, confident that he would be taken last night at 'The World's End' with the other plotters, and that when taken he would be discovered to be Captain Gaynor."

A footman entered and came to proffer Mr Templeton a letter bearing an official seal. He took it abstractedly.

"An extraordinary error," said Sir Richard, smiling. "I would we knew the source of it. I vow that Harry Gaynor will be vastly diverted when I tell him – yes, and grateful to you, Ned, for a judgment and perspicacity which have saved him this annoyance."

"Oh, but for obstinacy, commend me to his lordship – commend me to him!" cried Mr Templeton. "When he learns that no Captain Gaynor – no Captain Jenkyn in any form – was taken with the plotters – if, indeed, they are plotters, which is yet to prove, does he admit, think you, that there has been an error? Not he. 'The Captain must have escaped,' he says. 'These rogues have done their work badly.' There is no arguing with such a man."

He had broken the seal of the letter whilst speaking. He scanned now its contents, and as he did so his face was seen to empurple. He struck the table with his clenched hand.

"Now sink me into – ahem! There is no answer, Jones. Say that I will answer it myself, in person, later." The servant vanished.

"What is it, Edward?" asked Mrs Templeton, who had observed the alteration in her husband's countenance.

"What is it?" he echoed. "It is – But listen for yourselves? Egad! If I had required a proof of what I was saying this could not have come more opportunely to my hands. Listen." And he began to read:

DEAR MR TEMPLETON, – Acting upon the opinions which you know me to entertain, I despatched last night a messenger to Sir John Kynaston's place in Surrey to ascertain whether Captain Gaynor continued there. This messenger has just brought me the information that Captain Gaynor left Chertsey in the afternoon of yesterday and has not yet returned. I shall be obliged if you will take such measures as may be necessary to ascertain not only Captain Gaynor's present whereabouts, but also the particular business which brought him yesterday from Chertsey. It is greatly my fear that as a result of my having lent an ear to your assurance that this person is not the Jacobite agent I am informed, he may slip through our hands and escape the country. I shall be surprised, indeed, if he is not on his way to the coast or even at sea by this time. Believe me to be your obedient servant,

CARTERET.

He flung the missive down with an oath. "Blister me!" he bellowed, and he was by no means a man addicted to such expletives. "He blames me already, you see. I have enabled a Jacobite agent to win clear, and this is coldly stated with no more proof that Captain Gaynor is a Jacobite spy than that I am. The man may not leave Chertsey but it is a proof to his lordship that he's a Jacobite and on his way to the coast if not at sea already. Here, my dear Tollemache, you may observe for yourself the mind of one of the world's great men – ah – dissected, as it were, for your inspection. What do you think of it?"

Sir Richard was frowning. "I am certainly of opinion that my Lord Carteret is a man of very rash and hasty conclusions."

"How long, I ask you, Tollemache, how long do you suppose that such men could keep their positions were it not for such as I who do their work like moles underground where none perceives them? Pah!" He flung himself back in profoundest disgust.

"Is it impossible that his lordship should be right for once?" quoth Mrs Templeton.

The question was as a cold douche to her husband. He cringed under it.

"Right?" he gurgled. He tossed his arms to heaven. "Is he ever right?"

"He is certainly wrong in this case, I'll stake my life on't," said Sir Richard, carrying conviction to Mrs Templeton and extinguishing her nascent doubts.

"Ay, and in every other case," pronounced the fuming Second Secretary. "You may stake your life on that too – with confidence. I told him yesterday that if he was entirely – ah – positive, he might issue the warrant himself and take the consequences. Did he? Bah!

He answered me that that was my function. My function – to run all risks and stand between ridicule and this man who takes all the glory that is shed."

Sir Richard rose from the table. "The situation may be awkward for my friend Gaynor," he said.

"You have to find him," Mrs Templeton reminded them.

The door opened, and again the footman appeared. Again he was the bearer of a letter, and Mr Templeton frowned prodigiously upon perceiving it.

"What now?" quoth he.

"A messenger, sir, from the Gatehouse, Westminster. He stays for a reply."

"From the Gatehouse? What a plague have I to do with the Gatehouse? Am I at the beck of every magistrate's clerk?" He snatched up the letter peevishly, and cut the thread that bound it. It bore no seal.

He spread the sheet, read, frowned, then dropped it from hands that were suddenly limp. He bore those hands to his sides. He seemed to breathe stertorously for a moment, then he exploded; and never in the experience of living man had the solemn, decorous Second Secretary been heard to laugh as he laughed then. Peal upon peal of it reverberated to the ceiling. Gradually, at last, it weakened to a splutter. Mrs Templeton, Sir Richard and the very footman regarded him with eyes of increasing alarm. At last the power of speech was restored to him.

"He – he's found!" he cackled weakly. "Oh – oh! He's found! He's not at sea – not even on his way to the coast. He's – he's – Oh, sink me! Where do you think he is? Where do you think he has been all night?"

"Where?" quoth Sir Richard, staring; but having no doubt concerning the person to whom Mr Templeton was referring.

"Listen!" The statesman took up the letter. "It is from the magistrate, Sir Henry Tresh." And once more he read to them:

HONOURED SIR, – There is brought before me this morning a gentleman who has spent the night in the Gatehouse, having been found early last evening by the watch dead-drunk in the neighbourhood of Whitehall Steps. He gives the name of Captain Harry Gaynor, claims the honour of your acquaintance, and presumes to say that you will speak for him. I venture to send you a note which he himself has penned to you, to inform you of his circumstances, and I shall be honoured by a word to guide me in dealing with him.

He paused to wipe his eyes, still faintly tittering at the thought of Lord Carteret's discomfiture. Sir Richard, too, was smiling, as was even Mrs Templeton.

"But listen further to what the rascal writes, himself. The rare impudence of this rogue to desire a Secretary of State to go bail for him! Listen:

DEAR MR TEMPLETON, – Such muddled memories as I retain of what befell me yester evening at 'The Cock' in Fleet Street are at your disposal when I have the honour of meeting you, for I judge that you may require to know more of how I am come to such a pass as this. What concerns me chiefly at present is the circumstance that whilst I was in an unconscious condition some rogues cleaned out my pockets of such monies as I had, my watch and seals, the silver lace on my coat, and everything else of value. But for this I should make shift not to disturb you upon so trifling a matter. I shall be vastly your debtor if you will send a line to Sir Henry Tresh, as warranty that I shall pay the fine imposed so soon as my liberty is restored me. Your most obedient –

"And that," cried the jubilant Second Secretary, "is the Jacobite plotter, the agent who yester evening was conspiring in a tavern, the desperate Captain Jenkyn!" His laughter swelled again, and it was joined now by his cousin's.

"That should answer my Lord Carteret, egad!" cried Richard.

"It should. It shall – ecod! it shall. I'll send him these letters forthwith, and then straight to the Gatehouse to release this rogue of a plotter."

He pushed back his chair, and rose. He turned to the waiting servant.

"Say to the messenger that I shall follow him in person to wait upon Sir Henry so soon as I am dressed."

"By your leave, I'll go with you, Ned," said Sir Richard.

"So you shall." He strode briskly to the door in the wake of the departing lackey. "Oh, 'slife!" he cried over his shoulder. He was most flippantly profane that morning. "I'd give a deal to see his lordship's countenance when he receives this testimony of an alibi – and such an alibi!"

He went out laughing, overjoyed at the discomfiture in store for his superior, and loving Harry Gaynor as a son for having provided him with so very apt and crushing an answer to that haughtily couched imputation.

Chapter 11

PAUNCEFORT'S MOVE

Captain Gaynor, duly enlarged from durance by the good offices of Mr Templeton, and looking somewhat jaded and hollow-eyed as a result of his unpleasant night in the Gatehouse – an appearance which lent colour to the debauch of which he claimed to be victim – was an object of mirth and the butt of a deal of spurious wit on the part of the very jubilant Second Secretary.

When this had somewhat spent itself, the Captain explained the object of his visit to town.

"I was on my way to wait upon you, sir, when this befell me," he announced unblushingly. "I am hoping that by now you may have found some commission for me."

The statesman's face lengthened. In Lord Carteret's present mood it would be worse than futile to approach him on such a subject. But he refrained from saying so. He contented himself with deploring that so far naught of a quality worthy of the Captain's high attainments had offered itself; but he protested that it was a matter he must not be thought to be neglecting, and soon he hoped to have the good fortune of offering Captain Gaynor something that he would consider acceptable. The Captain expressed his profound indebtedness.

"Meanwhile," said he, "I am for Scotland. I have friends there whom I desire to visit, whom I have not seen for years."

His destination, as a matter of fact, was Rome and his master's Court, to report his failure. But to announce that he was returning abroad at such a moment must call for explanation, might even savour of flight, and were therefore imprudent in the extreme.

"You will keep me advised of your whereabouts?" said Mr Templeton.

"I shall be roaming," was the answer. "So perhaps 'twill be best, should you have letters for me, that you address to me at Childe's – my bankers here, with whom I shall be in communication. I shall report myself to you immediately on my return to town."

On that, with the compliments which the occasion called for, they parted.

Mr Templeton hired a chair, and went to wait upon Lord Carteret, whilst Gaynor and his friend Sir Richard sauntered off together.

Upon the pretence of repairing the loss he had suffered by the picking of his pockets yesternight, Captain Gaynor paid a visit to Childe's, upon whom he had a letter of credit. He drew there a sum sufficient for the journey that lay before him. Next, towards noon, they looked in at "White's"; and for an hour or so they lounged there in amiable talk of the pleasant season they had spent in Italy in each other's company, and of other matters.

At the end of that hour they parted, the Captain to return to Chertsey and Sir Richard announcing that upon the morrow he was for his seat in Devonshire, where he hoped that Harry would visit him ere he left England for the post in the colonies that was to be obtained him.

Captain Gaynor detested the deception he was practising upon his friend, detested having used him in his need. He would have liked at parting to tell him the truth of matters, but he dared not for his very life's sake.

He walked from "White's" to the post-house at Charing Cross and thence rode post to "The World's End" at Chelsea, where he but stayed for a word with Maclean and to recover his own horse.

Heavy-hearted, now that the adventure was at an end, with all the burden of a sense of failure upon him, he rode on to Chertsey; and heaviest of all was the knowledge that tomorrow he must look his last upon that sweet lady he had met in the enchanted garden. Never again, it seemed to him would he ride fancy-free, never again find the cup of adventure all satisfying, never again be content to wander and take pleasure in the wandering. All was changed. All was very dark ahead in a world that but a little week ago had been so full of sunshine.

Meanwhile Mr Templeton had gone to lay before Lord Carteret the desired evidence of Captain Gaynor's whereabouts, together with conclusive proofs of the error under which the Secretary of State had laboured.

This he performed with an abundance of smirks, an occasional chuckle and many a "Did I not tell your lordship how it was?" Finally he withdrew in magnificent, dignified triumph, his knowledge and perspicacity entirely vindicated, leaving his superior not only discomfited but extremely raw at his discomfiture. For to be guffawed over in such a manner by your underling, and to be forced almost to admit that you have sneered at warnings which an intelligent man would have heeded, is not to be endured complacently by any. Least of all is it to be endured by a Secretary of State when the chastening falls from such soft, pompous hands as those of a Mr Templeton.

Lord Carteret, as is the wont of men in high office, looked about for someone upon whom he might visit his ill-humour and to whom he might impart some of his own rawness. To him in this questing mood comes that morning my Lord Pauncefort, very resplendent in black periwig and saffron-coloured coat.

"Good morning, my lord!" the statesman greeted him, in a tone that implied that he wished the viscount anything but a good morning. "I was about to send for you." Lord Carteret – a man of a comfortable habit of body, with a hooked nose, a crafty mouth, and small round eyes that were singularly penetrating and level – scowled upon his visitor. "What cock-and-bull tale was this ye brought me concerning one Captain Gaynor?"

"Cock-and-bull tale?" echoed Pauncefort, taken aback by the question and still more by the tone of it. He drew himself up to the full of his magnificent height, and stared down haughtily upon the Secretary of State. He was not accustomed to being addressed in the manner that Lord Carteret employed this morning.

But he did not long maintain his stare or his haughty poise. The thin lips of the minister wore a sneer and the round little eyes flashed a contempt before which Lord Pauncefort was forced to lower his own. A slight flush crept into his swarthy cheeks.

Men such as Lord Carteret may use men such as Lord Pauncefort; but from the moment they so use them equality ceases between them and is never again to be resumed. To Lord Carteret, the viscount was just a vulgar spy, to be used with contempt, paid his dirty wages and scorned as was his proper due. All this he showed in that faintly sneering mouth and disdainful eyes.

"Those were my words," he said steadily, and he repeated them. "Cock-and-bull tale. This Captain Gaynor was not at Chelsea last evening, and it has been made plain to me that it is impossible he should be Captain Jenkyn, as you have said. It was made plain to me yesterday; but I persisted under your assurances, and as a consequence I have enabled that coxcomb Templeton to laugh at me this morning. Now his Majesty's Government, my lord," he continued mercilessly, "is not paying you for fictions, but for exact – for scrupulously exact – information."

"And you have had it," answered Pauncefort in a dull voice.

The statesman rapped the table impatiently with his knuckles. "In this case we have not."

"In this case more than in any other," Pauncefort insisted. "What should it profit me to accuse an innocent man who can prove his innocence as soon as he speaks?"

"Yet that precisely appears to be Captain Gaynor's case."

"Appears to be – ay. The fellow is slippery as Satan himself."

Lord Carteret pooh-poohed the statement. He proceeded to relate where and how Captain Gaynor had spent the night. Pauncefort listened attentively.

"At what hour did the watch discover him?" he inquired.

"At nightfall, I am informed."

"That would be at about half-past nine. And at what time were the arrests effected at Chelsea?"

"At something before nine. He can hardly have been in both places within the time and drunk himself into a stupor in between. Besides, why should he?"

"To set up an alibi, in case it should be necessary. Was he drunk at all?"

Lord Carteret shrugged impatiently. "The watch affirm it: they should know, and Templeton swears he still stinks of brandy."

"And yet, that he is Captain Jenkyn I know; and that he was at Chelsea last night I'll make oath."

"Had he been taken with the others, the fact that he is an agent of the Pretender would have been established, and we could have dealt with him. As it is – why, as it is, I must believe that Templeton is right and that he is – "

"He is Captain Jenkyn, my lord," Pauncefort insisted still.

"You are becoming plaguily monotonous, sir," snapped Carteret. "If you would prove a little more and affirm a little less I should be better pleased with you. Ye see, we can't hang the fellow on your bare word. Indeed anybody's word would be almost better in the ears of a court than that of an informer. You understand?"

That he understood his countenance showed. "My lord," he burst out angrily, "you are putting an affront upon me!"

The minister surveyed him coolly. "I am calling things by the names that belong to them," he answered icily. And my lord was compelled to swallow that added insult – his very proper and inevitable wage.

"I'll wish your lordship a good morning," he said stiffly. He bowed curtly and gained the door. There, a thought striking him, he turned. "You said, I think, that Sir Henry Tresh was the justice before whom Captain Gaynor was brought at Westminster?"

"That is so," said his lordship. "Come to me again when your information stands upon better foundations."

The viscount went out raging, and kicked a flunkey out of his way to vent a little of the fumes with which he was swollen to bursting-point.

He straightway sought the magistrate upon a pretence of being a friend of Captain Gaynor's who had just received news of his arrest. Sir Henry informed him that the Captain was already at large, whereafter his lordship lingered in talk concerning the erstwhile prisoner, and in the course of their entertainment Chance favoured Pauncefort in a manner entirely unexpected. He learnt that Sir Henry had been at "The World's End" at Chelsea last night when the arrest of the plotters was being effected, and he learnt something further, something which was imparted that evening to Sir Richard Tollemache Templeton by his cousin.

"What, think you, is my Lord Carteret's present view of your friend Gaynor?" inquired the Second Secretary.

"Does he hang there still?" quoth Sir Richard in surprise.

" 'Tis an obsession with him – an obsession! Oh, 'tis incredible that fatuity should go to such lengths – incredible! And the story itself would be incredible to any but a man who is – ah – lost to all sense of the ridiculous. Why, listen to't. It transpires that by an odd chance Sir Henry Tresh was at 'The World's End' last night when the arrests were made. He was sitting over his wine with a friend when the stir took place. Having witnessed it he goes to his wife's room, finds the door locked, and believes that he hears voices within the room. He knocks; there is a delay, and finally the cuckold is admitted. He demands an explanation of those sounds, of the delay and of the extraordinary agitation in which he finds her. Whereupon she tells him that a gentleman unknown to her entered her room and locked the door, leaving thereafter by the window.

"Sir Henry – a most obliging husband, this – believes her implicitly, assumes that like enough the fellow would be one of the Jacobites who escaped the general arrest. Today my Lord Carteret hears the story, and concludes – can you credit it? – that here, at last, is the explanation of why Captain Jenkyn was not taken with the others. If he were to pause there, I could credit him still with an – ah

– with a remnant of sanity. But straightway Captain Jenkyn becomes Captain Gaynor again, in spite of the alibi, the credentials and all else. What, I ask you, Tollemache, can you say to such a man?"

"God help England, I think," answered Sir Richard. "And the worst of it all is that he threatens to execute the warrant for Captain Jenkyn upon Captain Gaynor."

"Is he quite mad?" asked Tollemache.

"Quite – oh, quite!" And Mr Templeton shook his great head. "He'll be in Bedlam before the year is out. But I've washed my hands of the affair. I have told him so. I have warned him. Let the consequences of it – if indeed he goes so far – recoil upon his own head. I shall take measures to protect mine. I shall publish it broadcast that in this blunder at least I am not concerned, that indeed I have done all in my power to avert it. Then, when his lordship rightly becomes the – ah – laughing-stock of the country for an alarmist who sees Jacobite agents in every shadow, then we shall see – we shall see." And Mr Templeton washed his hands in the air, his eyes glowing upon a vision of power that should be transferred to his own more capable hands as a proper and fitting result of his chief's disgrace and downfall.

Chapter 12

NATURE TRIUMPHANT

On the morrow Captain Gaynor made his preparations for leaving England.

He had learnt upon returning to Priory Close of the messenger who had sought him there, and thus realised how narrow had been his escape. For the present, however, he had obtained – thanks to Mr Templeton and his own wit – a temporary respite, and that respite he proposed to employ in giving my Lord Pauncefort his quietus. He looked upon this as a sacred duty, and he could not account himself at liberty to depart out of England until he had discharged it. His intention, therefore, was to return to London, and that very day seek out his lordship and, wherever he found him, force upon him a quarrel demanding immediate adjustment. He reflected that the affair would serve him well, and would leave Mr Templeton with an obvious explanation of his subsequent flight from England. He should be glad of that, for he had no reason to embroil the Second Secretary, who had been so very good a friend to him.

He began that morning by desiring his valet, Fisher, to pack his few belongings, and by informing Fisher that once London were reached he would be obliged by circumstances to dispense with a body servant. The valet, who in the week during which he had served the Captain had found him not only a kind and considerate master, but further had been drawn to him by that magnetism which the Captain's strong personality irradiated, was so distressed as to seek the reason of this.

"I am very sorry, sir," he said. "I hope your Honour has no cause to be displeased with me. I have done my best, but there has been little opportunity – "

"It isn't that," said the Captain. He laid a hand upon the little man's shoulder, and looked kindly into his sharp face. "You have done very well, and I am sorry to part with you. But – to take you into my confidence, which you'll respect, I know – I have an affair on my hands."

"Oh, sir!" the fellow cried, with quick understanding, and Gaynor was moved by the look of concern that leapt into those keen eyes.

"If it end one way, Fisher," the Captain continued, "I shall require no more servants. If it end the other – as I am trustful it will – I shall be put to it to fly the country, and I cannot take you with me."

"But why not, sir?" cried the valet. "I've travelled aforetime. I was in France and Italy with his Grace of Wharton when I had the honour to serve him. I know foreign ways. I – "

"I do not doubt it at all, my friend," the Captain interrupted him. "But there are reasons why I cannot take you, reasons for which you must not press."

"I shouldn't dream of such a liberty, sir."

"Then we must leave it there. I am sorry, Fisher, sorry to part with you."

"And I am sorry, sir," said the little man with profound sincerity.

"Thank you, Fisher."

"Thank you, sir."

Then the Captain went downstairs. He was touched a little by the valet's manner. It seemed to increase the burden that was upon him. He was almost obsessed by a sense of imminent evil, born, no doubt, of the impending farewell that he must make to one with whom he must leave, it seemed, a part of himself – and that the better part – when he rode away that day.

He was exercised, too, by the continued absence of Sir John Kynaston. There was news that, Sir John's brother being now out of all danger, the baronet would be returning on the morrow or the day after. But Captain Gaynor dared not wait and the abruptness of his departure demanded an explanation; more, the events which had transpired in these last few days made it necessary to convey a warning to the baronet. Yet how was he to accomplish it? Write, he dared not; for letters are ever dangerous and liable to miscarriage, and the things he had to say might, if written, come to prove a deadly witness against Sir John. Thus he was driven to the decision that he must entrust his messages by word of mouth to Evelyn – by whom, of course, he meant Damaris.

He reflected that Sir John might prefer her to remain – like the rest of the household – in ignorance of her father's slight association with the Jacobite Cause; but he had no alternative. It was a choosing of the lesser of two evils; and, after all, he had perceived in this sweet lady such admirable qualities of head and heart that he was comparatively easy in his mind at the thought of confiding in her. Moreover, be would so put it as not to betray Sir John even to her in any unnecessary degree. With this intent he sought her now.

He was informed by a servant that Miss Kynaston was with her ladyship in the latter's withdrawing-room. Thither he went, to find, of course, Lady Kynaston and Evelyn. They accorded him a pleasant, friendly welcome. He hesitated to ask for the lady whom he sought, and he was spared the need, for through the window he espied her walking in the garden.

Yet for all his haste to join her there, he must linger awhile in a properly deliberate exchange of courtesies with his hostess. She had been perusing *The Daily Courant* of yesterday when he entered, and, presumably for lack of other matter, she alluded to something she had read.

"Did you hear aught in town, sir, of these knavish Jacobites who are again attempting to undermine the peace of the realm?" she asked him, and in the main, she was quoting words that she had read.

"I heard something, madam," he answered lightly.

"Ah!" said she. "You do not treat the matter with a proper seriousness."

"Is it very serious, ma'am?" he asked her.

"Serious? Why, the notorious Captain Jenkyn is in England again."

"Pooh! A rumour, no doubt."

"Nay, sir, no rumour – a report."

" 'Tis all one, mother dear," said Evelyn from the window, where she was standing. "I hope they will not take him," she added, and paid that gallant unknown the tribute of a sigh.

"You hope they will not take him, Evelyn!" Her ladyship was outraged by such a sentiment. "The man is a dangerous and pernicious rebel. And they'll take him, never fear."

"I wonder!" said Captain Gaynor.

"Look at this," she bade him, and held out *The Courant.*

He took the news-sheet, and followed the indication of her finger. But there was not the need of it. The bold announcement at the foot of the second column challenged every eye:

ADVERTISEMENT

WHEREAS it is reported to his Majesty's Government that the notorious rebel and Jacobite spy and agent who is known as Captain Jenkyn is at this present time in England, his Majesty's Secretary of State hereby gives notice that any who shall bring such information as will lead to the arrest and conviction of the said rebel shall receive from his Majesty's Treasury the sum of TWELVE HUNDRED GUINEAS in REWARD.

"His value is increasing, it seems," said the Captain, returning the sheet to her ladyship. "Poor devil!" he added, and soon afterwards found an excuse upon which he might withdraw and go to join Damaris in the garden.

"Madam," he said, bowing formally before her, "I am come – alas! – to take my leave of you. But ere I go there is something I desire to say for your private ear, if you will so honour me."

He saw the quick blood leap to her cheeks and ebb thence again, leaving her very white; he saw that droop of the brown eyes, the sudden agitation of her breast, the little quiver of her hand upon the briar from which she had been about to break a rose.

He knew then how she misunderstood his aims; knew that she cared; and the knowledge was as a sword in his flesh.

"Yes," she answered faintly. "I am listening, Captain Gaynor."

He hesitated yet a moment. Then: "Will you walk, madam?" he invited her, his voice oddly subdued, faltering a little even.

She turned at his bidding, and together they took their way at a gentle pace towards the plantation; they crossed the bridge, and followed the main valley of the glorious garden; and all this with no word spoken between them, yet such a communion of soul and soul as gladdened her and left him sick with fierce despair.

She imagined that she understood why he led her to the garden. She remembered how he had spoken of it as enchanted, a place wherein a man might be content to lay down ambition and have done with strife. It was here, too, that they had first talked to any purpose. It was almost as if they had met there, under the apple-blossom, for until that talk they had been as utter strangers. There it was that he had first revealed himself with all that stark honesty which she found so admirable in him, that it more than made amends for his avowed lack of great ideals. She was touched by his desire that they should talk now in such a place; that he should have chosen this garden of enchantment, in which he had erst revealed himself, to reveal himself yet more fully unto her alone.

Rejoicing, she went with him thither, as she would have gone with him wheresoe'er he bade her. Was she not his to claim? And in that hour she was glad indeed of the deception that had been practised, glad that he had not known her for the heiress, Damaris Hollinstone. For thus was she brought to the sweet and tranquil conviction that here was one who desired her for her own self and not for aught that she might have to give. She was glad, too, that she was Damaris Hollinstone and rich, and glad that he was poor. Thus should be increased the joy and blessing that would be hers in giving

– for she was of those selfless ones who, where they love, desire to give and give. She knew that she was good to look upon; and in this too she took joy that morning, since this too had she to give.

She was dreaming as she stepped along beside him, a happy dream whose fulfilment she deemed impending. Why did he not speak? she wondered. Did he hesitate, poor lover? Did he doubt her? God wot, there was but little need for that. Furtively, shyly she glanced aside at him, to observe at last his haggard look and wrinkled brow.

Dear heart! How needlessly was he torturing himself! How fondly she longed for the uttered word that should give her the right to drive forth his fears, to transfigure his face and smooth away those lines. Yet she loved him the more for this most sweet timidity towards her in one whom she judged of a nature that normally was bold and fearless.

And then, at last, he spoke, his voice singularly small and quiet; and his first words shattered that dream-paradise of hers so abruptly that for an instant she was stunned and numb.

"It is of Sir John that I desire to speak to you, madam," he said. "I have a message for him of gravest import – so grave that I dare not write it, lest an ill-chance should put it into hands that might use it against him."

Mechanically she walked on. She was choking. Her face was deathly pale; her eyes seemed suddenly enlarged in it and very dark; her mouth was trembling. But he observed naught of this. He did not observe her at all. He was looking away through the sundrenched orchard on their right.

Followed a little spell of silence, in which they came to the first of those courts enclosed in their tall, boxwood settings. He stood aside to let her pass first through the narrow archway in that massive hedge. He followed, and they stood in the rose-garden, which was now all fire and snow with petals red and white.

"You will tell him, madam, that I am grieved beyond all mention that I may not stay another day for his return, to take my leave of him in person; that I dare not; that with every hour I tarry now in

131

England the shadow of the gallows falls more heavily across my path."

She came out of her stupor, awakened by the sinister image he had employed.

"The gallows?" she cried, horror in every line of her lovely face. "You are in danger!"

Deliberately had he spoken so, hoping that his words would convey not only the intended message to Sir John, but a message to her too that should explain his need to preserve silence upon the subject on which she looked to hear from him. Yet now that he saw and interpreted her alarm, his soul was torn with sobs unuttered. His eyelids flickered. But beyond that he gave no sign of the terrible ordeal he was sustaining, must sustain for honour's sake. His every nerve and fibre shrieked imperatively that he should take her in his arms, and claim her – who stood so ready for surrender – for his own. But the calm, cold voice of Honour warned him not to heed those treacherous behests of heedless Nature – of Nature, who knows naught of honour and such human shibboleths.

What manner of knave would he be, Honour demanded, to return the good that Sir John had ever done him by the evil of such a deed? To repay the baronet's trust and affection by stealing away his only child and bearing her with him upon his hapless wanderings?

Were Sir John here, things might be different. Captain Gaynor could have gone to him and loyally spoken what was in his heart, loyally abided by the baronet's decision. But without the baronet's consent – a consent which Gaynor deemed extremely unlikely – he must not speak to her of this thing with which his heart was bursting. And linger until Sir John's return, he dared not; not merely for the danger that he ran – that danger he would have faced most gladly – but because his presence in England might place in jeopardy those arrested Jacobites, against whom little could be enacted if he remained undiscovered, he must depart at once. The voice of Honour was very clear, and not to be misunderstood. It bade him be silent, and so depart.

So in that swift flicker of his eyelids he determined. He brushed aside with a disdainful gesture the suggestion that the danger he ran was one to occasion concern.

"The danger is naught," he said, "or will be naught so that I depart at once. And I mean not only danger to myself but danger to others who would be implicated were I taken. Please remember this that you may tell him. And that the principal ones of my master's friends have been prematurely arrested; that no great harm threatens them, but that for the present I have been obliged to abandon my mission; that I shall not go to Rochester, nor indeed take any further steps, but shall return immediately to Rome.

"That, I think, is all that I need say. The rest he will infer. But add that there is a warrant out for my arrest – though not in my own name, as the Government is not yet assured that my identity and that of the person sought are one and the same. And before the Government has such assurance – if indeed it ever has it – I hope to be very far away. Bid him spare himself anxieties on my account. My plans are soundly laid, and I have a friend at Court upon whose offices I am depending.

"Tell him just that, madam," he concluded, his eyes ever avoiding hers, "just that and my deep devotion. He will understand why I was forced to this precipitate flight, and he will know how to guard himself from any consequences of having sheltered me in the event of my being ultimately identified with – with the man for whom the warrant has been issued."

"I will remember all," she said – indeed, every word of it was seared upon her memory – "and I will tell him. But you, sir" – her voice dropped a little, and her tone by its gentleness seemed to belie the words she uttered – "you have deceived me."

He looked up sharply. "Deceived you – I?"

"You represented yourself to me as an adventurer, a follower of Fortune's banner, a mercenary who sold his sword to the highest bidder."

"All this I have been – all this I am," he answered. "I practised no deceit."

133

"You practise it still," she said, her pride in him increased a thousandfold by her discovery. "You spoke but now of a mission and of your master in Rome. You are a Jacobite, that much you have made plain – one who in the pursuit of an ideal imperils his life and moves, in your own words, under the shadow of the gallows. Yet," she reproached him almost fondly, so caressingly protesting was her tone, "you represented yourself to me as a hireling; you provoked and submitted to my scorn."

He trembled, looked at her, then looked away across the flaming roses. His first impulse was to say that in this too he was a mercenary; that what he did, he did for gold. First the falsehood stayed him; then the reflection that even that falsehood could not serve him now. He had won her love; her every word and look assured him of it. Should he then be so ungenerous as to maintain this hateful pretence that she was nothing to him? Could that serve any but a hurtful purpose? Was it not better that he, too, should let her see how it was with him? Was it not better that she should know that where unwittingly he had conquered he had been conquered also? That she should hold this knowledge would, he felt, comfort him; and her too it might comfort. Some day – who knew?

But there he went too fast. He would convey it, but not utter it. To utter it were to break down the barriers which Honour had raised up.

"You are right," he said gently. "I crave your pardon."

"My pardon?" she echoed. "My pardon – for being noble where I deemed you base!"

"Nay, for the deceit I put unworthily upon you."

"Why did you?" she asked him, the intimacy between them growing now with an odd and alarming swiftness.

"To be consistent in the part I played. Had any known my secret, all must know it. Yet there was no untruth in my deceit. I was a mercenary in all other services but this. And of this I dared not speak – at least not then."

"And now?" she asked him without shyness.

"Now?" He looked at her, full into her steadfast eyes that were drawing his very soul from him. "Now to make amends I will place my life in your gentle hands. God knows it is all I have to give." He laughed a little ruefully. She was trembling. "I am he whom the Government knows by the name of Captain Jenkyn."

She fell back with a little cry. She needed no explanation. She, too, had seen *The Daily Courant* that morning and the Secretary of State's announcement. She turned white to the lips, realising at last to the full the overwhelming peril in which he stood. She clasped her hands.

"Oh, God of pity!" was her moan. And then, in an agony: "Why – oh, why did you tell me this?"

The appeal was more than he could endure. Impulse shattered Honour's barriers at a blow, and struck Honour herself silent, whilst Nature swept on triumphant and irresistible.

He strode to her, caught her in his arms and crushed her to him. His voice shook with mingled pain and exultation.

"Because I love you, oh, my lady!" he cried. "Because all that I have, all that I am I would place in your sweet hands in pledge of it."

"I asked not any pledge," she sobbed in a gladness that mounted and overrode her terror. His head drooped to her upturned face, and they kissed. "Dear love," she murmured, as she lay there happily upon his breast, "I, too, must make confession."

"Confess, dear sinner," he replied, "and be very sure of shrift."

"I am glad that you deceived me, for I too have practised a deceit on you."

"Deceit – thou?" his voice was scornful.

"I am not Evelyn," she confessed, watching his face, observing the cloud that gathered on his brow. "I am Damaris Hollinstone."

The cloud grew darker, then suddenly it vanished utterly and he laughed.

"Faith, then, I'm glad," said he, "for Damaris is a sweeter and more fitting name."

"And for no other reason?" she inquired.

"What other could there be? You are you under whatever name you please."

And so they hung there, the world and all its perils sunk many a fathom deep into oblivion, conscious of naught but each other – just man and woman in a garden.

From behind the boxwood hedge stepped, soft-footed, a hidden watcher. Another – a golden-headed, fragile slip of womanhood, fled, shuddering and weeping softly in an agony of remorse at the catastrophe she had invoked, a catastrophe that overleapt her every expectation and spread grim tragedy where she had thought to set a comedy with a spice of malice.

Through the archway into that Eden stepped the inevitable Satan, wearing the handsome outward seeming of my Lord Pauncefort. He paused an instant, himself unobserved, to consider the idyll that he came to shatter with a bloody hand. And what time he paused, he set upon his seething rage the mask of a sardonic humour.

"Soho!" he announced himself. "Here is not merely a rebel, but a rebel in arms, it seems."

Chapter 13

IN THE ROSE-GARDEN

Alarmed, confused, the lovers sprang apart; yet not so far apart that the Captain's arm continued to encircle – protectingly now – the waist of Damaris.

There followed a spell of silence during which the two men measured each other with their eyes, like swordsmen about to engage. And there was something more in the Captain's glance; there was satisfaction to see before him the man who was become his quarry. No need now to go afield in search of him. With a smouldering eye, with something that was almost a smile on his lips did Gaynor ponder now his enemy.

But it was Damaris, standing tense and white, who was the first to break the silence.

"By what right, sir, do you thus insolently thrust yourself in here?" she challenged the intruder.

"Do you, madam, question my right?" quoth he, eyebrows raised.

It was Captain Gaynor who supplied the answer to her question. "By the right of his nature, Damaris. He can no more help being a spy than the fox can help its smell."

137

His lordship's eyes swung back to the Captain's face, and betrayed by their startled look how shrewdly this blow had caught him. But he made a swift recovery, throwing back his handsome black head in arrogance.

"What shall that mean, sir?"

"Mean, you base Judas!" The Captain's passion was overmastering him at the sight of this man whose falseness had wrought such fearful havoc, had ruined for a season his beloved master's every hope. Thus that fierce burst of rage escaped him. But he controlled himself almost at once.

"Let me present to you, Damaris," said he, in a cold, sneering voice, "the most infamous spy in England, who in the discharge of that office has thrust himself here upon us. You may have conceived that in my Lord Pauncefort you beheld a nobleman, a gentleman, a man of honour. So have others thought to their undoing. Instead, you behold there a broken gamester who for a handful of gold has betrayed the men who trusted him and counted him their friend, has sold the Cause in which he himself believed, has bartered his honour and brought everlasting shame upon the name he bears."

"Be silent!" thundered Pauncefort, advancing a step and checking there, his countenance writhing. "It is false, I say!"

"You perjured hound! False, is it? Ay, the deed was false and foul as hell, in which it shall be expiated."

"Was it he betrayed you?" quoth Damaris, her voice most singularly calm and quiet.

"Ay was it. Look on him, Damaris." He flung out an accusing arm. "Look on him, for you may never again see such another – a man who was born a gentleman and is reduced to infamy, a man who has pawned his soul to keep his body in luxury."

Pauncefort was livid, stricken by the unexpectedness of this attack, for he had been very far from dreaming that his treachery was detected.

"And now, sir," said Damaris, "now that you have received what was here your due, perhaps you will depart again?"

Her contempt struck him more keenly than the Captain's bitter denunciation. It stirred him, awakened him from his stupor. Swiftly he mastered himself to play his part in this game; and he was suddenly heartened by the knowledge that he had a card in his pack should trump this whirling Captain's trick.

He turned upon Gaynor very haughtily, every inch of him the great gentleman.

"Sir," he said, "base as you are and as I know you to be, you have said that to me here which is not to be borne by any man, however high-placed, from another, however low. Elsewhere we will continue this discussion."

"We shall, by God!" said Gaynor. "I so intend it."

"And," his lordship added, "you shall eat the lies you have uttered." Upon that his gesture signified that he had done with him. "But you, Damaris – oh, that you should have lent an ear to this infamous defamer! that you should have believed these things against me, myself unheard! This is what stings and cuts me to the very soul!"

She surveyed him with an eye that pierced this miserable artifice. She disdained him any answer other than: "Will you go now, sir?"

He stared at her as if this fresh dismissal were beyond belief. He played his part with vigour and intensity.

But it was quite futile. Yet in the face of his indifferent audience he maintained it, enheartened by the confidence that his finest line was yet to utter; saving this skilfully for his climax, a climax that should overwhelm and conquer her for all her present scorn of him.

"No," he answered, "I will not go. My place is here beside my affianced wife."

"Your – ?" She checked, her cheeks aflame. "You do well, I think, to remind me of my shame. But that is past. I am your affianced wife no longer."

"Ah?" he said. He was quite himself by now, betraying no least sign of heat. "Since when this change?"

He got his answer pat. "Since you, yourself, failed in wit to conceal from me that it was my fortune, not myself, you wooed."

He considered her, and his eyes were melancholy. He sighed. "I feared you had thus misunderstood me!"

"Oh, I did not misunderstand you," she answered. "I understood you for the first time. And that is how it happens that Captain Gaynor's further revelation of your ways does not surprise me."

This was a blow between the eyes. But his lordship did not stagger under it. He preserved a calm front. "For that, too," said he "you shall contritely and of your own free will yet seek my pardon."

"I?" Her contempt withered him. "Oh, will you go!"

And seeing him still making no shift to depart: "I think," said the Captain, "this lady bids you go. Must I compel you to obey her?"

"Very well," he said to Damaris, entirely ignoring the Captain. "Very well." He bowed to her. "Another season will perhaps serve me better. I should indeed prefer to clear myself in your eyes when there are no witnesses at hand. Yet ere I go, I will ask you to remember that however you may have misunderstood my motives, you are pledged to me, and I have not redeemed you from that pledge."

"Myself have cancelled it," she answered him. "I will not wed a thief."

"Ha!" cried the Captain. "'Tis the very word – the very word I sought. A thief! Ha!"

The swarthy face flushed heavily, the eyes were venomous in the glance they flashed upon the Captain. My lord drew a deep breath with a little hissing sound, thereby acknowledging the hit.

"How wanton can a woman be when her mood is cruel!" he exclaimed. "How wanton is her injustice! This injustice, madam," he continued sadly, his head bowed, "yourself shall come to acknowledge. As I know you to be a true and generous woman where you are not misled, so do I know that you will sue for pardon to me. You think to fling me aside because you imagine – oh, so mistakenly, dear God! – that I was a fortune hunter, that (in your own cruel words) I wooed your fortune and not yourself. And yet – and yet, such is a woman's blindness – you replace me by one who is an avowed adventurer, a self-confessed fortune-hunter, a mercenary in all things; one who openly and without disguise or shame sought to win you for what you're like to bring him in worldly estate."

He had begun at last to play his trumps, and Captain Gaynor stiffened as he listened, stiffened in sudden horror of a picture that leapt before the eyes of his memory.

"Have you quite done?" was all Damaris' acknowledgment of his lordship's scathing words.

"Quite, if you do not believe me," he answered with grim confidence.

Had she but preserved silence, had she but maintained her haughty indifference, all might yet have been well. There would have been no more to say, and, his rebuff complete, he must have taken his departure. But, woman-like, she must have the last word in this; she must come down a little from those frosty heights to utter it, and in uttering it must open the door to more.

"I do not believe you," she said, to which he returned the obvious answer:

"And if I could prove it to you?"

"Prove it?" she cried, and now her pride and confidence in her lover were as much to blame as any other sentiments. "Prove it? You poor deceiver! Why, I can prove the very contrary. Until this hour, until he knew that he had won me – for I am his, my lord – he did not know my name; he deemed me Evelyn Kynaston, as a result of a poor deceit we put upon him; and for that I thank heaven, since it gives me this easy means of showing how fully I account you what Captain Gaynor says you are."

But his lordship brushed the insult aside. It was insignificant, then; a mere piece of detail. The fact to which it was attached arrested him. For a second it checkmated him. And then he saw how it might be turned to account.

"He thought you Miss Kynaston?" he cried. "He has succeeded in making you credit even that? Now what a most complete and finished liar have we here!" Then, in a voice of thunder, a voice whose very weight and volume seemed to increase the burden of his overpowering words, he let her have it.

"Why, this man" – and he shook a quivering finger at the Captain – "this dastard came here of set intent to woo you, ere ever he had seen you. In his own words, ma'am, he knew not whether you were tall or short, dark or fair, plump or lean, neither did he care; he knew you for the wealthiest heiress in all England, and in no other way did he desire to know you." He swung upon the Captain, smiling grimly. "You see that I have treasured the remembrance of your every word, sir."

"You hound! You jackal!" said the Captain through his teeth.

But my lord ran on: "And because he knew me betrothed to you; because he knew me in straits for money, in the clutches of a merciless usurer, a debtor's goal awaiting me, he availed himself of my despair to propose to me that I should play him for the right to wed you, which was mine. To my undying shame, I confess that I succumbed. He set you against ten thousand guineas, and he lost. Yet in spite of that, so false a dastard is he, he cannot abide by that issue of the cards, but comes here to steal a thing which is doubly lost to him in honour. And yet you call me a thief, and fling yourself into the arms of such a thief as that!"

He paused, and still she answered nothing. Her calm was impregnable. She just looked at him with eyes of coldest scorn, eyes that seemed to say she but suffered him to talk that he might be done the sooner, that she but waited to be rid of his unwelcome presence. Yet he had not quite done. The card was played; but its force and value were not yet realised.

"I have been in a very hell of shame since I lent myself – induced in my despair – to such a thing. But however shameful you may deem me, I am not shameful as is he. I at least desired you because first and last I loved you. It was not your fortune that I staked upon the board when I gambled for my right to wed you – not your fortune, but my very life, my every hope. But he – Well! I have told you what words he uttered. He will not deny them if you ask him. He cannot, bold liar though he is."

142

He had finished. If he had ruined himself, at least he had ruined the Captain. And yet for himself he had a glimmer of hope. If on the recoil from himself she had tumbled into the Captain's mercenary arms, might he not win her yet upon this second recoil that must inevitably follow now? It was just possible, and he had the means, he thought, to compel Sir John's assistance. He could not think that he had talked in vain. He preened himself upon his knowledge of the ways of women, and here he was confident of having taken a course that no woman could disregard. Yet, it seems, there was one woman whom he had not gauged. For all that Damaris answered him even now was: "Will you go at last, sir; or can you think of aught else to say – though I warn you twill be so much wasted breath."

He gasped and blenched. His eyes bulged as he stared at her.

"You – you do not believe me?" he cried, as he had cried before, but without the confidence that had informed the earlier question.

"Believe you?" she said, and smiled. "I see that you have thought me mad."

"Ask him!" he barked, and flung out a hand again towards Gaynor.

"There is not the need," she said, with quiet confidence.

For a moment he continued to stare at her – her loyalty – her foolish, headstrong loyalty had defeated him, he thought. How she must love this fellow Gaynor that no doubt of him could find admittance to her mind however spurred.

"You are right," he said at last. "There is not the need to ask." And he, too, was smiling, never so wickedly. "You have but to look. Look!" he commanded. "Look in his face and see for yourself what is written there; see for yourself whether I have lied. Oh, indeed, there is no need to ask."

She looked as he bade her. Captain Gaynor's continued silence under that long and formidable accusation occurred to her, perhaps, to cause her at last to do his lordship's bidding and turn her head to look upon her lover's face.

What she saw there struck all her proud confidence to earth, left her frozen and panic-stricken. His face was as the face of a dead man;

the very eyes were gone lustreless, and they could not meet her own.

"Harry," she said, and the steadiness of her voice surprised her. She considered that steadiness almost critically, just as she considered the circumstance that this was the first occasion on which she used his name; and to think that she must use it to ask him – to ask *him!* – to refute a grotesque and foolish accusation. Yet ask him she must, which meant that the accusation had ceased of a sudden to seem to her grotesque and foolish. She was as one who looked on at herself and at her fellow-actors in this scene. It was as if her spirit were disembodied, to become a cold and critical spectator.

"Harry, you will tell me that he lies. That is all that you need tell me."

"Were I the man to have done what he says I have done, then I should be a liar, too, and I should not scruple to answer you as you desire," he said. His voice was husky and unsteady.

She did not understand. There was a confusing paradox in his words. She weighed them in her mind, repeated them to herself, and found them meaningless. She said so.

"But you mean that it is untrue?" she pleaded.

"Untrue, as there is a God above me," he answered, "yet every word of it is true."

She drew away from him. In the half-benumbed condition of her mind she could set but one interpretation upon his stricken condition, his husky, vibrant voice; she saw nothing but subterfuge and quibble in his words.

"True?" she echoed. "You gamed for me?"

He did not answer. He stood rigid, with hands clenched at his sides. The temptation to explain assailed him for a moment; but he allowed it to pass on unheeded and despised, as she must despise it did he attempt to offer it. It were, he realised, but to make himself seem viler and more pitiful. It could not be believed, could carry no conviction; rather must every word of such explanation as he had to offer seem the obvious pretence put forward by a rogue and liar; every word and act that had passed between them since his coming must add confirmation to the thing that Pauncefort told her, since fundamentally that thing was true – the blackest, foulest, untruest truth that was ever uttered.

She waited, then, in vain, waited until his silence bore the only answer.

"O God, pity me!" she wailed. She stumbled, and put a hand to her brow. He flung out a hand to save her, and that act revived her; with fresh panic she shrank from the touch of it as though it had been redhot iron, and in shrinking she stiffened and regained a wonderful composure.

Torn, lacerated, anguished, she stood before these beasts who had fought for her and mangled her very soul in the strife, and she determined in her pride to let them see nothing of her hurt.

She turned very quietly, and with figure erect, though her head drooped a little, she passed down the narrow alley of that court.

"Damaris!" cried Pauncefort as she approached him, his flaming eyes devouring her. But before her glance he quailed and fell back. There was something awful and forbidding there that he dared not brave.

She continued on her way unhindered further. But as she was passing underneath the archway in the hedge she heard her name again.

"Damaris! Damaris!"

It was the cry of one in mortal agony. It was a voice that had grown more dear to her than any human voice, than the sum of all other human voices. She might account him vile and faithless; but his call could still, it seemed, compel her. For she paused and turned her head – turned to him that lovely, stricken face, those deep brown eyes in which so lately he had seen his own reflection, those pale trembling lips that so lately he had kissed. Thus, her head turned, she waited, hoping madly even now against all reasonable hope.

"One thing, at least, believe, O Damaris!" he cried. "One thing I swear – and it is a thing that should efface all else. Until this hour I did not know that you were Damaris Hollinstone. That much I do swear by the God above us, Who is my witness."

If that were so, then indeed did it efface all else, as he had said. If that were so, then all else could matter nothing. She tried to think, to weigh his words. And then, to help to falsify her scales, came a little wicked, scornful laugh from my Lord Pauncefort.

"Of course," scoffed his lordship, "the gentleman must be believed. Has he not deserved to be? Is he not the very soul of honour?"

That gave her the right perspective, she opined; and listlessly she continued on her way, and so out of their sight.

Like a sleep-walker she made her way to the house and ascended the broad steps. Straight and evenly she held upon her course, up the great staircase, to her own chamber. By the narrow white bed she sank down upon her knees. Then pent-up nature had its way at last and, kneeling there, she swooned away. And thus, perhaps, she saved her reason.

Outside, in the rose-garden, my Lord Pauncefort and Captain Gaynor eyed each other in silence for a moment after Damaris had vanished. The Captain listened to her footsteps intently until they had faded in the distance. Then, as if some arresting influence were removed, as if a spell were shattered, he shook himself and his sword flashed lividly from its scabbard.

"Now, you – you lackey!" he snarled. "It is my turn." And on the words he sprang, trampling a bed of roses in his haste to come upon his enemy.

Pauncefort would have avoided this. He was no coward, but to fight a man in the Captain's white-heat of rage were utter suicide. He saw his death in the blazing eyes that looked out of that livid, distorted countenance.

He flung up a hand to arrest the other's attention. "This is neither time nor place," he cried, "and the man that prevails will be indicted for murder."

The Captain laughed.

"Send your friends to wait upon me," his lordship insisted, "and you shall have what satisfaction you desire."

But as well might he, like Canute, have attempted to arrest the tide.

"Draw, damn you," was his answer. "Draw, or I spit you as you stand."

As my lord still hesitated, that long, thin blade flashed up and its point came level with his heart. The sweat broke out cold upon his brow. He drew perforce, and threw himself on guard.

The Captain pressed him wildly, a maniac, panting, sobbing, jeering as he fought. He was terrific, and terror of him went deep into his lordship's soul. He was vengeance incarnate, a bloodhound upon its prey; and in imagination already my lord felt that bright, cruel steel tearing at his throat.

"What place or season could be better?" the Captain mocked him, as he drove his lordship back into a rose bed, across it, and plump into another, that dancing point hovering ever with its deadly menace along the line of his lordship's Adam's apple. "You are fastidious indeed, if my lady's rose-garden will not suit you for a death-bed; a dunghill would better meet your merits."

His lordship crashed backwards through a rose-bush, stumbled, recovered and fought on in desperate defence. He had caught a sound of running feet to hearten him. The Captain heard them too, a moment later.

"You hear them running," he mocked the other. "So run your sands. Your wages are due, my lord, and shall he paid you – thus!" He beat aside the other's impotent blade, and his own point leapt out to end the matter. But as it leapt, his lordship leapt too, back and aside, and then fled in utter panic.

"O coward!" roared the Captain. "Coward that cannot even face his death. Take it, then, from behind." And he sprang to follow. His foot caught and tangled in the root of a brier. He plunged forward, and fell upon his face. As he struggled to rise a hand came to help him, a hand which retained its hold upon his arm after assisting him to his feet.

As through a mist he saw the weather-beaten face of one of the gardeners; another stood on his other side. He strove to throw off the grip that held him. But the second man came to the assistance of the first. Between them they overpowered him and deprived him of his sword, muttering apologies the while for the force they were employing.

My Lord Pauncefort, limp and breathless, leaned against a hedge, and looked on, until one of the gardeners respectfully advised him to be gone. Acting upon that excellent advice, he sheathed his sword and withdrew, mopping his livid brow.

"You may go now," Gaynor called after him, "but do not think to escape. It is but a postponement."

Lord Pauncefort, something recovered by now, turned to his antagonist.

"In a regular manner I will meet you when you will," he panted. "I shall expect you." And upon that he took his departure.

Chapter 14

THE ROAD TO TYBURN

That afternoon Captain Gaynor, once more completely master of himself, and showing no least outward sign of the storm through which his spirit had so lately passed, of the rage that for a while had so entirely governed him, took his leave of Lady Kynaston, informing her that business of some urgency compelled him to depart at once without awaiting Sir John's return.

Her ladyship made no allusion to the fracas in the rose-garden, of which her servants had brought her word; but she did not doubt that his departure was concerned with it, and that this urgent business which he pleaded was the continuation of that quarrel. Upon what grounds it had arisen she had formed the obvious opinion, but dared not ask its confirmation. The Captain's manner was respectfully forbidding. She did not go so far as to connect with it the fact that both her daughter and her niece had kept respective chambers since the event.

Unquestioned, then, he was permitted to go his ways. He did not see Damaris again, which caused him no surprise. To the circumstance that he did not see Evelyn again he gave no thought, perturbed as he was.

He put up at an obscure inn in the neighbourhood of Charing Cross, and there he dismissed Fisher. That done he cast about him for a friend who would wait upon Lord Pauncefort on his behalf, and he bethought him of Sir Richard Templeton, whose residence in St James's Street was within a stone's throw of Pauncefort House. It was possible that the baronet had already departed for Devonshire. But he would ascertain.

He went, then, to make the discovery that in St James's Street he was already expected – not, indeed, by Sir Richard, who had, in fact, departed already, but by the tipstaves set to watch for him by Lord Pauncefort, who counted upon a visit to himself. As the Captain was turning out of Pall Mall he was suddenly confronted by a couple of burly, coarsely garbed fellows, the foremost of whom desired a word with him.

"With me?" he said, stiffening haughtily, yet more than guessing their business.

"I have a warrant for you here," said the taller of the twain – the very man who had been the leader of that raid at "The World's End." He produced his parchment, and thrust it under the Captain's very nose.

"I think ye'll be the person mentioned there – Captain Jenkyn."

What, Captain Gaynor asked himself, could it avail him to deny? They held him, and they would not be like to let him go upon a denial, however emphatic. Moreover, it came to him suddenly that he did not want to go. The cause he served was ruined for the time being, set back for many a year, perhaps, if not for ever. The woman he had come to love – he, who hitherto had held himself aloof from all women, being wholly wedded to his master's service – deemed him base and unworthy, and must so deem him. What, then, remained in life? – the avenging of their betrayal upon that traitor Pauncefort; and that, he knew, another hand than his would execute ere long.

This arrest seemed to him in that despondent hour to resolve his difficulties, to remove from him a heavy burden. He had sickened at the very thought of returning to Rome with the dismal report of his failure; he had sickened further at the thought of living on, a dastard in the eyes of the only woman whose esteem he courted.

He considered his captors, and his glance was almost friendly. Were they not good friends of his, the best he had ever known, friends who came to him in the hour of his most urgent need?

"'Tis so," he said quite simply. "I am the man you seek. I am Captain Jenkyn."

The trial of Captain Jenkin – which, under instructions from the Secretary of State was hurried forward, so that it took place within three days of his arrest – attracted little notice at the time.

As in the case of all matters relating to Jacobite plottings, it was the desire of the Government that it should be disposed of as quietly and speedily as possible. Therefore the news of his capture was not allowed to transpire until his trial was over, and he himself under sentence of death.

The prisoner's admission that he was Captain Jenkyn had saved the court both time and trouble, for all that it was exercised not a little by this sudden supineness in one whom they had every reason to believe bold and resolute. They accounted for it upon the assumption that, being caught, his resourcefulness and courage had deserted him, and that perhaps he had hoped by pleading guilty to the charges preferred to earn the clemency of his judges. Lord Carteret was relieved to learn that the fellow had, himself, admitted his identity, since that disposed of the necessity of unmasking so very valuable a Government spy as Pauncefort. Under the circumstances sufficient evidence was afforded by the three tipstaves who had arrested him, and Sir Henry Tresh's lady, who came forward to identify him with the man who had invaded her chamber at "The World's End" on that evening when the plotters were taken there.

The affair was a very brief one, summarily dealt with, as you may see by consulting the "State Trials," where you will find all the details of it if you have a mind for them. The prisoner himself seemed intent upon assisting the court at every turn, readily admitting, one after another, the charges brought against him – whether concerned with previous visits to England or with the present one – charges which had long been drawn up in preparation for and awaiting such a day as this – a preparation which explains the Government's ability to expedite the affair.

On one point only was the prisoner stubborn. Whilst ready to admit that he was Captain Jenkyn, he would not admit that his real name was Captain Gaynor. He did not deny it; but he refused to admit it. They had arrested him, he said, as Captain Jenkyn, and as Captain Jenkyn he was indicted. Let that suffice them.

This apparently curious attitude was based upon the reflection that to admit his real identity might be to assist the Government in proceedings against many of those who were known to have been the associates of Captain Gaynor and against whom there was no independent evidence of Jacobitism. He did not know to what extent the absence of positive knowledge would hamper the Government; but, in any event, he was resolved to make no admissions that might assist it.

The court did not press, obedient always to its instructions. It could have done so, obviously. It could easily have produced witnesses to swear that he was Captain Gaynor; it could have fetched Sir John Kynaston and his family from Chertsey; it might even have thrust the discomfited Second Secretary Templeton into the humiliating position of saying by what name he had known this man who had so imposed upon him. But the Government desired, above all, that the matter should be swiftly and quietly determined, with as few witnesses and as little stir as might be necessary to procure the conviction and sentence of so very desperate and dangerous a rebel.

So the court waived this minor point, and as Captain Jenkyn our Jacobite was duly sentenced to be hanged at Tyburn like any common cutpurse.

There was calculation even in this, and wise calculation. He was to die obscurely, at the hands of the common hangman; this, too, it was deemed must prove a deterrent – that is to say, not merely the death, but the inglorious manner of it.

There were few people in court when the sentence was passed, and no single face did Captain Gaynor see with which he was acquainted. Pauncefort, he imagined, might have looked in to gloat over his plight. But Pauncefort wisely had kept away. Templeton, he had fancied, might have desired to come there and satisfy himself of a thing that to him must seem incredible. He marvelled at the Second Secretary's absence; but then he did not know that the Second Secretary found the ridicule which he had sought to heap upon Lord Carteret concerning Captain Gaynor all recoiling upon himself; that he had taken to his bed, announcing himself assailed by gout. (When Templeton came to hear that sentence had been passed upon the prisoner, he immediately resigned his office as the only possible step remaining to his tattered dignity.)

Sir John Kynaston, the Captain had thought, would surely have come. For he did not know that Sir John, like all the rest of the world, was in ignorance of the fact that the trial was taking place, conceiving that a trial upon charges so complex and difficult to establish must be long in preparing.

Captain Gaynor heard his sentence entirely unmoved. He had expected nothing else. He was no trivial foolish plotter, but an accredited agent, the disturber – as the indictment had it – of the peace of the realm, a man who aimed at the overthrow of the dynasty and, if necessary, at the death of the reigning sovereign, a man who was looked upon as a spy of the Pretender's, and for whom there could be no fate but the spy's.

Nor was his immobility merely external, or born of pride as it is with so many who show themselves outwardly undaunted at the prospect of an early death. His pulses remained calm, his heart tranquil. It was no more than he desired. Standing in the face of death he was enabled to do a thing he could not have done with life before him – a thing to be done at all costs, even at the cost of life itself, as he was doing it.

His trial took place on a Monday – the last Monday in June – and he was informed that same evening that he was accorded three days in which to set his affairs in order and make his soul. On the following Thursday he was to hang.

The time was more than he desired; certainly more than he required for what remained him to do. Relatives who mattered, he had none. With his friends he did not dare to communicate for fear of implicating them. To his master in Rome it would have pleasured him to send a dying message of devotion. But he knew that no such message would be allowed to reach its destination. There remained, then, but the letter to Damaris to indite. When that was done, he would be done with all matters of this world, and that was the thing which the near approach of death enabled him to do, the thing he could not have done had the way of life been open still before him.

But it was not until the evening of Wednesday that he asked for pen, ink and paper. He desired to make that communion with her almost the very latest act of his swiftly ebbing life, setting at last to paper the thoughts that since his trial had almost entirely occupied his mind.

He headed his epistle: "From my cell in Newgate, on the even of my death."

That done he was fretted awhile, as he sat pen in hand, to know how to address her. He solved the riddle, at last, by confining himself simply to her name.

Damaris [he wrote], when you read these lines I shall have gone where neither execration nor compassion can pursue me, and for that reason if for no other I have the consolation in these my last hours of hoping that you will read what assuredly you would not read were I still living and at large. For that reason alone I think that I am glad to die, since death gives me certain privileges and rights that are denied the living. Further still, since I stand upon the dread threshold, since the gates of doom are opening to admit me, and I am on the eve of facing my Eternal Judge, I have a claim to be believed when I write of things that might seem to you incredible did I still walk the great highway of life. For it is not to be thought that I should in such an hour and for no possible temporal profit sully myself with faleshood in matters whereupon I might without temporal loss continue silent to the end. When you consider, then, how little falsehood can avail me now, when you consider how repellent it is even to the most abandoned to deal in falsehood with the cold eye of death upon him, the icy scythe severing him already from all earthly hopes, desires and aspirations, I die content in the knowledge that what I am writing here you must believe, and believing will come to give me dead that treasure of your loving thought which living I could never have claimed again.

All that my Lord Pauncefort told you was true, yet no less true was my assurance, when you asked me to deny his story – that only were I the dastard he represented me could I have saved myself by the falsehood of such denial. You did not understand. You do not yet. For in these words, until all is known, must seem to dwell nothing but confusion. Yet in them dwells the whole and absolute truth. For never, 0 Damaris, was truth more untruly told than by Lord Pauncefort on that evil day.

It is true, then, that I played with him that ill-considered game. It was on a night when he had lost to me some eight thousand guineas, and he was bewailing that he stood upon the brink of utter ruin and in peril of a debtor's gaol. In that ill-omened hour, I bethought me that he had something yet to stake – his right to wed you – for I believed him still betrothed to you – and it is true that when I made him that proposal I had no thought of winning your own self, and that your fortune was the real stake I saw upon the board. But it is not true that by this – assuming that I succeeded with you did I win that game with him – I was an adventurer seeking your fortune for myself. My only thought was to devote that fortune to the service of my master, who is in such dire straits for means to his high ends. It was for him that I played that game, as my Lord Pauncefort well knows. That I should sacrifice you to a cause to which already I had sacrificed myself, in which I was imperilling the life that at last I am about to lose, did not then – nor does it yet – seem so heinous and unforgivable a thing.

His lordship won the cut. I paid him his guineas, and there the matter ended, or would have ended but for the deception which for reasons that I cannot fathom you thought it well, with your cousin, to play upon me. For here we touch upon a truth which should efface all other things in this mistaken enterprise, a truth which already I have uttered. I did not know, nor ever dreamt, that you were other than you represented yourself to be. I did not know, nor ever dreamt, that you were Damaris Hollinstone until you told me so in the garden a moment before his lordship came upon us. I looked upon your cousin as the heiress – as, I suppose, you intended that I should – and from the hour in which I met you I was glad that it was not you – you, Damaris – whom I was pledged by the fortune of the cards to abstain from wooing. I was glad in that hour to think that I had not won a game, whose stakes my honour must have compelled me to take up – for my honour is so bound up with the service of my king and master that I must account dishonourable all measures that do not aim at its advancement.

There, my beloved, you have all the truth, and it is my hope as I write – nay, it is my certainty – that the knowledge will help to comfort you. You need not take shame in any thought that you were the mere prey of an unscrupulous fortune-hunter, that you gave the pure and holy treasure of your love to an adventurer, a mercenary and a scoundrel.

The thought that you will come to know and to understand enheartens me and irradiates a season that must otherwise be very dark indeed. It warms and gladdens me in this hour, and I shall go blithely to my end, knowing that it is the modest price I pay for the sublime good of sending you this undoubtable assurance.

Tomorrow, for as long as thought can hold a place in this poor head, that thought will be of you. What is to follow after I do not know, nor do I fear. But if memory of life is still to be retained in the great beyond, one memory will linger to make my heaven – the memory of you, the consciousness that, knowing all, you will hold the memory of me in tenderness until we meet again, if there be meetings yonder.

And so, my sweet lady, my dearest love, goodnight!

It was late when the letter was concluded. He folded the sheets, tied them together, sealed them and placed them in his breast-pocket. Then he lay down, and soon was very peacefully asleep.

Before the hangman's minions came to seek him in the morning, he had given the letter into the hands of a friendly gaoler, together with his purse, containing some twenty guineas in recompense for the service the fellow had promised to do him.

Soon after eight the ordinary was introduced. He was a short, stoutish man with mild eyes but a heavy jowl, and the stubble of beard – a week's growth at least – that blackened his face lent him an almost ferocious aspect. He wore a soiled surplice; there was a peck of snuff hanging about his bands and in the stubble of his upper lip.

Captain Gaynor gave him a very courteous if somewhat distant welcome, presuming upon which the parson straightway fell to talking of the Captain's soul. In this the Captain cut him short.

"By your leave, good sir," said he, "I am of opinion, look you, that I know more of my own soul than any man can tell me. So leave me, I entreat you, to search it for myself. Meanwhile I can minister to your body. You'll find some passable Hollands in that jar, and there is a bottle of Burgundy which the gaoler has just procured me. Pray honour me." And the Captain waved him to the rude table where stood the vessels and a couple of drinking cans.

Thereafter he was but little troubled as he paced to and fro in his cell, awaiting with some impatience the coming of those who should take him for his last ride. They arrived at last, at a little before eleven.

They conducted him to the courtyard, where the cart was waiting, a company of redcoats drawn up about it, and every window of the gaol packed with villainous faces, their eyes greedy of as much of the coming spectacle as it might be theirs to witness.

He leapt lightly into the cart, and the ordinary, somewhat flushed with Burgundy, clambered after him. Gladly would he have dispensed with the fellow's company; but the rules did not permit it. The parson must be with him to the end – must, indeed, intone the psalm that would be sung at the turning-off. So perforce he submitted with the best grace possible.

The driver stood up and turned to the prisoner. He held a length of whipcord in his hand, and with this he pinioned the doomed man's wrists behind his back. Then he took up a length of hempen rope with a running noose in it, and deftly flicked this noose over the Captain's head, leaving the end of the rope to hang behind him. That done – and with the utmost nonchalance, the ruffian puffing, meantime, a short and very foul pipe – the gates were opened. The Sheriff's Deputy, a splendid figure in a gold-laced, scarlet coat, gave the word of command, and the procession formed up and started.

Ahead went the military in their red coats and mitre-shaped hats, opening a way with their musket-butts through the mob that had collected about the prison gates. Out into that seething, human ocean rolled the cart. With dispassionate, almost pitiful eyes the Captain looked upon that surface of upturned faces. One bestial fellow was singing an obscene song allusive to the Captain's grim condition. The Captain's eyes fell upon him in a look so profoundly compassionate that the rascal broke off short in the middle of his ditty, and after a moment's silence loosed a volley of lewd oaths at him.

Looking, the Captain had wondered in what circumstances death would come to find such a man, and he had seen – with that extraordinary vision which is vouchsafed to men who stand upon the Threshold – an image dreadful beyond words, an image that had informed that profound compassion of his glance.

They pushed on. Crowds everywhere along the cart's way; every window held a little mob, assembled there to see a man pass to his death. To Harry Gaynor though ever dispassionate now and beyond resentment of such trifles, there seemed something foul and obscene in this curiosity.

He turned his gaze from it at last and met the mild eyes of the ordinary. They were full of tears. This he deemed very odd. He was almost touched by it, forgetting entirely the amount of Burgundy which the chaplain had consumed and in which his heart had been softened so that the death of a stray dog would have rendered him maudlin.

"Sir," he said very gently, "I beg that ye'll not weep for me who do not weep for myself."

"That is the very reason of my weeping," the parson answered him, and a tear detached itself at last, ran down his ample cheek and joined the snuff on his neckband, all of which the Captain observed with extraordinary interest.

"This is very odd," he said. "Do you, then, not believe in what you teach? Do you not believe in a joyous and glorious hereafter?"

The ordinary stared at him, and in his surprise forgot his weeping.

"Or is it that in your own experience this world has proved it so extraordinarily delectable a place that you will not barter it for any other?"

"Nay, nay, sir. But you, so young –" the fellow mumbled inconclusively.

"Am I not fortunate therein, since I shall be spared the infirmities of age?"

"But to be cut off in mid-life, thus! It is so monstrous pitiful. Oh, sir," he implored, "turn your thoughts, I beg, to other things."

"They are so turned," the Captain answered quietly. " 'Tis yours, sir, that seem to be earth-bound, else why this grief in which I cannot share? Sir, I do think you lay too much store by this little moment we call life." And lo! it was the doomed man who set himself to offer spiritual comfort to the parson.

159

"Since go we must in the end, what shall it signify that we go today or tarry until tomorrow? Shall we bewail a day? Let me tell you a story I heard once in the East."

"God forbid!" ejaculated the ordinary. "In such an hour!" he cried, all scandalised. "Would you still dwell upon your past when your thoughts should be all of the future?"

The Captain smiled a little, and said no more. Still overlooking the Burgundy, he accounted this fellow unfit for the ordeal of bearing solace to the doomed. The task, it was evident, confused him. There fell a silence between them. The cart, at a snail's pace, was crawling up Holborn Hill, and everywhere surged the same brutal, unfeeling crowd, staring, shouting, jesting, jeering.

Do not suppose that in this was any political rancour. Few, indeed, had any notion of the offence for which the Captain was to suffer. He was just a man going to be hanged, and a man going to be hanged was ever an interesting and often a somewhat amusing spectacle, always sufficient to justify a holiday.

The ordinary, watching his face, saw its almost contemptuous wonder, and misinterpreted it.

"I marvel vastly, sir," he said, "that you did not get leave to come in a coach."

"Could I have done so?" asked the Captain, with but indifferent interest.

"At your own expense," the parson assured him.

"Ah, well, 'tis little matter."

But now another thought occurred to the ordinary. He had just observed that the cart contained no coffin.

"Have you no friends?" he asked abruptly. He was obliged to shout almost that he might be heard above the din.

"Friends? I hope so."

"Where are they, then?"

The Captain's brows were knit in an instant. "Would you have them here to swell this dreadful throng?" he asked.

"Nay, nay; but what provision have they made?"

"Provision, sir?"

"Ay, for your burial. Have they obtained leave to bury you?"

The Captain looked at him, and smiled. "The thought has never engaged me. I had imagined, if I imagined anything, that all this was the concern of those that hang me."

"Then ye were mistaken, sir."

"Does it signify so much?" he asked. And before the extraordinary calm of the soldier's eyes, the ordinary became suddenly aware that he was very far astray from the path of his duty, that his thoughts were all for this wretched, perishable body instead of for the imperishable soul.

He uttered some commonplaces of religion, some of the minor currency that it was his trade to circulate. The soldier sat silent, his thoughts far away, thankful for this respite from the man's more trivial chatter of trivial things. He turned his head to look forward, and he heard the ordinary's sudden, alarmed "Don't look!"

But it did not deter him. They were trundling downhill now, the mob growing more and more dense, the houses thinning. Below there, at the hill's foot, the ground was black with swarming humanity, and from the midst of it, a dark triangular object reared itself – the sinister triple beam.

Captain Gaynor eyed it steadily, then turned him to the ordinary once more.

"We approach the journey's end," he said, and smiled. "It is very well, for the journey itself is none so pleasant."

Chapter 15

EXECUTION

Often has it been written that death is life's greatest adventure. A paradox lurks subtly in the statement, which may be the reason why the phrase has been esteemed of so many writers. But of the death Captain Gaynor was to die that day at Tyburn, the statement can be made in its literal meaning, and without paradox, that it was the greatest adventure of his life.

I am tempted at this stage of my history to interpolate here a memoir from the pen of the somewhat famous Dr Emanuel Blizzard. And if upon due consideration I have resolved not to quote this document verbatim, it is because, despite its wealth of detail, this record is, after all, an incomplete one; for there was, of course, much concerning Captain Gaynor's history with which the famous professor was never made acquainted.

I write, however, with the doctor's memoir before me – indeed, in its absence, it would be impossible for me to fill in the details of this most extraordinary part of the history I am relating. Much of that memoir – and my reader will be quick to discern the passages – I transcribe almost literally, save that here and there I have been able to elaborate from other records at my disposal certain points which to the doctor remained perforce obscure. Moreover, it will better contribute to the lucidity of my own narrative if I marshal the events in the order of their happening – an order by no means observed by the professor.

As the cart bearing Captain Gaynor came under the fatal beam, the vociferations of the crowd abated. They sank to a mere murmur, to a subdued hissing whisper, as of a breeze stirring through a forest, and lastly into an absolute and deathly silence – the impressive, expectant hush of nature when a storm impends.

The ordinary was reading aloud the Office for the Dead. Jack Ketch, the ruffianly driver of the cart, was on his feet. He took the end of the rope that hung from the noose round Captain Gaynor's neck, swung it a moment to gather the required momentum, then threw it over the beam and deftly caught it again as it came round and down. In an instant he had knotted it. In another he had resumed his seat, taken up his whip, and with a stinging cut sent his horse at a half-gallop down the lane which the military had opened out for him in the mob.

Captain Gaynor found himself alone now in the cart. The parson had vanished, though he could not remember at what precise stage of the journey the fellow had left him. All round the vehicle seethed the crowd, yelling, shouting, cursing, laughing once more, but they seemed no longer to heed him.

Onward the cart rolled, with a thundering rumble now, which increased in volume as they went, and the Captain observed with faint curiosity that those who were not quick to avoid it went down under its wheels. Theirs were the curses and foul oaths with which his ears were being deafened.

Soon, however, these and all other sounds began to fade. They had left the crowd behind, about that triangular structure which he knew stood some way in the rear. They were coming into the open country. The wheels of the cart still rumbled, but less noisily now, and as they rolled presently over a soft spread of emerald turf this sound faded almost entirely.

The Captain discovered that his hands were no longer pinioned, and this was as mystifyng as that sudden disappearance of the parson, for he could not recall at what particular stage of his progress the bonds had been removed.

He turned, and saw before him, sitting upright upon his plank, the immobile figure of the driver in his ragged three-cornered hat and coat of rusty black. The fellow still puffed his short clay pipe, for the smoke of it hung in wreaths about his head. He marvelled at his unconcern and apparent disregard of his prisoner.

They were ambling gently now down a lane between hedgerows that were aflame with extraordinarily rich blossoms. The sunlight was dazzling. It shone upon the waters of a pond, which he perceived through a gap in the hedge, so brilliantly that his eyes were hurt and dazzled.

It occurred to him then that since Jack Ketch was so unobservant and unconcerned, and since there was none other by to hinder him, he need not continue in the cart. He threw a leg over the rail at the back, and leapt lightly to the ground.

The vehicle rolled on. He stood watching it as with incredible swiftness it diminished in size down that interminable avenue. When it was no more than a speck in the far distance, he turned and went through the gap in the hedge with that unbearable reflection of sunlight on water beating upon his eyes; and turn which way he would he could not avoid it. There was water all about him now, and it all shone fiercely, like a mirror in the very eye of the sun. At last he perceived a bridge. He advanced towards it, and crossed it, shutting his eyes to exclude that fierce glare, yet still conscious of it even through closed lids. He opened them again to make the discovery that this bridge which he had crossed was the rustic structure leading into the garden of Priory Close. Strange, he thought, that he should never before have observed what a deal of water flowed down the little ravine it spanned. And then he ceased to wonder about anything, for before him stood a radiant Damaris with arms held out in welcome.

He plunged forward with a cry, and sank into her embrace.

"My dear," she said, "why have you left me so long to my bitter thoughts of you?"

He sought to answer her, but could not; her arms were laced so tightly about his neck that he could not speak. She was strangling him. Had he been able to speak he would have told her so. But he could not. Yet although the choking was hurting him, he did not attempt to struggle. It was so good to lie there. He was very, very weary. He nestled his head more closely upon her breast. A great drowsiness overcame him, and he fell asleep.

Between two of the three uprights of that triangular structure, the body of Captain Gaynor swung gently to and fro, as if the warm summer breeze made sport with it.

About the foot of the gibbet there was an open square, maintained by a hedge of men in scarlet coats and mitre-shaped hats. The drums had long since ceased to beat.

Came a sharp word of command, and a line of muskets flashed up and rattled to rest, each upon the shoulder of its owner; another word of command, and the redcoats manoeuvred into marching order, four abreast. Then the drums rolled out again, and the scarlet phalanx swung briskly away through the tumultuous crowd.

The show was at an end.

Into the open square which the military had maintained at the gallows' foot sprang now some half-dozen resolute and bustling ruffians. The crowd surged after them, like waters suddenly released, and a cart pressed forward with the foremost.

The tallest of these ruffians, with a knife between his teeth, shinned up one of the vertical timbers and threw a leg over the cross-beam from which the Captain's body was swinging. With his knife he slashed through the rope, and the body tumbled into the arms of his companions below. Two of them bore it away. The others plied elbows and tongues to force a passage through the rabble with their prize. They gained the cart, flung in their limp burden, and as one of them vaulted after it, the driver cracked his whip and cursed the people volubly and obscenely. A way was reluctantly opened, and into this the little cart pressed, driven forward like a wedge. Slowly it won through.

Some little distance from the gallows a chaise had been drawn up. In this sat an elderly gentleman, who, with a grey face and dull, pain-laden eyes, had watched the execution. His aspect was so profoundly grief-stricken that the crowd about his carriage had felt the influence of it, and had preserved an almost utter silence. They resented being constrained to this despite themselves, for they felt that their enjoyment of the show had been marred; but for all their resentment they had not been able to shake off the spell of that anguished old countenance.

Suddenly, as the body was being borne away, Sir John Kynaston – for he it was – seemed to rouse himself from his trance. He uttered a cry and carried a trembling hand to the carriage door. He fumbled at it for some moments, opened it at last, and sprang down, shouting. But his voice was lost in the terrific uproar. He attempted to struggle through the crowd. But, spent as was his strength by grief, he was unequal to the effort, and after a quarter of an hour's striving he had got no farther than the foot of the gallows, whilst the cart was vanishing into the Edgware Road.

He implored those about him to pass the word along that he would pay the snatchers handsomely for their booty. An attempt was made to do his will, and the message travelled some little way, but it was scattered and lost at last.

In the end he was forced to give up the attempt. Blaming himself for not having thought of the matter sooner, he made his way with feeble, unsteady steps – his vigour all sapped – back to his carriage. The crowd was growing thinner now. He regained his chaise, and so returned in sorrow to Chertsey, deriving, if possible, an added grief from the reflection that he had neglected to perform the last rites by the body of his old friend's boy.

Priory Lodge in those days was haunted by an atmosphere of gloom. Evelyn and Damaris remained both invisible even to Sir John, both pleading indisposition.

Evelyn was overcome with terror at the ruin she had wrought, for she accounted that Captain Gaynor's arrest and execution had all resulted from the disclosure of his identity when Lord Pauncefort spied upon the lovers in the garden. She it was who had fetched his lordship to Chertsey by her letter, and she, herself, had conducted him to the garden that he might surprise his betrothed in the arms of another.

It had been with her no more than an act of petty vengeance, she could scarce have said for what. But she had intended that it should remain petty; she had never dreamt of such tragic consequences as these. She was prostrated by them and by her consciousness of guilt; and it went as near to making a woman of her and arousing her dormant intelligence as anything could do. She had not seen Damaris since the happening – now some ten days old – in that garden. She had been afraid to face her, and now her fear had increased to terror since Sir John had brought word three days ago of the sentence of death that had been passed upon their whilom guest. That had been terrible enough. But now came the still more terrible news – again brought by Sir John – that Captain Gaynor had been hanged.

In her anguish, in her overwhelming panic, Evelyn wanted to die. She could never again meet the eyes of Damaris. She was – she told herself that night, as she lay wide-eyed upon her bed – a murderess. Once, in the grey hour of dawn she rose from her bed, fell on her knees beside it, and prayed – not to heaven, but to the spirit of Captain Gaynor – for forgiveness. Conceiving that this spirit being disembodied must be now all knowing, she cried out to it that she had not meant to work this havoc, that her deed had been light and heedless, that never would she have performed it could she have dreamed of such consequences to himself as these.

Some comfort she took in the reflection that he must know, and that knowing all he must forgive, as all must who know all.

It was on the morrow that Sir John brought himself to question his wife on the subject of the Captain's sojourn at Priory Close. His wife, with habitual irrelevance and her passion for the unimportant, related to him the deception that had been practised by the girls. He gathered from this and from what else she added that Harry Gaynor had wooed Damaris under the impression that he was wooing Evelyn; he learnt that Pauncefort had been at Priory Close on the very morning of the day upon which the Captain had been arrested; and he was able for himself to piece together the event, save that he knew nothing of the revelations that had driven Damaris away in a loathing of Harry Gaynor as great almost as had been that which earlier had turned her from Pauncefort.

He sat in the library pondering it all, and thinking of the elder Gaynor who had been his friend, his more than brother, and thanking God that he had not lived to see this day of sorrow. He pondered the hope he had nourished of wedding his only child to Harry. That hope must, he saw, in any case have been frustrated. It mattered little now. For Evelyn, indeed, it was better as it was; better that she had not loved him. And then he sat up sharply with a sudden, a terrible thought. It moved him to rise and go in quest of his wife again.

"What ails Evelyn?" he inquired.

"I do not know, my dear. The child is very odd always, and very headstrong." Lady Kynaston sighed. "I never had her confidence."

"How long has she been ailing? How long has she kept her chamber?"

Her ladyship considered a moment. "Why, ever since Captain Gaynor left us," said she.

He was answered, he thought. His daughter, too, was stricken by the same blow. She had conceived for the Captain an unrequited passion. His heart bled for her, and in his compassion he went at once to seek her.

He found her sitting listlessly by the window of her room, her hands idle in her lap. The roses had all fled from her cheeks; she looked haggard, so haggard and woebegone that even her air of intense femininity had departed from her. She raised heavy eyes to her father's face, and he observed the dark lines under them that told the tale of sleepless nights.

"My dear!" he said. "My poor child!" He held out his arms to her, and there were tears in his old eyes.

His pity stabbed her. She did not understand it, but she understood that it was sprung from some misapprehension.

"Ah, don't touch me, father!" she cried. "You don't know, you don't know!"

"I think I do," he answered very gently.

"You do?" He saw horror in the eyes so suddenly lifted to stare at him. At once she realised that he had no knowledge of the truth, that something very different was in his mind. He came upon her very ripe for confession, at a point where, did she not share her burden with another, she must sink under it and die, she thought. She rose, flung herself upon his breast, and there, through a storm of sudden weeping, in a voice broken by sobs, she poured out her miserable story.

He listened, frowning awhile. But when the end was reached he did not put her from him in aversion, as she had feared. Gently he stroked her golden head.

"For the unworthy thing you did, Evelyn, you have been punished enough," he said. "Do not torment yourself with the supposition of a greater sin. It was not you who gave Captain Gaynor to the hangman, nor did Lord Pauncefort do it in consequence of what he witnessd here, nor yet did he, as you suppose, discover Captain Gaynor's identity as a result of what you enabled him to overhear. He knew it already. He was himself a Jacobite who had betrayed his fellow-plotters. So comfort you at least with the knowledge of that."

She comforted herself very speedily and completely, as such natures can. She slept soundly that night, and on the morrow when she made her appearance at the breakfast-table she had resumed much of her habitual air.

Nor was she any longer oppressed by the fear of meeting Damaris, since in no degree now did she account herself guilty towards her cousin. It was true that she had done a meanness in writing to Lord Pauncefort and bringing him to spy upon the lovers, but for the rest she had her father's word for it that her action had nowise altered the inevitable course to which the events of these last days had been fore-ordained. But if she no longer feared to meet Damaris, yet she could not go the length herself of seeking Damaris, nor for that matter could Sir John, despite the urgings of his deeply sympathetic nature.

There was not, however, the need. Damaris, of her own accord, came forth on the following evening from her retirement, and sought her uncle.

He was in the library, writing to his brother, when suddenly she stood before him, almost ghostly in her intense pallor as she paused among the shadows by the door for his leave to intrude a moment. He sprang up at sight of her and went to meet her, and even as he was shocked by the change that grief had wrought in her, so was she shocked by the greyness of his face, the haggard air where joviality had ever sat and the dullness of those blue eyes that usually were so bright and smiling.

He held out his hands and she took them, her fingers tightening upon them. But for this man who had been more than father to her, her loneliness must be utter now.

"How cold you are, my child," he murmured. Then his voice broke. "Oh, my poor Damaris!" His voice told her that – no matter how – he was informed of all, or, at least, of all that mattered.

"I came to talk to you of him," she said quietly, her voice, as controlled as her face, like her face showing, despite her, the suffering through which she was passing.

He led her forward to a chair, and when she was seated he went to stand by the overmantel. So had he stood, she remembered, on that day when at Pauncefort's side by the window there, she had looked upon him as her enemy, and defied him. How bitterly, now, she repented her that momentary defection! How profoundly she loved him, since today, in his affection for Harry Gaynor, she discovered a fresh and very solemn bond between them.

"He desired me to give you certain messages when he was on the point of setting out," she said, and neither of them deemed it strange that she should find no need to mention any name. "They do not amount to very much, but he dared not write them, he said, lest his letter should miscarry. As it is, you no doubt will have guessed what he would wish to say." And she repeated with a rare fidelity the words he had entrusted to her.

"Yes," he said heavily, when she had done. "All that I understood."

"I – I have since had a letter from him," she said.

"He wrote to me from Newgate, on the eve of – on Thursday last. You – you were with him – at the end?" she asked.

"I was there," replied Sir John. "But he did not see me."

She swayed on her chair. She passed a hand over her brow, her face strained with the effort of self-control. "How – how did he die?" she asked at last.

"Happily, I think," Sir John replied. "He was smiling at the end, when – when he stood up. What had he to fear?" cried the baronet, a sudden vigour returning to his voice, a defiance almost. "What had he to fear? He was as brave and gallant a gentleman as ever drew the breath of life, a man whom all honoured and loved, and he died a martyr to truth and right. What then, had he to fear in death?" The tears ran down the old man's cheeks, and his voice sank again, as he concluded: "Had the poor lad been my own son I should have been as proud of him as I was of the affection with which his father honoured me."

She rose and came to him. She reached up to put her arms about his neck, drew down his head, and very gently kissed him. And so, quietly, her sorrow ever silent and contained, she left him.

Chapter 16

RESURRECTION

For almost all the matter contained in this chapter I acknowledge an indebtedness that will presently he apparent to that memoir of Dr Blizzard which I have mentioned, and upon which already I have drawn for those dream-sensations experienced by Captain Gaynor when he was turned off and left swinging after the cart had drawn away from under him.

I closely followed that portion of the memoir up to the point at which the Captain lost consciousness, or – to adhere strictly to his own impressions – at which he sank to sleep, his head pillowed upon the bosom of Damaris.

When next he awakened it was in surroundings vastly different from those under which he had sunk to slumber, as he believed. Here was no sunlit garden, but a square, whitewashed chamber, lighted not only by a window in one of its walls, but also from another – and a very large one this – in the ceiling immediately above him.

Someone was bending over him, and a face was peering into his. But it was not the lovely, beloved face of Damaris. Instead, it was a keen, lean, almost wolfish face, with leathern cheeks and very piercing little eyes that were considering him through horn-rimmed spectacles.

He lay quite still and only half conscious as yet, looking up into that face, and neither wondering nor caring to whom it might belong. Then, as his awakening proceeded, he was conscious that his body was cold and stiff and that there was a strong taste of brandy in his mouth. His left wrist, he discovered, was in the grip of this wizened-faced man; but it was a very gentle grip, with a finger pressing lightly upon his pulse.

Then, quite suddenly, memory like a flood poured in upon his consciousness, and his awakening was complete.

He attempted to rise from his recumbent position, and the effort set a thousand hammers swinging in his brain. His head, he found, was just an ache, a globe of pain, no more. The window above him appeared to slide to and fro, the couch upon which he lay heaved under him, and the wizened face of his companion dilated and contracted horribly as he watched it. He groaned and closed his eyes. The pain spread downwards through his body, which lay stark there upon a table – for such was the nature of his couch. Then, at last, the tide of torment slowly ebbed again, leaving him bedewed from head to foot with sweat.

He opened his eyes once more. He attempted to speak, and this fresh effort centralised the pain in his throat and tongue. They seemed swollen to elephantine proportions.

The leathern mask of a face above him appeared suddenly to crack across. A very wide and quite lipless mouth had opened, and from it issued a queer, clucking sound.

"Tut, tut! Tut tut! Better keep still! Better keep still!"

The hand had already left his wrist, and now the figure turned and moved away a little to another table under the window in the wall. Captain Gaynor was able to follow it with his eyes without moving his head. He observed the man to be of middle height and very thin. He wore black velvet breeches, black silk stockings and shoes with steel buckles. He was without a coat, and the sleeves of his waistcoat and shirt were rolled up to the elbows of two long, thin, sinewy arms. His waistcoat itself was concealed by a coarse, yellowish apron in which there were several dull, brown patches. This apron covered him in front from chin to waist; the remainder of it had been rolled into a rope and was twisted round his middle. The table to which he had moved was of a good size and of plain deal. Part of it was encumbered by phials of all forms and sizes; but in a clear space in the middle, upon a spread cloth, was an array of very bright instruments of queer shapes, whose purpose the Captain could not have guessed had his mind been in a condition to attempt the task.

Dr Emanuel Blizzard – for this was the identity of the man – took up a short-stemmed lily-shaped glass, and held it up in one of his enormous, bony hands. From one of the phials he poured into it a ruby-coloured liquid; from another he added something else that was quite colourless, and he did this with great care, pausing, adding another drop or two, pausing again, and yet again adding a drop. Then he set the phial down, and carrying the glass he once more approached the table where the Captain lay.

He thrust his left hand under his patient's head, and raised it very slowly and gently. But for all his gentleness those great hammers were set to swing again, and they crashed forward and backward in Harry Gaynor's brain. The rim of the glass was brought to his lips.

"Drink this," said the gruff voice, and obediently, without any will of his own, the Captain painfully swallowed the fluid. He was not conscious of any flavour in it at the time. But afterwards, when his head had been lowered once more, and the room had ceased to swing about him like the cabin of a ship, he became aware of a fresh pungency in his mouth, soothing and cooling and seeming to reduce its inflammation.

In the moment that his head had been raised, he had perceived in a subconscious way that he was quite naked, that there was blood on his left leg, that a ribbon of this blood ran to the little puddle reaching to the table's edge. Now, as he lay back once more, he noticed a faint dripping sound, recurring at very brief and very regular intervals. Dimly, and without much interest, he connected this sound with the puddle he had observed.

The events of the morning were coming back to him now in detail. He remembered the cart, the crowd, his pinioned wrists, the parson who had ridden with him, the glimpse he had of the gallows when he had turned his head as they were going down the hill. What happened afterwards, he could not remember until he came to that point where he had found himself in the open country, still in the cart at first, and later crossing a bridge over a great expanse of glaring water to find Damaris awaiting him.

He could not distinguish between the real and the imagined. That all this had happened to him he never doubted; but he could not explain it, any more than he could explain how he came to be lying stark naked upon a deal table with blood flowing from his leg and dripping into some vessel on the floor whilst a stranger tended him.

It would seem as if he had not been hanged after all, and he wondered why was this. But he did not wonder with any great activity; there was no vigorous mental effort to resolve this mystery. His brain was too tired and indolent for the exertion. The indolence gained upon him; it became a torpor, and very gently he sank once more into oblivion.

His next awakening was very different. It took place some twelve hours later, early in the morning of the following day. He was abed now in a solid furnished room that was full of sunlight, and for some moments he lay still, staring up at the white, flat canopy overhead. Then quite suddenly he sat up. Pain shot through his head once more, to bring back a dim memory of his last awakening. But it was endurable now, though still acute.

His sudden movement had been answered by another. From a chintz-covered settle ranged against the wall on his right sprang now the slender figure of the doctor. An arm went round the Captain to support him in his sitting posture; the little piercing eyes considered him again through those spectacles with their great horn rims, and Gaynor observed that, for all its wolfishness, the face was genial and kindly.

The wide lipless mouth opened, and as before it emitted that clucking sound; but the leathery, close-shaven countenance was wrinkled in a smile.

"Eh, and how do we feel now, eh? Better?" And as he spoke, the professor stamped his foot three times upon the floor – an obvious signal to someone below.

"Who are you?" the bewildered patient asked him.

"Eh? My name is Blizzard – Doctor Emanuel Blizzard, professor of anatomy, eh. And you're safe and snug in my house."

"In your house, Doctor – "

"Blizzard, sir – Emanuel Blizzard."

"And how came I here?" the Captain asked, his wonder and bewilderment increasing. His voice was so husky that he could not speak above a whisper, and he was conscious still of a numbness of tongue and throat.

The professor clucked again. "Tut-tut! 'Tis a long story that, and a strange. You shall hear it when you are more recovered. Ye're weak, eh? Ye will be. I bled you very thoroughly. But we'll soon renew what's lost."

A knock fell on the door. The anatomist set the pillows behind his patient so that they supported him in an upright position. Then he sped to the door, opened it, and returned with a tray on which was a bowl, a flagon of red wine and a glass. This tray he placed upon a table by the head of the bed. He took up the bowl, which was filled with steaming broth.

"Ye'll be hungry, eh?" he said, his head on one side. The Captain nodded weakly. "Aha! 'Tis very well."

He approached the patient, and with a horn spoon proceeded himself to feed him. Then he carefully measured him a half-glass of Burgundy, and he held it to his lips, what time the Captain slowly drained it.

"Another?" he asked. "Tut, tut! Better not. Better not, eh? We must go slowly. *Piano si va sano*, as the Italians say. For the present – *ne quid nimis*, eh?"

Gently as a woman might have done, he replaced the pillows, and induced his patient once more to lie down. Captain Gaynor obeyed him, too feeble, too utterly bewildered to resist. Something had happened to him; something altogether inordinate; but what that something might be he had no faintest conception, and least of all could he conceive how he came into the house of a professor of anatomy who treated him with such tenderness and solicitude. There was one point, however, that so plagued him that he must have enlightenment upon it. He looked up into that wolfish yet kindly countenance.

"Then – I was not hanged?" he inquired feebly.

"Hanged!" cried the other. "Tut, tut! Go to sleep. You'll be stronger when next you wake. Go to sleep now."

The prediction proved true enough. The broth and the wine spreading warmth through that debilitated frame bore a torpor with them, to which the Captain very shortly succumbed, notwithstanding the question with which he still plagued himself.

When next he opened his eyes upon that room, the sunshine had left it. By the mellow light and the tepid air that came through the open casement he knew it to be eventide. A stout, middle-aged woman with red polished cheeks, that gave her face the appearance of a giant apple, occupied a chair near the bed. She smiled reassuringly when she encountered his questioning gaze, and she rose at once.

"Better now?" she greeted him.

Captain Gaynor was better indeed, and he was conscious of an appetite that was keen as a razor's edge. He said so, and found his voice much stronger, whilst there was hardly any of the sensation of pain in tongue and throat. His head, too, was clearer, and it no longer ached when he moved it, as he did by way of testing its condition.

"I'll go call the doctor," she said. "He's resting below."

In a very few minutes the anatomist was at his patient's bedside. In another few minutes there was more broth and Burgundy for the

Captain, and even a few slices of capon's breast and a little wheaten bread.

"And now," said Captain Gaynor, reclining comfortably among his heaped-up pillows when he had consumed a meal which he found all too spare, "will you tell me how I come here, and how it befell that I was not hanged? What happened to me?"

The professor looked at him, meditatively stroking his smooth chin.

"It did not befall that you were not hanged," he said slowly. "Ye were hanged – two days since."

"Hanged?" The Captain started up. Horror and incredulity were blent in his countenance.

"Tut, tut, now!" clucked Dr Blizzard. "Let us be calm, eh! There's not the need to start and cry out. It's over, and it's not to do again. *Nemo bis punitur pro eodem delicto*, remember. That is the law, eh?"

But the impossibility of punishing a man twice for the same offence was the last thing that exercised the Captain's thoughts just then.

"But if I was hanged," said he, his face an utter blank, "how – how come I to be alive, for I am alive, am I not? I am not dead and dreaming, perchance?"

"Eh! Why, to be sure you're alive, and in a week or so I make no doubt but ye'll be about again as sound as ever you were."

"But how – how, if I was hanged?"

"Because if a man won't drown who's born to hang, neither will a man hang who's born to drown, eh? 'Tis the best reason I can think of, faith! And, faith! it's reason enough."

Still understanding little or nothing, the Captain stared at the doctor.

"I – I don't understand even now," he said weakly. "How came I here?"

"Eh? Ah, that is another matter, and well may it exercise you. It was this wise." The doctor took snuff in prodigious quantities, then snapped and pocketed his box, and sat upon the edge of the bed facing his patient. "It was this wise. When you had hanged for the term of twenty minutes – as by law prescribed – you were cut down by a couple of rascals who know where to obtain a guinea or two for the fruit of the leafless tree, as they humorously term it. And here let me say that ye were mighty fortunate in that ye gave no thought to your own burial and that no friends of yours saw to the reparation of that omission. He, he!" he laughed on a thin high note. "But for that – faith! – ye'ld not be sitting there drinking Burgundy. Ye'ld have been snug under a tombstone by now, eh!

"Well, then," he pursued, "these rascals brought you hither in a cart, and never was there living man who looked more dead. Ye deceived even myself, when I had you lying stark upon my table, for you'll understand that I had bought you to dissect you, and I never so much as suspected how I'd been swindled – that ye were not a corpse at all – until I had run my scalpel across your breast; you'll feel the sting of the scratch belike. It was not a cut; 'twas no more than skin-deep, to mark the line I was to follow. But behold! this line I had drawn turned suddenly bright crimson. If I say that I was amazed, I say nothing. I ran my finger along it and withdrew it moist with blood.

"There could be no doubt then that ye were not dead, eh? But whether you had travelled too far into the dark valley ever to be dragged back again to the world of the living was what I could not say. I held a mirror to your lips, and found it filmed with moisture after a moment. I set my finger to your pulse, but could discover no movement in it. So I opened a vein in your leg to stimulate the heart by setting the blood a-flowing; and within ten minutes you had opened your eyes and were endeavouring to sit up.

"Since then I've done little more than leave you to the *vis medicatrix naturae*. For Nature, sir, has endowed you very richly; so richly that I could almost regret the loss of the two guineas I gave those rascals for your anatomy – for ye've defrauded me, sir, in a most heartless fashion, eh!"

The Captain smiled feebly at the jest. But it was something that he was able to smile at all, now that he had the full account of this most extraordinary adventure.

"But you repay me richly in another way," the anatomist pursued.

"I can assure you, sir, you shall not be out of pocket in any way," said the Captain.

"Pish! Tut, tut!" The professor waved one of his great bony hands contemptuously.

"Tell me," said the Captain presently, "is it not a very extraordinary thing to have happened?"

"Extraordinary? Godso! Ye're not supposing that it happens every week, oh?"

"Have you ever known such another case?"

"As to that, why yes – though never in my own experience. Did ye never hear of John Smith the housebreaker – a few years ago – who was reprieved after he had been turned off and hanged for a quarter of an hour? When the reprieve arrived it scarce seemed worth while to make haste to cut him down, he looked so dead. Yet to all the world's amazement the rogue revived to return to his house-breaking trade. Then there was the case of Anne Green at Oxford, over fifty years ago. She was hanged for over half an hour, and like yourself fell into the hands of an anatomist – a Dr Petty – who revived her. And there have been others. Still, the event is rare enough – so rare that a man should be thankful when it serves him, eh!"

The Captain lay back among his pillows and abandoned himself freely to his amazement, and to the thoughts and speculations born of his astounding situation.

As the doctor had said, "*Nemo bis punitur pro eodem delicto*"; and so from the law of England he had nothing more to fear, even should his identity be discovered. But he did not think that it need be.

Very soon his thoughts turned to Damaris, and it was with a sudden fearful doubt that he asked himself what result his revival would have there. How had she received his letter? There was, he thought, but one way in which she could receive it. Yet his being alive again, or alive still, must alter everything and might modify her feelings if they were – as he thought they must be – of forgiveness.

The doubt was most cruelly tormenting. He turned suddenly to the doctor.

"How soon," he inquired, "shall I be in case to depart?"

"Tut!" clucked the professor. "Here's a great haste, now! Why, if you are quiet and obedient to me, perhaps in a week or a little longer you will sufficiently have regained your strength. You're healthy, amazing healthy. But I've half drained your veins, ye'll remember, and ye'll need wait until they are replenished, eh."

"A week!" he groaned.

"Tut! 'Tis but a little while. Be thankful ye're not dead and buried. And if ye've any friends with whom you'ld wish me to communicate – "

"No," said the Captain. "My friends can wait. It will be better." Then, shifting the subject: "Sir," he said, "there is a debt between us that it would tax my wit and my resources to liquidate."

"It need not. Tut! No. What else could I have done? Carved you up, as it was? Faith! every doctor is not a murderer, whatever the vulgar may say. Besides, ye're a more interesting experiment alive. Tell me now, d'ye not actually remember hanging?"

"I do not," said the Captain.

The anatomist nodded. "Ay, ay; 'twas just so with John Smith when he revived. Tell me what you remember."

Readily the Captain complied, relating those dream sensations that had been his, and suppressing no more than the name of the lady who had awaited him in the garden and in whose embrace he had seemed to choke.

"A warning that," snapped Dr Blizzard, "a warning of the perils that may lie in a woman's arms. Still, men will run the risk. Tut! the pity of it!"

But the anatomist treasured those details of the Captain's perilous passage through the gates of doom, and he incorporated them in that memoir he prepared of the curious resurrection of Captain Jenkyn, a memoir which – as I have said – has supplied me with most of these particulars.

Chapter 17

PAUNCEFORT THE SOWER

On the Monday of the following week – four days after the execution of Captain Gaynor – came my Lord Pauncefort to Priory Close for the first time since that encounter in the garden in which his lordship had all but lost his life.

Of that encounter, too, Sir John was informed by now, and of the intervention of the gardeners, which had saved Lord Pauncefort – an intervention which Sir John deplored as profoundly as any of the events of the past week. Indeed, but for that intervention Harry Gaynor might still have been among the living, and the world would have been the sweeter for being purged of a villain.

It was again in the library that the interview took place between Sir John and his unwelcome visitor. The baronet's first impulse had been to deny himself to his lordship. But he had thought better of it, and had repaired to that lofty, book-lined chamber where his visitor awaited him. Yet his greeting had been sufficiently uncompromising.

"Do you not think, sir," he said, "that you have wrought evil enough here already and that so you might have spared us this intrusion upon the grief you have occasioned?"

His lordship, hat under arm, and leaning lightly upon his amethyst-headed cane, had looked the very picture of injured innocence.

"Sir John," he protested quietly, "assuredly you speak under a grievous misapprehension."

"Is it a misapprehension that you delivered Captain Gaynor to his death?"

"A gross one," cried his lordship instantly. "Though I can see upon what grounds you base it. I am the more glad I came since I may now dispel your error. You have supposed, I see, that Harry Gaynor's arrest was the result of his unfortunate quarrel with me here. That is not so, sir. The warrant had been out some days already, and he must have been taken when he was. And the real fact is I came to warn him."

"To warn him that you had betrayed him?" Sir John's blue eyes were hard and cold as they played over his lordship's handsome, swarthy face, which flushed now under that regard.

"You use harsh words, sir, and untrue."

"In that you lie, my lord," answered the baronet. "Do you hear me – you lie!"

His lordship stiffened. He drew himself up very rigid, and Sir John watched him with eyes that gleamed almost wickedly.

"Were you twenty years younger, Sir John, I should ask you to prove your words upon my body. But you are an old man," he added, in tones that became a very insult of tolerance, his tall figure relaxing its menacing rigidity, "and so I must even bear with you and attempt to prove to you in more peaceful ways the ineffable injustice of your words."

"Spare me more of this," flashed Sir John impatiently. "You may disregard my insult on the score of my years, and I may lack the means to force you to regard it – for you would swallow a blow even as you swallow all else – "

"Sir John!" the other cried, suddenly roused. "Do not urge me too far or I may forget the years that lie between us."

"There is not the need. There are younger swords in plenty to call a reckoning with you. What of O'Neill and Leigh, your sometime friend, Harewood, Clinton, Brownrigg, and Mr Dyke, who is said to play the deadliest sword in England? Have you bethought you what will happen when presently these and the others you have betrayed into gaol are restored to liberty? – as restored they must be for lack of satisfactory grounds upon which to impeach them. Do you think they will be slow to avenge upon you the base treachery you performed in selling them? Or do you perhaps consider them in ignorance or doubt of their betrayer?"

Ever since his encounter with Gaynor, Pauncefort had been plagued by the thought of this; for Gaynor had made it more than plain that his lordship's treachery was revealed, and it was odds that what Gaynor knew was known to all the plotters. And yet it was possible that it might not be; and, Gaynor being dead, his lordship had clung to that possibility. As for Sir John, he was aware of the source of the baronet's suspicions; he knew that they sprang from the veiled threat he had uttered at their last meeting.

Slowly now he shook his head under its heavy black periwig. His large eyes looked almost sorrowful.

"How sadly are you mistaken," said he. "As for those you name, I cannot think they would so misjudge me. But if any should, he will find me ready for him – ready to satisfy him in any manner he desires. Meanwhile, however, Sir John, there is the business upon which I am come."

"Ah, true!" snapped the baronet. "I detain you, no doubt. Pray state this business. Thus shall I be the sooner rid of you."

"I bring you a warning," said his lordship.

"Such a warning, I make no doubt, as that which you bore Harry Gaynor," was the stinging answer.

Lord Pauncefort considered him with those sorrowful eyes of his. "Even so," he said quite simply. Then he sighed. "Indeed, I think that I had better go my ways, leaving you to the fate that hangs over you, since you have naught but insults for me. And yet, sir, I will beg you to consider – since there is no other way of convincing you of my good faith – that I can stand to gain little or nothing by my warning to you, and," he added with slow emphasis, "that I might gain a deal by your impeachment."

"You mistake," said Sir John, "I am in no danger of being impeached."

"It is you who mistake, Sir John; for you are in danger, in grave danger, not only of impeachment but of conviction. Against those others whom you have named I gladly admit that the Government can take no proceedings and will be forced to let them go for lack of evidence, and also because such is the Government's policy. But you, sir, are in far different case."

"I am," Sir John agreed, "because against me there is not even the shadow of an accusation to be produced."

"Ah! You build on that?" said his lordship sadly, and again he shook his handsome head and sighed. "There is something you've forgot. You have forgot that you harboured here one Harry Gaynor, the notorious Jacobite agent and spy – I use the Government's terms – who has been convicted and hanged."

It was quite true. If Sir John had not overlooked the fact itself, at least he had overlooked the consequences it must have for himself did the Government elect to move against him. It was a matter to which he had never given thought, and finding it thrust upon his notice thus abruptly by Lord Pauncefort, he perceived his danger as clearly as one may perceive a chasm that has opened in one's path.

He stood with hands clasped behind him, his tall, portly figure somewhat bowed and his face suddenly troubled, all the fine arrogance gone out of him. For there were not only the consequences to himself to consider, there were the consequences to his wife and child – the consideration of which had made him cautious to the point of lukewarmness in his support of that Cause in which at heart he believed. Were he convicted of treason – as it was very clear now he might be – part of his punishment would be a fine that must leave Lady Kynaston and Evelyn all but destitute.

A deep silence ensued. Sir John stood pondering with bowed head. When at last he raised it, and his troubled glance once more rested upon his visitor, Lord Pauncefort observed that his countenance was ashen. But if there was no longer any arrogance in his bearing, it was still in his tone and his uncompromising words.

"And it is of this that you are come to warn me?" he asked.

"Indeed, I would that were all," replied his lordship. "I am come to tell you that my Lord Carteret has at present under consideration the issuing of a warrant for your arrest upon that charge."

Sir John smiled bitterly. "Your information would serve, at least, to resolve any doubt that might linger in my mind concerning your own connection with the Government."

A shadow crossed his lordship's face, but he remained quite unmoved.

"You persist in your opinion of me. It is so deepseated that all things must serve to confirm it. But you are mistook, Sir John. My information springs from my personal relations with the Secretary of State, relations which have permitted me aforetime to serve my friends, and which have permitted those – such as you, sir – who are not my friends, to misconstrue my aims. I will add, sir, that in your own case this warrant would already have been issued but for the exertions which I have used with his lordship. I have played upon his friendship for me by drawing his notice to the fact that I must, myself, suffer by your arrest since I am hoping for the honour of becoming related to you by marriage before long."

"Ah!" said Sir John dryly. "I thought we should come to that in the end!"

Pauncefort frowned. "The disinterestedness of my motives must be so apparent, even to a mind prejudiced against me, that I marvel you still remain in doubt, sir. You conceive, I fear, that I am come to bargain with you. You expect me to say: 'Sanction my wedding with your ward and niece, and my influence with my Lord Carteret shall be employed, to obtain the suppression of this warrant.' That is what you expect of me, is it not?"

"Some such proposal, I admit," answered the baronet, "though I am sure you will cloak it in more specious terms."

His lordship stroked his cleft chin thoughtfully, and his eyes narrowed as they surveyed Sir John.

"Let me," he said very gently, "let me beg you to observe, Sir John, that to serve such aims as you impute to me, I need in this matter but to stand aside and suffer the warrant to be executed. Nay, more: Were I first and last the self-seeker you account me and do not scruple to pronounce me, I should be employing such influence as I have with the Secretary of State to urge the warrant's instant execution. For reflect, I beg, that upon your inevitable conviction of treason must follow your outlawry. The powers conferred upon you by the will of the late Mr Hollinstone will be determined; you will no longer have any voice at law in any matter whatsoever, and for sanction to my union with your ward may be dispensed with, for it is a thing you will have power neither to confer nor to withhold. That, Sir John, is a reflection which may lead you to judge me in a spirit of some justice."

But Sir John did not seem at all disposed to do so, notwithstanding that he perceived the irrefragable fact to which his lordship drew his attention.

"I see," he said slowly. "I see! What you have to propose then is that subject to my giving my sanction you will so exercise your influence with my Lord Carteret as to achieve the suppression of the warrant, eh? And thus – "

"Not so," Pauncefort interrupted, loud and imperiously. "I make no bargain. I have nothing to propose. I merely desire to indicate that by serving me you will best serve yourself. In any event my efforts can never be addressed to any end but that of saving you from your impending fate – and this, notwithstanding the insults you have heaped upon me now. But those efforts, which would be almost certain of success if exerted by one who is become your relative, are almost equally certain of failure coming from one who is no more than your friend."

The impudence of it struck Sir John speechless for a moment. He found in it matter for laughter almost, despite the overwhelming peril at which his heart was sickening.

"My friend?" he said, and his lip curled ominously. "Too great an honour." And he bowed ironically. "And there is one trifle that has escaped your attention, too, in this. You have forgot to consider Miss Hollinstone herself and her inclinations."

His lordship was on the point of answering that those inclinations might easily be swayed when she knew of Sir John's peril. But from that false step he saved himself betimes. He was none of your clumsy, superficial intriguers, but one who went to work skilfully in the depths. He contained himself and bowed, his face wearing an expression of concern and sorrow.

"It is true," he said. "I have not sufficiently considered how those inclinations will have been swayed against me in a household so permeated by a spirit hostile to myself – in a household where, despite all that I can protest and all that I can do, I am looked upon as a man who has not kept faith. It is monstrously unjust; but it seems there is naught I can do to combat it."

Suspicious of this half-resignation, Sir John eyed his visitor shrewdly.

"You betrayed yourself to her, my lord, in this very room," he answered slowly. "You betrayed the true fortune-hunting motives by which you were animated. Can you wonder that she looks upon you now with – with the contempt you merit?"

His lordship sighed. He dabbed his red lips with a flimsy kerchief ere he answered. Then he shrugged despondently.

"I was mad that day," he said. "That infamous money-lender, Israel Suarez, had been almost violent, and I was driven to the verge of despair. But, Sir John, if I showed myself eager for control of your ward's fortune, it was not thence to be construed that I was not eager for herself, that I did not love her for herself." He turned his large, handsome eyes upon the baronet. They were heavy with sorrow. "I would give my life to efface that hour," he said.

"Do so, then," said Sir John, "and perhaps you will efface it. If not, being dead, it will signify less to you. You will cease to suffer."

"You rally me, sir!" was the indignant cry.

"Neither yourself nor the Government," said Sir John, "can deprive me of the right to laugh. Soon it may be the only right remaining me."

His lordship took up his hat from the table, tucked it under his arm, and drew on his heavy riding-gloves. His face was set, his lips tight-pressed. But all this was purest comedy. He realised that he had said all that need be said. He had sowed his seeds, and it were well now to depart without further disturbing the soil, leaving those same seeds to sink in. He was fairly sanguine that they would put forth roots ere long. And, meanwhile, as some recompense for his services and some compensation for the injustice done him in the case of Harry Gaynor, Lord Carteret was willing to delay Sir John's arrest until Pauncefort should give the word. So that there was no desperate haste.

"In spite of all, Sir John," he said, "I cannot forget that for a season we were good friends."

"My memory is not so good as yours," quoth the downright, uncompromising baronet.

"So I perceive," said the viscount, smiling bitterly. "Mine is not only long, but grateful. And so, despite the unworthy manner in which you have used me today, I shall continue to strain every effort with my Lord Carteret to procure your immunity from the consequences of your meddling with treason."

Sir John strode to the bell-rope, and tugged it with a violent hand.

"I should loathe to be beholden to you," he said. "Pray leave my affairs to care for themselves."

"I understand, Sir John," replied the other, with a resumption of his air of resignation. "Oh, I understand." Then he bowed stiffly. "I have the honour to give you good day."

Sir John waved a hand in almost contemptuous dismissal. A footman, summoned by the bell, stood in the doorway. "Reconduct his lordship," said the baronet shortly.

But once alone, his manner changed as abruptly as if he had thrown off a cloak in which he had been wrapped. He walked heavily to the writing-table, sank into the chair, leaned his head upon his hand and stared dully into vacancy. Then something that was almost a sob shook his massive, vigorous frame.

"My poor Maria!" he groaned aloud. "My poor Evelyn! God help you both!"

But he had been wiser if, instead of groaning impotently there, he had retained awhile his cloak of defiant self-possession, and himself escorted my Lord Pauncefort to the chaise which awaited him in the avenue. Thus might he have averted the ill-chance which came to serve his lordship. For as Pauncefort was descending the steps, he encountered Miss Kynaston herself.

He paused a moment to give her greeting. His air was gloomy and preoccupied. But what engaged him now was a new thought that had flashed into his opportunist mind. True, he had accounted ample the seed he had sown; and yet he knew that Sir John could be very obstinate, that he might immolate himself out of that obstinacy upon the altar of what he accounted a sacred trust from the dead. There could be no harm his lordship opined, in sowing a little more seed in this very pretty and fertile soil so opportunely thrust before him.

"Alas, Miss Kynaston, I fear that I have been the bearer of but indifferent tidings to your father," he said, and the gloom of his face was most tragically deepened.

It alarmed her, as that subtle gentleman intended that it should. He noted the flutter of colour in her cheeks, the startled look in her eyes.

"What is it?" she asked him a little breathlessly.

He glanced aside at the footman who stood by the door. She read the look, and understood his meaning when he invited her to walk the length of the avenue with him.

"Drive on," he bade his coachman. "Stay for me at the gates."

Down the avenue of elms, in the dappled shade, stepped dainty Evelyn beside his handsome lordship.

"It is well, perhaps, that I should tell you," he was saying musingly, "most opportune, indeed, that I should have met you. You may be able to accomplish something in which I greatly fear me that I have failed, and in which my failure involved your father in grave peril."

Piqued, alarmed, flattered by the suggestion that she might achieve something in which he had failed, Evelyn's sweetly timid eyes fluttered him an upward glance of inquiry.

"Your father, madam, has involved himself very seriously by having harboured here one who has been convicted and hanged as a traitor and spy. Such an action subjects a man to penalties scarcely less grave than those imposed upon the actual traitor, because in itself such an action implies an almost equal degree of guilt."

"What do you tell me?" she cried, now all alarm.

"The brutal truth, ma'am. But there is not yet the need for alarm. What friend can do I am doing to obtain the suppression of the warrant which the Secretary of State has already signed for your father's arrest."

"For his arrest!" She stood still, one hand clutching his lordship's sleeve, and her lovely empty face was blenched.

"Nay, now, nay!" he soothed her. "I entreat ye, ma'am, do not give way. I am hopeful that I may prevail. I have much influence with my Lord Carteret; he listens to me, and you may be sure that all such influence shall be employed to serve you."

"What – what could they do to him if he were arrested?" she asked.

"Ah!" he said, and rubbed his chin. "They would hardly hang him, I think. No, no, there is no danger of that. But they will mulct him very heavily – so heavily that it may almost amount to a complete confiscation of his estates and possessions."

A vista of poverty, of destitution, was instantly opened out before the eyes of her imagination. It terrified her, for all that the picture was far from lifelike. She had looked upon so few of the realities of life that she was incapable of adequately conceiving this one. But she conceived enough of it to undergo almost an increase of terror.

"Oh!" she moaned, and again: "Oh!"

"But you are not to be alarmed," he repeated. "Oddslife, now, did I not say that I would exert my influence, and that my influence is great? Bear that in mind to set against your fears." He spoke cheerfully and confidently, and, reflective as she always was, she felt herself cheered and her confidence returning. Then his face clouded. "If," he ran on, "your father had but chosen the way I showed him, I could make his immunity a certainty. Unfortunately – "

"What way was that?" she questioned eagerly.

He looked down at this frail slip of womanhood, observed the elegantly coiffed golden head that scarce reached the level of his shoulder, and he sighed.

"As you know," he said, "I am betrothed to Damaris."

"Yes, yes," said she, for even now she had not learnt of the grounds upon which that betrothal had been dissolved. The readiness of the "yes, yes" informed him of this fact, and made things easier for him. His eyes glowed a moment with satisfaction.

"You may not know that your father is opposed to the marriage; that he will not allow it to take place until Damaris is of full age."

"But why?" she cried.

"Some trifling scruple of adherence to her father's wishes," he answered lightly. "This scruple I have begged him to put aside. I have assured him that were I his relative, instead of his friend, it would strengthen my hands to serve him, it would render Lord Carteret's suppression of the warrant certain. For, you see, madam, he loves me too well to wish to hurt any who might stand in a degree of relationship, however slender, towards myself."

"Then – then it is easy. He is safe, and there is not any cause for fear," she exclaimed, and her face was upturned to his.

He gloomed down at her sorrowfully, and shook his head.

"Unfortunately, your father will not waive his idle scruples," he said. Then he brightened again. "But do not let it concern you. After all, I do not doubt but that I shall be able to prevail even as it is. Still, the other way would be safer. But I dare not press your father on the point; nor yet dare I press Damaris, because – This is a confidence that you'll respect, Miss Kynaston?"

"Yes, yes," she assured him eagerly.

"Because," he resumed, "Damaris once did me the injustice to think that I wooed her out of mercenary motives, and I could not for all the world give her cause to think so again."

"How could she in this?" cried simple Evelyn.

He smiled the bitter, knowing smile of the man of the world, of the man who has looked into the human heart and studied its proneness to unworthy suspicions.

"It might be construed that I sought to make a bargain, and I could not suffer that. Therefore, I may not insist. Perhaps, indeed, I have failed to represent to your father the full extent of your peril. If I tell it you, it is because, thinking highly as I do of – of your wit, you may perhaps consider well to give a hint in the proper quarter. But do not on any account say that I urged it, and – and perhaps you had best say naught to your father."

It was as plain an invitation to tell Damaris as he could well have uttered; yet she did not perceive his subtleties.

"I understand," she cried. "Oh yes, I will do what I can."

"I am sure of it, and thus you will bring me the happiness of having served not only your father, but yourself – for it involves your own future as well!" Doffing his three-cornered hat, he bowed low over her hand. He kissed it in farewell, and also, as it were, to seal a bond between them.

They had reached the chaise by now. He entered it, whilst she stood by the gate-post watching him, somewhat bemused by all that he had said. The coachman gathered up his reins, when suddenly his lordship checked him. He thrust his head from the carriage window.

"Upon second thoughts, Miss Kynaston, perhaps it were best if you said naught to anyone. Leave the matter in my hands to deal with as best I can. I" – he faltered, and shrugged his shoulders helplessly. "I so dread the danger of unworthy motives being imputed to me. So best forget what I have said."

Again he gravely saluted her, and without waiting for an answer he sank back into his chaise. But as the carriage rolled away he smiled, well satisfied to reflect that his meeting her had been a most fortunate chance, and that he had sowed more than he had looked to do when he came, and some of it on very fertile soil.

Chapter 18

IN CHECK

As my Lord Pauncefort calculated so did things fall out. No sooner had she seen his carriage roll away in a cloud of dust towards London than Evelyn went in quest of Damaris.

She found her seated by the window of her room – she would sit there by the hour now in apparent idleness – and in her hand Damaris held Captain Gaynor's letter, which already she had read so often that its every character was seared indelibly upon her memory. She thrust the epistle into the bosom of her corsage when Evelyn entered, still pale and breathless now from the haste she had made, and she listened quite calmly to the tale that Evelyn brought.

At the mention of Sir John's danger her gentle face had hardened and she had frowned. Her quick mind perceived it instantly. Whatever else might be false in the message of which her cousin was the bearer, there could be no question as to the truth of that part of it. Yet she remained singularly quiet.

"I see," she said, when Evelyn had done. "And of course Lord Pauncefort bade you tell me this." The faint sneer gave the words their intended meaning, and Evelyn grasped it instantly.

"Not so," she cried, her cheeks flushing with indignation for one whom she felt it her duty – since he had so openly and honestly confided in her – to champion. "Not so – though he feared that you would think so."

"Then, of course, he did intend that you should tell me."

"He did not!" Evelyn stamped her foot. She was angry now.

"Why all this heat, my dear?"

"Because you are so unjust, so meanly suspicious. And you go too fast in your suspicions. It was just because he feared that you might impute unworthy motives to him that he begged me as he was setting out to forget all that he had said and to mention it to no one."

"Being quite confident, of course, that you could not keep it to yourself," said Damaris. "Nay, Evelyn, be not angry with me. My scorn is not for you, child."

"I am as old as you are," flashed Evelyn back, with something of her mother's irrelevance.

"But you have been saved some of the bitter experience which has been mine," added Damaris, with a pale smile, "else my Lord Pauncefort would not so easily have made a tool of you."

"A tool of me? Lord Pauncefort?" Her indignation was out of all proportion to the charge. For she magnified it into an insult – a slight upon her shrewdness.

"Do you not see, Evelyn dear, that if he had no ends to serve by telling you this, he would not needlessly have harassed you by showing you your father's peril? It is precisely because he sought to strike a bargain with Sir John, and because Sir John failed him entirely, that he sent me this message by you."

"He sent no message," Evelyn insisted. " 'Tis hateful to be so suspicious. He told me not to mention what he had said, just because he feared you would so construe his ends."

"That fear, at least, was shrewd in him."

"I see that it is idle to make you understand." And on that, with flaming cheeks, Eveyln swung on her heel and left her cousin.

To have been told that Lord Pauncefort had made a tool of her, as though she had no wit of her own! It was monstrous, and it sent her very angry to her chamber. Had she known in what frame of mind she left poor Damaris, perhaps her own had been less bitter.

To the burden, already almost overwhelming, of her grief was added this fresh horror – the knowledge that over her only remaining friend hung this terrible peril in which his very life might be involved, and the further torturing, agonising knowledge that it lay within her power, by self-immolation, to rescue him.

She rose, and remained standing for some time by the window, her hands pressed against her brow, as if seeking to stimulate the numbed brain within. Did it greatly matter what befell her now? Did it greatly matter that she should deliver herself to Pauncefort as a ransom for Sir John? Was it not, perhaps, the best use to which she could now devote her otherwise wasted and useless life?"

Heavy-footed she went below in quest of her guardian. She found him still seated at the table in the library, bowed down in expectation of the descent of that impending sword. He looked up as she entered, and the sight of that grey face, and the dumb pain investing those eyes that were wont to gleam so clear and jovially, strengthened her in her purpose by showing her the great good to be achieved.

She came to him, and set an arm about his shoulder, her smooth warm cheek against his own.

"Father dear," she murmured – and since it was not her custom to address him by that name, her present use of it lent her a greater tenderness. "Father dear, you are troubled, and I have come to help you if you will let me."

"Trou – troubled!" he faltered, with a poor attempt to bluster. "Nay, now, what should be troubling me?"

"This thing that my Lord Pauncefort came to tell you. You see that I know all."

He attempted to swing round in her embrace that he might face her.

"Who told you?" he growled. "Did you see Pauncefort? Did he make you this infamous proposal?"

"No," she answered. "He saw Evelyn."

"And he told her to the end that she might tell you!" His voice was shaking now with indignation.

"Be not angry with her, father dear." Her cheek pressed his own yet more closely. "Evelyn is but a child. She never realised that my Lord Pauncefort used her to this end. I do not think that she fully realises your danger even now."

"Indeed," he answered bitterly, "it is well written that the father of a fool hath no joy." For in his mind at that moment was the fact that his child, informed of this horror that menaced him, had never given a thought to the condition in which it must have left him, had never attempted to seek him out, to bring him at least the comfort of her affection and sympathy. It had been left for Damaris to discharge a consoler's duty, and more, to seek him with the offer to immolate herself that she might rescue him – for already he guessed, with heavy foreboding, the nature of the help which she announced.

It must be as Damaris said. It must be that this frivolous, irresponsible child he had brought into the world had not the wit to understand his position. He sighed heavily as he reflected that she was, after all, his offspring – his and his foolish wife's – and that he had not the right to complain.

"Do not grieve, my sweet Damaris," he said presently. "Your sympathy has consoled and cheered me. It makes me realise that perhaps all may not yet be lost."

"Nothing is lost," she answered him, "since we have it in our power to – to ransom you."

"Not that!" he cried, in a voice of thunder. "I forbid it. Do you hear me, child?" He disengaged himself from her arms, and threw back his great head that he might regard her fully. Then in a milder, tender voice, he pursued: "Ah, it is sweet in you to offer it; it is noble in you, and I am proud and happy in this earnest of your love, my dear. But it may not – it shall not be."

"I am but a husk," she said slowly, her voice a little wistful, her eyes resolute. "All that was Damaris Hollinstone perished at Tyburn a week ago – all save this little of me that I have kept for you. What, then, can it signify? Let my lord have this husk. It is all that he seeks of me – more than he seeks, since my fortune is his real desire. And how better could that fortune be applied than to ransoming the man whom today I honour most in all the world. Ah, father dear, you'll not deny me. Did you know how gladly I will – "

"No!" he roared again, and his great hand crashed heavily upon the table. "It shall not be. I would not permit it were it to save me from being quartered alive. What manner of knave should I be, Damaris? What respect for me could linger with you or with any honest soul did I become a party to so infamous a bargain?" He waved a hand of peremptory dismissal. "Let come what will. I am an old man, and in any event I should not have many more years of life before me. The Government will get but little, when all is said, and for such a little the ransom you propose were altogether absurd and disproportionate."

"Can it be that you think only of yourself?" she asked him.

He stared. "My dear, I hope I think of you as well."

"There are those who have a prior claim to mine upon your thoughts."

She saw the sudden spasm of pain that crossed his face; noted the little pause before he spoke again. But when he did speak his tone and manner were unshaken.

"And am I so base that I will purchase their welfare at the price of your prostitution?" he asked her.

But she did not flinch. "I have told you that I am but a husk," she said. "Do you not believe me?"

"O my God!" he groaned, and for a moment he was limp and helpless. But in the next he had mastered himself. "Not another word of this, my child," he said, and his voice was now one of utter finality. "As you love me do not attempt to pursue this subject further. I will not listen. Ah, don't think me harsh, don't think me slow to perceive your nobility, your greatness, my sweet Damaris." He rose, took her in his arms, and kissed her very tenderly. "For that I thank you from my soul. You have brought such comfort and gladness to my grey hairs this day as I have never known. To the end I shall thank God for the treasure of your affection."

"Ah, but, father dear!" Her face was upturned to his, and he saw the tears brimming her eyes.

"No more," he said gently. "No more of this. You cannot constrain me, for even if you consented of your own accord to the sacrifice, even did you in your foolish nobility seek that hound Pauncefort and announce your readiness to pay the price, yet should I withold my consent to the union, and exercise my rights under your father's will. I must, as I believe in God and in honour."

She perceived then how irrefragable was his resolve, perceived with her true-sightedness that did she urge him further he might perhaps make an end by impaling himself upon the sword that threatened him. So she went her way, praying heaven to afford her the means of saving him yet, despite himself. Indeed, so engrossed was she in the thought that she realised but indifferently its meaning to herself, had little leisure in which to dwell upon the horror of the price that she must pay.

One day, a week later, she thought that her chance had come, when Evelyn brought her word that my Lord Pauncefort was again closeted with Sir John in the library.

Again as on the occasion of my lord's previous visit, Sir John's first impulse had been to deny himself. But he reflected that it were best to receive his lordship and learn – as he supposed he would – the precise present degree of the danger threatened. Yet his reception of Pauncefort was again as uncompromising as before.

"You are not welcome, my lord," he said, rising to receive his visitor, and keeping him standing throughout the interview, "and if your visit has the same object as your last you had been better advised to have spared yourself the trouble."

"I deplore, Sir John," returned the viscount, with his almost miraculous equanimity, "to find you still in the same obdurate humour. But I think I shall have the felicity of mending it." He advanced slowly, gracefully into the room, whilst Sir John took his habitual stand with his shoulders to the carved overmantel. "Had I not conceived," he continued, "means of removing your unworthy suspicions, of proving to you how disinterested is my action, how dictated purely by my profound affection for your ward I should not again have intruded where – as you do not omit to tell me – I am unwelcome."

He had waited from hour to hour in London, confident that there would come to him a letter from Damaris. Unable, however, longer to endure the suspense; knowing, too, that he could not much longer delay action in the matter of advising Sir John's arrest, lest it should occur independently to Lord Carteret to order it (from which will be gathered the falsehood in which his lordship had been dealing), he had returned to the attack, armed now with a fresh weapon.

"I am listening, my lord," was the baronet's cold answer. "But I warn you that the matter will need a deal of proof, and I conceive that your invention is more like to be strained than my credulity. But proceed, my lord."

"You have said, sir, that to the end you would withhold your sanction to my marriage with your niece?" His lordship's statement was interrogative rather than affirmative.

"I have said so," answered Sir John.

"And I hope," said his lordship, "that you adhere to that resolve."

"You are justified of that hope, at least," was the dry answer.

The door opened gently and, unobserved by either of the men, Damaris appeared under the lintel.

"I rejoice in that," answered his lordship, his face lightening suddenly, "since thus I can prove to yourself and to Damaris my penitence of my past attitude and the sincerity of my feelings. I am willing, Sir John, willing and eager to marry your niece, as you once invited me, without your sanction. And so, the devil take her fortune!"

"And the devil take your offer!" was the imperturbable reply.

"No, no, Sir John!" It was Damaris who spoke. She advanced quietly into the room.

"Damaris!" cried Sir John, and his brows grew dark. His lordship, a fine figure in bronze-green satin, bowed until the curls of his periwig almost met across his face.

"Since his lordship offers this proof of his sincerity – " she began, and Lord Pauncefort's eyes were aglow with triumph. But this triumph was not yet complete.

"His sincerity!" the baronet interrupted. "Are you deceived by these smooth words?"

"Sir John, you go too far," my lord reproved him, very haughty now. "Consider, pray, that I do no more than take you at your word, as I should have taken you when it was uttered but that I was a fool. Thus, at least, I had saved Damaris and myself much fruitless pain. I am here, sir, to repair a fault for which I have never ceased to feel the most profound contrition, and if there is deception in my words I challenge you, sir, to unmask it."

He flicked a handkerchief as he finished, applied it to his lips, and with head thrown back, gallant defiance in every line of him, he waited for Sir John's answer. It came hard and swift.

"Why, what a foolish rogue is this! It passes belief! That he should think, Damaris, to cozen us with transparent falsehoods that would not deceive a child! And you would listen to him. Be it so; but at least let me help you to understand him. He will take you without my sanction, he says; by which he means that he will take you without your fortune, and that in withholding my sanction I am to dispose of your inheritance as your father's will directs. But am I? Shall I be allowed to do so? If they arrest me and make an outlaw of me, what power have I to execute any such deed? And that, Damaris, is what my lord is counting on. Oh, he is subtle but not subtle enough to match his villainy."

Lord Pauncefort's face was black with anger. "Your injustice, sir, is the only thing that passes belief." He swung to Damaris. "I am employing every effort of which I am capable to restrain the Secretary of State from issuing a warrant against your uncle as I have told him; and all that he can find for me on his side is insult. I think I had much better wash my hands of the affair, and leave him to his fate."

"No, no!" she cried. "Wait, my lord. Do you undertake that Sir John shall have complete immunity from any proceedings?"

"From any proceedings resulting from his having harboured Captain Gaynor," said his lordship. "That is what I have promised. I do not wish this to be a bargain between us, Damaris. In no sense do I make it a bargain. But loving you as I do," he continued, affecting not to observe how she winced under those words, "loving you as I do, how can I refrain from pointing out that, were I Sir John's relative by marriage, my Lord Carteret, out of his affection for me, would be more easily induced to refrain from proceedings against him? This I can promise."

"Ay, and prove as false to your promise as you have proven false to all else," stormed Sir John. "Oh, do not heed him, Damaris."

"Nay, you must heed me, mistress," said his lordship. "You were right to – to have despised me once for an altogether unworthy hesitation. That hesitation I am now amending, and I implore you not to make me suffer more for it than I have done. I am ready and eager, as I have said, to waive Sir John's sanction, and thus consent that your fortune be bestowed elsewhere. What greater proof can I afford of the sincerity of my intentions?"

"He waives my sanction," said Sir John, "knowing full well that once I am laid by the heels he can dispense with it at law to appropriate your inheritance. Do you not see, Damaris, that, far from helping me, as you suppose, by such a sacrifice, you will but imperil me, you will make my doom doubly assured?"

This was checkmate indeed; and his lordship saw it – saw it reflected on her face. Her shrewd wit had straightly followed Sir John's shrewd indication.

"Then you must give your sanction, Sir John," she cried. "You must!"

"Never!" he answered, and his lips closed firmly, his face became a stone.

Lord Pauncefort perceived the doom of his hope as far as the present line of attack was concerned. But from her attitude he perceived where and how a flanking movement might be made that should carry him to easy victory. At once he flung off his hypocritical mask of resignation, and showed now a countenance that was evil and menacing.

He bowed. "There is no more to be said at present," he murmured. "You are too old a man to call to account for your words. It but remains for me to withdraw from further insult."

As on the former occasion Sir John pulled the bell-rope. "I am glad, sir, that you perceive it," was his scornful answer.

Deliberately his lordship turned his shoulders upon him, and with bowed head he stood respectfully before Damaris.

"I will beg you to judge more mercifully than does your uncle. Believe me," and his voice vibrated with an apparent sincerity that almost deceived her, "I have not deserved so much opprobrium, and I am honest in my love of you."

He swept her a profound bow, and was gone.

She ran to Sir John, and put her arms about his neck. "Why did you refuse?" she wailed. "You have doomed yourself."

"Not more than I was doomed before," he answered gloomily. He stroked the dark head, and looked wistfully into her brown eyes, that were now so troubled for his sake. "Indeed, my only chance is to stand firm," he said, to comfort her. "If I give way I am destroyed. But as long as I refuse him, I may hold him off; he may hope and, hoping, may not denounce me – for it is upon his denunciation that my arrest depends. The rest is all a fable of his own. He has convinced me of that today."

"Oh no, no; never that!" she cried.

"I know my Lord Carteret. We have been almost friends. And I know that he is not the man to stand like a lackey at that fellow's beck. Pish! It is as I say. He pretends to stand between me and arrest. He does – by not denouncing me. He denounced all the others. He denounced Harry Gaynor."

She cried out at that. It was a shrewd thrust, well calculated to pierce her armour of self-sacrifice, as Sir John intended.

"Ay, it is true enough, as God hears me," he insisted. "And that is the man you would have married! You see how impossible 'twould be? You had not quite understood this until now, eh? But do not fret, dear child. By opposing him we may still weather this."

She was deceived. "You believe that?"

"I do," he answered, lying bravely. And so, somewhat comforted by his assurance, she departed.

But when alone he went again to sit at that table, as he had sat before after the last interview with Lord Pauncefort. And if on that occasion he had accounted himself in grave danger, today he accounted himself irrevocably doomed. The end would not be long in coming, and he wondered again what would betide his helpless child, and still more helpless wife, when the blow fell. From his heart he sent up a silent prayer to God to guard them.

Still sitting there, quite idly, a lackey found him half an hour later when he entered with a letter for Sir John, which a messenger had just brought from London.

Chapter 19

THE CAPTAIN GOES INTO ACTION

Sir John broke the seal, and spread a sheet of yellowish paper on which a crabbed and spidery hand had written:

HONOURED SIR, – I have a communication to make that I think you will consider of importance, concerning your friend Captain Harry Gaynor, and as I am in some haste to deliver it, which you will consider quite natural when you shall have received it, I hope that you will find it possible to do me the honour of visiting me here at once. The bearer of these present has my order to reconduct you hither should you desire to give my request the immediate compliance which I solicit. Should this not be possible or convenient, he is to bring me word on what day and at what hour I may look for the honour of your visit. My house is situate in the Gray's Inn Road, three doors from 'The Weeping Woman,' as you go from Holborn.

I am, honoured sir, your obedient, respectful servant,

EMANUEL BLIZZARD.

Sir John read the letter twice with knitted brows. A communication concerning Harry Gaynor! And the writer did not so much as say "the late Harry Gaynor." It flashed through his mind at the first reading that here might lurk some trap for him. But that omission of "the late" – with its inevitable suggestion that the writer was in ignorance of the Captain's death – was in itself almost sufficient to dispel any such fear. Assuredly, anyone preparing a snare for him would not have fallen into such an omission as that. A doubt still lingered. But he crushed it aside. What need was there to lay traps for him? If his conviction was desired, the grounds already afforded were ample.

He rose abruptly, his decision taken. He could form no conception of the nature of this promised communication, seek as he might; but it could not be his to be slow to inform himself. He looked at the respectfully waiting servant.

"What like is the messenger who brought this?" he inquired.

"Just a plain youth, Sir John," the man replied. "He came on horseback."

"Tell him I will accompany him. Bid them saddle Jessie for me, and send Bird to help me on with my boots."

He said nothing to Damaris, and to his wife no more than that he was summoned to London upon a matter of some urgency and that he would return that night.

A couple of hours later he was standing in a dark room on the ground floor of the doctor's dingy house in the Gray's Inn Road. Into this room came the slim little professor, moving swiftly and jerkily, as was his habit, and clucking as he came.

"Tut, tut! This is kind in you, Sir John. I should be distressed to think I had caused you inconvenience, eh? I trust I have not." He washed his great bony hands in the air, his gimlet eyes gleaming through his spectacles.

"I should not consider any inconvenience of account to receive a communication touching one who was almost as a son to me, Mr Blizzard."

"Doctor – Doctor Blizzard," the professor amended. "Your obedient servant. But, will you not sit, eh?"

Sir John took the arm-chair to which the doctor waived him, and set his hat and whip on the table at his side. The professor leaned against the table, clucking for a moment. He thrust his spectacles up on to his forehead until they almost joined the rim of his grizzled bob-wig, and he peered at his visitor with short-sighted eyes that had lost all apparent powers of penetration.

"The communication I have for you, sir, is very extraordinary – ve-ry extraordinary, eh; in fact, startling."

"Yes, yes," said the baronet. "I will beg you not to prolong my suspense."

"Tut! I should not dream of it. But it may be necessary to prepare you somewhat, eh?"

"To prepare me?"

"Godso! yes. Have I not said that my communication is of a startling character, eh? It amounts, sir, to this: that the gallows at Tyburn proved to your friend the gate of life in a sense other than that intended by the prophet, psalmist or theologian, or whoever it was, who made the phrase – *mors janua vitae*, ye know."

Sir John stared at him blankly. Had he to do with a madman?

"Will ye tell me Dr Blizzard, in plain terms, what ye mean?"

"In plain terms? Ah! In plain terms, then… But wait! I am a doctor, as I have told you, sir. I am a professor of anatomy, and therefore a student of anatomy. By great good fortune, sir, your friend's friends neglected to provide a funeral for him, and I bought the alleged corpse from the snatchers for a couple o' guineas, and – well, then, to put it in plain terms, as ye desire, I found that he wasn't dead at all."

Sir John sat very still. Slowly the colour faded from his face. His lips parted, but he made no sound. Then he began to tremble from head to foot.

"There, there! Tut, tut!" cried the doctor, slipping his spectacles once more on to his nose, and observing his visitor. "I told you 'twould startle you. Ye would have it in plain terms."

"I…" The baronet gulped. "I am quite myself, sir," he said, striving valiantly to master his agitation. He drew out a handkerchief, and mopped his clammy brow. "But I confess you startled me. In fact, I hardly understand you even now. Do you mean that Harry Gaynor is – is alive?"

"Not only alive, but almost well. Mending rapidly. In a day or two he will be in case to go his ways again."

There followed a silence which the professor did not attempt to interrupt. He understood that such news as this must be given time for assimilation by any ordinary brain.

"But this is a miracle!" cried Sir John presently, yet he spoke without heartiness. Obviously he was still incredulous; obviously he still but half understood the thing he had been told.

"Tut!" clucked the professor. "There are no miracles in nature. A miracle is a thing out of nature; and the thing I tell you is a thing in nature. Sufficiently rare to look like a miracle; but no miracle at all, eh!"

"Where is he?" was Sir John's next question, his voice trembling.

"Above stairs, awaiting you," was the answer, and it was an answer that seemed to dispel at last the mists that were obfuscating the baronet's understanding.

Harry Gaynor was alive, above-stairs, and awaiting him. Those facts he grasped clearly, and for the moment nothing more. He came instantly to his feet.

"Why was I not told of this before? Why did your letter convey no hint of it?"

"You must ask the Captain," said the professor, smiling. "I would have communicated with his friends at once. But he would not have it. A very cautious fellow for all his recklessness. But I detain you, eh? This way, sir."

He led Sir John from the room and up a steep, dark staircase. He paused on the narrow landing above, and after a preliminary tap he threw open a door. The baronet entered and then halted abruptly, as if in spite of what he had been told he still could not believe his eyes which showed him Captain Gaynor in a quilted bed-gown standing smiling to receive him.

Behind him the doctor had closed the door on the outside, leaving the two friends alone.

"Harry!" cried Sir John, his voice husky.

"My dear Sir John!" said the Captain, and he held out a hand in welcome. But the baronet, under the impulse of his overmastering feelings, thrust aside the hand, and, opening wide his arms, clasped the young man to his heart.

"My boy, my boy!" he mumbled brokenly, and the tears stood in his eyes. "We have wept you dead, and you are restored to us alive."

Presently, when the Captain had soothed Sir John's emotion and brought him by slow degrees to the full acceptance of this amazing state of things, they sat and talked at length, and Gaynor expounded his plans, which were concerned with little more than his immediate departure from England.

"The law may run that a man shall not suffer twice for the same offence," he said, "but I am by no means sure that an exception might not be made in the case of a dangerous Jacobite agent, that the Government might not find ways of disposing of me did it leak out that I have escaped my doom."

"Yes, yes," the baronet agreed. "You are wise in that. You will need money, perhaps?"

"I have," was the answer, "a letter of credit upon Childe's, under which I can draw something a little short of two thousand guineas. But I think it would he wiser not to use it. For all that the identification of Captain Jenkyn with Captain Gaynor might not have been complete, yet it is generally understood, no doubt that they are one and the same, and Childe's might account it their duty to advise the Government."

"You are right," said Sir John. "You must use my purse to any extent you need."

"Thank you, sir," the Captain replied, without hesitation. "A hundred guineas will suffice to get me to Rome."

"I will bring you the sum tomorrow."

"Then, I think, if Dr Blizzard will permit it, I will set out on the following day. And now of yourself, Sir John?"

Sir John looked at him, and marvelled that there had been so far no word of Damaris; yet he thought he understood the Captain's hesitation.

"Damaris," he said slowly, "will be as one born again when I bear her these glad tidings."

He saw the clear-cut young face grow white, and he observed the falter in the voice that asked him: "She – she has grieved?"

"Grieved, lad? She has been almost as lifeless as we deemed yourself. Oh, but this will be great medicine. It will bring back the roses to her cheeks, and the sparkle to her eyes. And" – he stopped short, smitten of a sudden by a great thought – " it will make an end of all danger of any such sacrifice as she has been contemplating."

"Sacrifice? What sacrifice?"

Too late Sir John perceived that his words had exceeded prudence. He could not now withdraw, and so he was forced to confide in Captain Gaynor, to lay his own troubles before him. Nor was he reluctant so to do; for upon the young man's resourcefulness he founded a faint hope that some way might yet be perceived, not apparent to Sir John himself, out of the danger that hung over him.

Captain Gaynor listened inscrutably to the tale that Sir John unfolded; the only outward sign he made was to nod shortly when the baronet pointed out the quality of the mesh in which Pauncefort was enfolding him. When Sir John had done the young man rose, and with hands clasped behind him, head bent in thought, he slowly paced the length of the chamber from door to window and back again. He was profoundly touched by the nobility of Damaris in her proposed sacrifice and the nobility of Sir John in his determination to frustrate her.

"For the present," Sir John had said, in conclusion, "I have succeeded in persuading her that, far from removing the peril, she will but increase it by consenting to marry that villain. If to this were added the knowledge that you have been so incredibly, so miraculously, spared, I think our work would be complete; for I am convinced there would be an end to the despair upon which her courage of self-sacrifice is founded."

"It – it amounts to that?" cried the Captain incredulously.

"My dear Harry, had you heard her say to me, 'I am but a husk – all that was myself perished at Tyburn,' you had so gauged the depth of that despair that you had been moved to tears."

He was not far from moved to them by the repetition of those words. He paced on, resolving all that Sir John had told him, seeking a way through this baffling tangle. At last, as he approached the window for the second time, he paused and his face lighted.

A course which he had earlier considered but which he had discarded as too desperate where it was only calculated to serve himself, recurred to him now. It was a reckless, adventurous audacious course, which yet might succeed by virtue of its very audacity. He threw back his head and laughed his full-throated, musical laugh. Sir John looked up, almost startled by the sound.

"I think," said the young man, "that it was high time that Captain Gaynor should come to life again."

Sir John, completely bewildered, continued to stare at him, whereupon that keen face became once more inscrutable.

"Look you, Sir John," he cried, "this danger of yours has been exaggerated to you. Let us say that they arrest you. To convict you they must still prove that Captain Gaynor and Captain Jenkyn were one and the same man, and that fact has not yet been entirely established."

"Pish!" said the baronet. "From the moment that it becomes necessary to advance proof of that, the Government can have no difficulty in doing so."

"Let us say that it can; let us say that witnesses could be found – though, I confess, I know not whence. The Government must still prove that you knew of my connection with the Jacobite movement, that you knew me for an agent of the King over the Water, and that I did not impose upon you as I imposed upon so many others – including Mr Second Secretary Templeton."

"Oh, Harry, Harry! These are but straws that will never float me through those waters, and you know it."

"I do not know it," said Harry, and he was smiling now. "But, even so, I have a sort of raft in the background that may serve you better."

"What is it?"

The Captain reflected a moment. Then – "I have yet a little work to do upon it to render it seaworthy," he said thoughtfully. "But I hope to have all in readiness by tomorrow, when you come again. I will tell you then."

And, despite Sir John's entreaties, not another word would the soldier add until the morrow, when Sir John not only promised to return but to bring Damaris with him, a promise which kept the Captain awake for most of the night in mingling joy and fear at the coming meeting.

But on the morrow, which was Tuesday, there was no sign of Sir John. The Captain had made the best of himself with the black suit in which he had been taken and hanged – the only suit he had. He had procured flowers – baskets of roses and tall virginal lilies – to deck his chamber for so wondrous an occasion. The morning went in preparation; the afternoon in expectation; the evening in sick disappointment and vain clingings to hope even after the candles had been lighted. Eventually he went to bed, still buoyed by the conviction that they must come tomorrow.

But the morrow again went by in the same manner, and still there was neither sight nor sign of Sir John.

On the Thursday morning, worn out by this suspense, utterly unable to bear more of it, the Captain borrowed the anatomist's apprentice, who, on that former occasion, had carried a message to Priory Close, and despatched him this time with a request by word of mouth for news.

The youngster returned with a tale of a desolated house and the information that Sir John had been arrested on returning home on the Monday night.

The Captain drew a deep breath at the news; not a breath of dismay, but of resolve, almost of relief. He thanked the messenger, and when the lad had gone he turned to the anatomist, who sat with him.

"Decidedly," he said grimly, "it is time I came to life again. What's o'clock?"

"Eh?" said the professor. "O'clock? Why, 'twill be nearly two."

"Then it is time I took my leave of you."

"Tut!" clucked the professor, rising. "D'ye mean ye're going, eh? Where are ye going?"

"Back to life," said Harry Gaynor.

"But in your condition?" cried the dismayed anatomist, who was reluctant to part with so amiable a guest. "Y'amaze me!"

"What ails my condition?" Gaynor asked him. "Look at me," he commanded.

Down came the spectacles from the professor's forehead to his nose.

"Ye've a somewhat feverish air," said he.

"That is anticipation," said the patient. He took the doctor's hand. "There is a debt between us, my friend, that it would tax me to discharge."

"Tut – tut!"

"Ye've been more than friend to me. And I hope that friends we may remain, and that if at any time Harry Gaynor has it in his power to serve you ye'll not forget to make him happy by acquainting him with the circumstance."

"My dear sir, my dear lad! Tut – tat! Tut – tut!"

"I leave your hospitable and kindly roof, sir, with profound regret. But this is not a parting. We remain friends, and" – he hesitated an instant – "there is the matter of the charges to which you have been put – "

"Sir!" the doctor exploded in the simulation of a towering rage. "Am I a vintner? Do I keep a tavern?"

The Captain pressed his hands. "Forgive me," he said. "My inability to repay the real debt rendered me the more eager in the matter of this other trivial one."

"Not another word or ye'll affront me, eh!"

They parted the best of friends in the world, and, after the Captain had gone, that lonely anatomist realised for the first time in all his absorbed and studious years that his house in the Gray's Inn Road was dingy, dull and dismal.

The Captain in his black suit and a hat that had been procured for him by the professor's apprentice, with a couple of guineas in his pocket borrowed from Dr Blizzard at parting, walked briskly down the road across Holborn and on until he came into the slush and filth of Temple Bar.

Here he hired him a chair, and was carried to that inn in Chandos Street where he had alighted a fortnight ago, and where his baggage would still he lying.

Chapter 20

MR TEMPLETON IN RETIREMENT

Sir Richard Tollemache Templeton, in his distant lonely seat in Devonshire, received from his cousin, the Second Secretary, a letter which produced in him the greatest consternation.

MY DEAR TOLLEMACHE [wrote the Second Secretary], – *De profundis* – out of the very depths of despondency I write to you, smitten down by a malignancy of fortune which I find it difficult even now to credit should have encompassed me. It has demanded of me the resignation of that high office which I held under the Crown, and today I am a man who hides his head in shame from the gloating stare of the vulgar, whose envy is ever gladdened by the spectacle of one fallen from high estate.

It is a full week since the untoward event befell which has been the occasion of this overwhelming disaster, yet it is only today that I am able sufficiently to take heart and summon the courage necessary to indite to you this miserable epistle, giving you, as is your due as the head of our honourable house, news of my condition. It solaces me almost, my dear Tollemache, that in such an hour, with the burden of ridicule and disgrace upon my shoulders, I am able to reflect that some of the blame for this attaches to yourself as well. You are not to suppose by this that I presume to censure you. We have both been the sport of malign Fate and of a villain who has already expiated on the gallows the perversity of his existence. But that you should have been cozened with me, that my cozening should in part have been a natural sequel to your own, rather than an independent error of mine, is a helpful reflection to me in this dark hour. But for this merciful circumstance I should never be able to show you my face again, I should not, indeed, have the courage to indite these lines to you.

The villain to whom I am referring, my dear Tollemache, is one who imposed himself upon you and abused the confidence with which, a little indiscriminatingly, I fear (though it is an error to which all men are liable), you honoured him. I speak of Henry Gaynor – or the man who called himself by that name. Strong in my faith in his loyalty, a faith rooted in your own absolute assurance of it, I defended him to the utmost of my strength when imputations were cast upon that loyalty, when it was first whispered that he was none other than the elusive Jacobite agent who has been known by the name – for want of knowledge of his real one – of Captain Jenkyn.

So positive, you will remember, were these assurances of yours that I stood between that man and arrest, pledging my credit and my very honour for his loyalty. But, as I have said, we have both been most grossly abused. There came a moment when it was impossible to defend him any longer. His arrest was ordered and effected and regarding himself as lost he took the course so common with desperate men who are cornered: he weakly confessed his treason and meekly submitted to his fate. He was hanged a week ago, as he more richly deserved than any man I have known of.

Need I add more? Need I tell you how this honour of mine which I had pledged was all but lost to me by my rashness, how nothing remained me but to resign my office and retire before the storm of contempt and ridicule which my lord Carteret directed upon my luckless head? I am a broken man, my dear Tollemache, and never was there one in greater need of sympathy and pity, never one more lonely. Though I hide me from the world, here among my books, I cannot hide me from Emily, whose tongue these days is as a sword of sharpness to my flesh.

I can write no more. But if you will take pity on my loneliness, and permit me to come to you in Devonshire for a season, until this matter shall be forgotten and I can again show my face among men, I shall be your deeply grateful as I am your affectionate and unfortunate cousin,

EDWARD TEMPLETON.

To Sir Richard this news had been altogether incredible. That Lord Carteret, persisting in the absurd mistake, or urged on by mistaken advisers, should, in spite of all, have gone the length of arresting Harry Gaynor as Captain Jenkyn was not perhaps surprising. But that Harry Gaynor – the Harry Gaynor he knew, of whose career he conceived that he was acquainted with every phase, whose every year, indeed, was accounted for by his credentials – that this man should have admitted himself to be the Jacobite agent in question was impossible to believe.

Sir Richard scouted the notion. His cousin was mad, or else some monstrous error lay at the bottom of the affair.

He did not trouble to answer the letter. So overwhelmed was he by its contents that two days after its receipt – so soon as he could set in order certain affairs on his estate that demanded his immediate attention – he set out for London. He arrived there two days later, having travelled post-haste all the way, and the very Thursday that saw Captain Gaynor leave the house of Professor Blizzard saw Sir Richard's dusty chaise drawn up before his cousin's door in Old Palace Yard.

He found the Second Secretary in his library. Edward Templeton was in deshabille, although it was already past noon. He wore a bed-gown of wine-coloured satin, and his cropped head was hidden in a nightcap of the same hue. His long countenance seemed to have grown longer, sallower and hollower in these last few days. His chaps hung dolefully. He looked uncommonly like a bloodhound that has been whipped, and his deep-set eyes were singularly dolorous. To look at him was to perceive that here was a fellow who pitied himself damnably.

He was standing to receive his cousin, and he went to meet him with both hands held out.

"My dear Tollemache" (his deep voice boomed like the note of an organ and was laden with a profound melancholy), " it is kind in you to respond so readily to my appeal; to seek me here in my – ah – tribulation."

"I could not wait for you to come to me," was the answer. "Your news was so wild and utterly beyond belief that I must come in person for its explanation ere I carry you back to Devonshire with me."

"Wild and utterly beyond belief it may be, but it is true none the less."

Sir Richard, still in his travelling clothes, flung himself into a chair.

"Tell me of it," he said impatiently.

"What remains to tell? My letter – "

"Yes, yes, but your letter gave me no more than the broad fact. I want the details ere I can believe."

"The details?" Mr Templeton paced the room with bowed head. He came at last to stand by the writing table where he could face his cousin. He looked through the window behind his cousin, and observed the grey sky and drizzle of rain under which the shrubs in his garden were drooping.

He told the tale with all that wealth of rhetoric that he used, thus rendering his cousin's impatience almost frantic.

"Is that all?" quoth Sir Richard, when the tale was done.

"Is't not enough?" demanded the sometime Second Secretary. "It has been enough to procure my ruin, Tollemache."

"And yet, weighed against my own knowledge of the man, it is not enough to carry conviction."

"Oh, he was deep – infernally, subtly deep," boomed Mr Templeton. "He completely bubbled you."

Sir Richard rose, and in his turn began to pace the chamber, whilst his cousin now let himself sink into a chair, and sat, knees on elbows and chin cupped in his palms.

"He was averse to coming to England," Sir Richard reasoned, "and it was naught but my own insistence fetched him hither. Even when I had prepared the letter for you, he must still idle there at Naples, and I'll swear he would be idling there yet but for the insistence which I employed."

"Ay – he was deep," was all that Mr Templeton could find to answer.

"But his credentials!" Sir Richard insisted. "His credentials! They were an almost complete record of his career, and not a year of it since he was nineteen but was employed in some service between here and the Far East."

"Forgeries!" growled his cousin.

"Forgeries? Not so. Did not yourself test two of them at the proper embassies here in London?"

"Two – ay. But what of the others?"

"*Ab uno disce omnes.*"

Mr Templeton crashed fist into palm. "The very argument I used to my Lord Carteret – the very words I uttered! 'Sdeath, how he has laughed at me since! Oh, blister me! you do not know what a butt for mockery I am become."

"You say that he confessed?" Sir Richard's voice was laden with ineffable incredulity.

"Abjectly."

"Y'amaze me! How did he bear himself at the trial?"

"Well, I am told. He was one of your cool, calm villains."

"Were ye not present?"

"Present?" cried Mr Templeton. "Do you not understand, man, that from the hour of his arrest I durst not show my face i' the town?

Do you think I would go to Court to be pointed at by every jackanapes as the man who was bubbled, the statesman who was this traitor's sponsor? I may count myself fortunate that I was not, myself, impeached."

And then Fate, that ironical stage manager, displayed its interest in this comedy.

There was a tap at the door, and a footman entered.

"Captain Gaynor is below, sir, and begs leave to wait upon you," he announced.

The two men stared at him, as if they were both stricken into stone.

At length, in a croak, came Mr Templeton's voice: "What the devil did ye say?"

The footman stolidly repeated his announcement.

"Captain Gaynor?" echoed Mr Templeton, with an accent on every syllable. "Cap-tain Gay-nor!" he repeated. "Are ye mad or drunk?"

"Neither, sir," replied the footman, his manner as near pert as any underling's manner dare be with the overawing Mr Templeton.

Mr Templeton screwed his face as he shot out the next question: "D'ye know Captain Gaynor? I mean – have ye ever seen him before?"

"Why, yes, sir; several times."

"And d'ye say this is he?"

"Yes, sir. Leastways, I think so, sir."

Sir Richard interposed. He was visibly as agitated as his cousin.

"Best desire him to step up, Ned," he suggested. Mr Templeton gave the order, and the intrigued footman vanished.

"What can it mean, Tollemache? What can it mean?"

"It seems to mean that I am right and that you and your Government are wrong. For if this is really Captain Gaynor, then, obviously, he is not Captain Jenkyn."

"You mean that Lord Carteret is mistaken!" cried the other, a dazzling vista of reinstatement with the last and the best laugh on his side opening suddenly before him. He heaved himself, excited, from his chair, to collapse into it again an instant later. "But it is absurd!"

he said, and sneered. "Impossible."

On the word the door reopened and Captain Gaynor was ushered in. He wore his close-fitting military blue coat buttoned to the chin, canon boots and steel-hilted sword, and under his arm he carried his looped and feathered hat.

Undoubtedly this was the man himself. Yet, as the cousins stared at him, Edward Templeton disbelieved the evidence of his own eyes.

The soldier advanced easily into the room, then bowed formally, his heels together. "I trust, Mr Templeton, that I do not intrude. Why, 'tis you, Dick!" he cried, perceiving who it was that stood there. "I am indeed fortunate. I was considering a jaunt into Devonshire, unless by now your cousin's efforts on my behalf have borne the fruit we hope for. But what's amiss?" he cried on a sudden, different note, looking from one amazed face to the other.

"Will you tell me who the devil you are?" asked Mr Templeton.

The Captain stiffened slightly; perplexity crept into his face.

"Who the devil I am?" said he. "Why, who the devil should I be but Captain Harry Gaynor, your obedient servant. I trust," he added, as if he suddenly suspected a possibility, "I trust, sir, that I have not unwittingly had the misfortune to offend you."

Mr Templeton looked at his cousin. "By God!" said he. " 'Tis the man himself."

"So it is," said Sir Richard, and on that he exploded into laughter.

Captain Gaynor looked from one to the other. His expression of perplexity changed to one of annoyance.

"Gentlemen," said he, very distant, "you'll forgive me if I say that I find you vastly odd. And you, Dick – "

Sir Richard sprang to him and wrung his hand. "Oh, my dear Harry," he cried, "although my manner seem odd, I swear I never was more pleased to see you – or any man."

"Nor I – oddslife! – no," roared Mr Templeton, who savoured already in imagination the triumph that was in store for him, his complete vindication and the turning of those malicious shafts of satire upon the fatuous Lord Carteret – their proper butt. "But can ye explain it?" he demanded.

"Explain what, sir?" asked the apparently bewildered soldier.

Mr Templeton changed his tone. "Where the devil have ye been this fortnight past?"

"Where? Why, did I not announce to you my departure for Scotland when last I came to take my leave of you? I should have tarried longer in the north, but that I was unable to find any of the friends I went to visit. So, as the north of itself has little attraction for one who's accustomed to softer climates, I came south again forthwith." He lied glibly and smoothly, and with little hurt to his conscience. Again he observed that his audacity had conquered completely here. Would it conquer as completely elsewhere? He had little doubt of it now.

"And you have had no news of London in your absence?"

"Who should send me news? I have so few friends in England nowadays."

"Then ye'll not have heard that Captain Jenkyn was taken and hanged?"

"Captain Jenkyn?" echoed the soldier, after the manner of one who searches his memory. "D'ye mean the Jacobite agent. Faith, then, the world's well rid of a meddlesome fool. But – " He paused to stare at them, bewildered. "You tell me this, I see, with some purpose."

It was Richard who interposed to tell him the story – suddenly become so monstrously comical – that upon Captain Jenkyn, whose real identity was unknown, had been thrust the identity of Captain Gaynor.

The Captain laughed a little at first. Then he checked himself, and grew very sober.

"But, 'tis a monstrous thing you tell me!" quoth he. "I cannot lie under so absurd an error. It must be corrected forthwith. I shall look to you, Mr Templeton, to do me justice."

"To me?" said Templeton. "Ye've further to learn that, as a consequence of my jeopardising myself by denying the possibility of your being Captain Jenkyn, I am no longer a member of the

Government. I have resigned my office. But there are reprisals in store – egad! Reprisals!"

"Then I must see Lord Carteret at once," cried the Captain.

"So you shall – and I'll come with you." Mr Templeton was recovering his habitual breadth of manner. "If ye'll but stay for me till I am dressed, we will go together. And you had best come with us, Tollemache."

"Faith! I ask no better entertainment," laughed Sir Richard.

But Captain Gaynor had yet a question to ask ere he would allow Mr Templeton to withdraw. "But how came this mistake about, sir? Was the fellow – Did he resemble me?"

" 'Tis more than I can say, and less than matters now. I think my Lord Carteret took too much upon assumption. It is all the work of that fellow Pauncefort."

"Pauncefort!" cried the Captain, and alarm flashed into his face. "Pauncefort! By heaven, then, I suspect some villainy here! Gad! 'Twas no mistake this; 'twas deliberate! I'll post to Priory Close and see Sir John Kynaston the moment I leave my Lord Carteret's. Heaven send I am not too late. I curse the hour I ever thought of Scotland."

"Sir John Kynaston!" exclaimed Mr Templeton very solemnly. "Why, what do you fear for him?"

"For him – nothing. 'Tis not himself I'm thinking of."

"Then d'ye not know – But of course you do not. Sir John was arrested two days ago."

Consternation spread on the face of that comedian. "Arrested? Sir John? Upon what charge?"

"Why, upon the charge of having harboured a traitor and spy – upon the charge of having harboured Captain Gaynor."

The Captain smote his brow with his clenched hand. "I see it all, then!" he cried. "Let us waste no time, sir. Sir John must instantly be restored to liberty."

"All things considered," said Sir Richard dryly, "I think my Lord Carteret will be very pleased to see you."

"He'll be the laughing-stock o' the town," said Mr Templeton, and he went out, chuckling, to make ready for that momentous visit.

Chapter 21

LORD CARTERET UNDERSTANDS

The arrest of Sir John Kynaston had been brought about, of course – like all the others – by the agency of the renegade Pauncefort. It was the last desperate throw he made in the game of mending his fortunes, a game which had reduced him to the treacherous infamy which he had perpetrated. But he intended that it should be no more than the means to his end. It was no part of his purpose that Sir John should ultimately suffer. That is to say, it was no part of his present purpose.

He had pointed out to the Secretary of State the grounds upon which Sir John should be arrested, and he had further informed against him out of his own knowledge of Sir John's association – however slight – with the Jacobite intriguers. But once the arrest was effected, he had come again to my Lord Carteret with the request that Sir John's fate should be placed in his own (Lord Pauncefort's) hands. He claimed this as part of the recompense due to him from the Government for the signal services he had rendered.

Lord Carteret had listened to his request with that frank contempt which the Secretary of State never failed to use towards this man who had turned informer. This contempt was rendered the more bitter on this occasion by the regard in which his lordship had ever held Sir

John Kynaston, against whom, indeed, he had performed his duty most reluctantly – a feeling this which Lord Pauncefort had omitted from his calculations.

The statesman pursed his thin lips and considered the viscount in silence with that cold glance of his, which my Lord Pauncefort found it so difficult to endure with equanimity.

"I find your request more than extraordinary, sir," said he.

Lord Pauncefort laughed. "If your lordship had my own unfortunate acquaintance with the requests of creditors, you'd find little extraordinary in mine."

"By which," said the minister quietly, "you remind me, of course, that you are my creditor; or, rather, that I am your debtor for services rendered to the State. Ah!"

"I think, my lord, that I deserve some recompense beyond the small sums of money which the Treasury has paid me."

Lord Carteret leaned back in his arm-chair, his finger-tips resting upon the edge of the writing-table before him. "These small sums, my lord, amount to close upon twelve thousand pounds. And in addition you are kept out of a debtor's gaol by my warranty to your creditors that your debts will be liquidated on your marriage. I confess, sir, that you appear to me to have been more than well paid already for the services that you have rendered. Some, indeed," continued the statesman, with the faintest note of scorn in his quiet voice, "would account that you have been paid far above the value of those services, although I am not of those. I recognise the position which you occupy, the estate to which you were born, and the fact, hence, that you require to be bribed upon a higher scale than does the ordinary – informer."

The viscount swallowed that last insult as best he could. He had swallowed so many of Lord Carteret's already, in the course of these very turbid transactions, that one more or less was of little account. He kept his head high, and preserved a smiling front.

"I will admit, my lord, that the payment has been generous, provided that it is completed. I mean, provided that I am enabled to redeem the warranty your lordship has given my creditors."

"I am not sure," said the minister slowly, "that 'warranty' is, after all, the proper word. But your creditors understand me, and so, I think, do you."

"Perfectly, my lord. You have honoured me by giving your word as bail for me to Israel Suarez and the others."

"And," Lord Carteret added, "it is entirely as a result of this that you continue to elude imprisonment for debt."

"And," Lord Pauncefort added on his own side, "it is precisely that your lordship may be relieved of your pledge for me that I prefer my present request touching Sir John Kynaston."

"You do not forget, I trust, that I retain the right of withdrawing my pledge at any moment, should it appear to me that you may no longer continue in the assurance of being ultimately able to satisfy your debts. But that is by the way. The thing you now propose is exceedingly distasteful to me. Indeed, I am not sure that I can honourably accede to such a request. I could do so only if I were satisfied that – " He broke off, and sat forward. "But we talk in the dark," he said more briskly. "Let me understand what ends you seek to serve by such a thing."

"Reasonable ends, my lord," replied Pauncefort easily. "I have already had the honour of informing your lordship of the terms of the late Mr Hollinstone's will, under which it is in Sir John Kynaston's power to withhold his sanction to his ward's marriage until she is of full age – "

"Yes, yes," the statesman cut in. "You have already told me all that. Moreover," he added, with another of his quietly incisive manifestations of mistrust, "I have obtained independent confirmation of the fact. Pray, continue."

"I have also had the honour of informing your lordship that my betrothal to Miss Hollinstone does not receive Sir John's sanction."

"Knowing and respecting Sir John as I do, I am not surprised," was the withering comment. "Well, what then?"

"Sir John, my lord, is under arrest."

"By your contriving – yes," said his lordship. "It is a matter, let me tell you, concerning which your true motives have never intrigued me. I was aware that your betrothal to the lady was not sanctioned by her guardian" (his lordship was not, it seems, aware that the betrothal had been cancelled), "and I perceived clearly enough that his conviction as a rebel would disqualify him from exercising his rights under the will. What I do not perceive is the reason of your present intervention. I hope you are attempting no double dealings with me, sir."

"Double dealings? I, my lord?"

"You don't know what they are, I suppose? Pshaw, sir! These virtuous airs are unnecessary here. Who has betrayed once will betray again. But I have no desire to recriminate, my lord. All I desire is to warn you to be frank with me. What is your aim? – briefly now, and clearly."

The viscount was forced to swallow this peremptoriness with the rest. He was a knave unmasked, dealing with a man of honour.

"My lord," he answered, "I should have thought my aim would have been clear. I have no ill-will against Sir John. If I am to wed his niece I would not be the one to compass his ruin. I hope, sir, to be able to induce him to change his mind on the subject of my marriage with his niece either before or after the marriage has taken place. I conceive, sir, that if I can visit him in prison and offer to use my influence to procure his release and pardon, natural gratitude should inspire Sir John no longer to – "

"Fiddlesticks!" the statesman interrupted. "Natural gratitude, faith! Why can you not be frank and tell me it is your intent to drive a bargain with Sir John."

Pauncefort permitted himself a wry smile. "It amounts to that, of course," he confessed. "And if I had the pardon in my pocket it would perhaps strengthen my hand."

The statesman sat back again, toying thoughtfully with a quill, and from that hesitation Lord Pauncefort gathered hope. He knew, as we know, that if there was one thing more detestable to Lord Carteret than these persistent Jacobite intrigues that simmered under the peaceful surface of the realm it was their disclosure. His policy was to stifle them; to strike alarm into the plotters and to disband them, effecting this with as little publicity as possible.

Now it was far from the Secretary of State's desire to procure Sir John's conviction, since that must mean an increased publicity for the Jacobite Cause. Ample for the Government's purpose was his arrest. He might now be liberated, sufficiently shaken, no doubt, to leave plotting alone in future. And if there were plausible grounds for his enlargement, so much the better would the Government be served. Now Lord Pauncefort's proposal afforded just those plausible grounds; through his agency Sir John might be left under the impression that his release had been the result of a personal intervention. Nothing, then, but the statesman's mistrust of Pauncefort caused him now to hesitate, whilst in his mind he cast about him for any other possible end which the informer might seek to serve. Presently a thought occurred to him.

"You do not by any chance require this pardon as an instrument with which to compel the lady?" he inquired in his cold, level voice.

Pauncefort was aghast at the minister's shrewdness, for Lord Carteret had dropped plump upon his real aims. That, indeed, was the last card that he proposed to play, confident that it was strong enough to win the game for him. But if his face showed anything it showed indignation of such a suggestion. That seeming indignation kept him silent for a moment. Then he smiled slowly, as it were in contempt of Lord Carteret's mistake.

"With the lady, sir, no compulsion is necessary, seeing that we are betrothed already, and have been these six months, as all the world knows."

It was a convincing answer, and yet it did not convince the statesman; for none knew better than Lord Carteret the crookedness of the man with whom he dealt. Slowly he shook his head, though for a moment he said nothing. At last: "When is this marriage to take place?" he asked.

"Tomorrow evening at my place in Surrey," replied his lordship promptly – and, indeed, subject to his production of the pardon in question, such was the agreement he had that very morning wrung from Damaris. His lordship fingered his quill a moment, then threw it down like one who has taken his resolve.

"Come to me again when you are married, then," he said, "and we will return to the subject. Very possibly I may do as you desire."

Almost Lord Pauncefort committed the imprudence of protesting, and thus betraying himself completely to one so shrewd as the Secretary of State. He caught himself betimes. There was no more to be said, and the more readily he professed his entire acquiescence the better must it serve him.

He was checked for the moment. A fresh difficulty confronted him. Nevertheless, he smiled as he rose to take his leave.

"Be it so, then, my lord," said he. "I shall have the honour of waiting upon you again betimes on Friday."

Lord Carteret nodded. "Give you good-day," he said coldly, and Lord Pauncefort withdrew, a smile on his lips and rage in his heart, to think out the situation and discover a means to surmount this obstacle which had presented itself where he had expected none. That means he was not slow in discovering, for a half-hour later he penned and despatched from his house in St James's Street the following epistle to Miss Hollinstone: –

MY DEAREST DAMARIS, – I have but left my Lord Carteret, and I take pen at once to send you these to dispel the anxiety in which I know you to be lying. The Secretary of State has lent an ear to my insistence, and is preparing Sir John's pardon. It will receive his Majesty's signature tomorrow, and it shall be my wedding gift to you when you come to Woodlands tomorrow evening.

This was followed by protestations of undying passion and delirious anticipation with which we are not concerned, but in which Lord Pauncefort must be done the justice of being acknowledged sincere. He did with most delirious anticipation look forward to his emancipation from Israel Suarez and this nightmare of a debtor's gaol that was with him day and night, and had made a villain of him.

Now all this happened on the Wednesday of that very momentous week.

On the Thursday his lordship departed for his seat in Surrey, to complete the preparations for the reception of the bride, and he took with him, to serve his needs, a poor hedge parson of the name of Pugh.

At about the same hour that his chaise rolled up St James's Street and turned into Piccadilly, another carriage drew up at Lord Carteret's door and deposited there Mr Templeton, Sir Richard and Captain Gaynor, who thus descended upon the Secretary of State.

Mr Templeton came to explain – a sort of chorus to this comedy, and something more; Captain Gaynor came to seek explanation; and Sir Richard came as an important witness to certain matters, should it be found that they required investigation.

They did not. The mountainous fact that Captain Gaynor stood there in the flesh entirely crushed the absurd allegation that a fellow convicted of being Captain Jenkyn, the Jacobite spy, and hanged at Tyburn a fortnight since, had been this same Harry Gaynor.

Obviously a most colossal blunder had occurred. Lord Carteret's consternation flamed quickly to anger under the deft fanning of Mr Templeton.

"Had your lordship but honoured me with attention, this – ah – deplorable mistake had not occurred; had not occurred." His voice rolled and boomed. "I strove with all my power, but your lordship would not be guided. Even when I produced unimpeachable evidence your lordship still – ah – preferred to give heed to other counsellors. If you should now incur the – ah – ridicule of the malevolent and of your political enemies, your lordship will perhaps feel some sympathy for me in what I have undergone most undeservedly."

"You are within your rights," answered his lordship bitterly, his little eyes like gimlets upon Mr Templeton, "to point out to me the error against which you warned me, and into which I fell, that warning notwithstanding. But I will beg you, sir, not to turn the sword in the wound."

"Oh, my lord! I should be the last to be guilty of such an – ah – inhumanity. If I have said so much it has been to justify the insistence of my warning."

"With Captain Gaynor before us it requires no justifying," said his lordship.

"I pledged my honour," Mr Templeton continued, "and I accounted my honour forfeit. I resigned my office under that assumption, and under that assumption your lordship accepted my resignation. I have been the butt of every scandalous tongue in town – of every scandalous – "

"It is possible," cut in his lordship, who felt it necessary to bribe Mr Templeton into silence not only here but hereafter, "that your successor in office might be – induced to resign to the end that justice be done and yourself reinstated."

"In that," said Mr Templeton, bowing, "I recognise your lordship's high sense of justice."

"To you, sir," continued his lordship, turning to Captain Gaynor, who stood stiffly at attention, "I shall see that proper reparation is made by publishing the error there has been – an error which even now, I confess, is entirely baffling."

Upon audacity Captain Gaynor now piled audacity.

"It is possible," said he, "that I may be able to elucidate the matter."

"Do you suggest one of those freaks of nature by which two men are given such identical features that one is not to be told from the other?"

"No such matter is in my mind. Though I am unable to speak as to a likeness between myself and this Captain Jenkyn, for I have never consciously stood face to face with him. I think, my lord, that the matter goes deeper. From what Mr Templeton has told me I understand that Sir John Kynaston has been arrested for having harboured me – always upon the assumption that I was the man who was hanged a fortnight ago."

His lordship grimaced. "Ay!" he said irritably.

"That will be another error to correct," put in Mr Templeton quietly. There can be no doubt that Mr Templeton was enjoying himself.

"And I gather further that this, as well as the confusion of the late Captain Jenkyn with myself, is the work of my Lord Pauncefort."

"Yes," said his lordship, and he confirmed the affirmative by an oath.

"I find this the more extraordinary in that I am perfectly well known to his lordship – at least, on that score I should find it the more extraordinary did I not believe that I hold the explanation of his most singular behaviour."

"What d'ye tell me?" demanded Lord Carteret sharply. "D'ye say that Lord Pauncefort knew you?"

"He knows me, my lord, as well as he knows Dick Templeton there, who is one of my oldest friends."

"Then – what the devil! – " His lordship paused. His friendship for Sir John Kynaston, combining with his mistrust of Pauncefort, spurred him suddenly to incredible conclusions. "D'ye suggest he did this thing – that he made a tool of me – to serve ends of his own?"

"I will suggest nothing," said Captain Gaynor. "I will state the facts."

He played boldly now. He saw that he held Pauncefort in the hollow of his hand, and he would have played as boldly and unwincingly had Pauncefort, himself, been present – for not all that nobleman's protestations and oaths could annihilate the overwhelming fact that the man whom he had alleged to be Captain Gaynor had been hanged a fortnight ago at Tyburn, whilst Captain Gaynor, himself, was alive.

"I shall need to trouble your lordship with some purely personal details," he said. "When, upon the instances of Dick Templeton here, I came to England a month ago with letters to his cousin, the Second Secretary, and in the hope of finding employment for my sword in the service of my own country, I sought the hospitality of one who had been my father's dearest friend. I am speaking of Sir John Kynaston. Whilst there, my lord, being in Sir John's confidence, learnt that a betrothal which had existed between his ward and my Lord Pauncefort had lately been determined in consequence of the discovery of – of certain unworthy motives in his lordship's suit."

"Determined?" cried the minister. "Determined, did ye say?" And swiftly his suspicions grew to certainty. "But I beg you to proceed," he added, almost grimly. "You promise to be very interesting."

Some vague fraction of what was passing in his lordship's mind was perceived by Captain Gaynor. It served to encourage him.

"It happened, sir," he resumed, "that I met the lady, and – and, in short, that his lordship had reason to behold in me a rival whom, under the circumstances of his own disfavour, he had cause to fear. Shortly thereafter, and in my absence from town, my name, I find, is given to a notorious rebel, the report of my execution set abroad, and my friend Sir John arrested for having harboured me."

Upon the faces of his listeners he saw clearly stamped the impression he had made and the conclusion to which all three had instantly jumped.

"Do you imply, sir, that it was to serve such ends as these that the villain so abused my confidence?" said the statesman in a voice that was like a knife's edge.

Captain Gaynor shook his head, his face inscrutable.

"Far be it from me to imply anything, my lord," he answered. "Naturally I must draw my own inferences; but those inferences you will permit me to keep to myself. It would be unfair in me to utter them, since I am an interested party, and – like all interested parties – subject to the sway of interest. Therefore I state the facts – no more. Your lordship must draw the inferences for yourself. You have acted in this matter upon certain information. You will hold, no doubt, that my presence here today, alive, is a sufficient proof of the falseness of such information. When in conjunction with that you consider what else I have now told you, you will be able to judge clearly for yourself the truth of this matter."

In his anger at seeing his every suspicion confirmed – at discovering, as he believed, that he had been so unscrupulously used – the Secretary of State came suddenly to his feet.

"Oh!" he cried, like a man who stifles, "it – it is incredible – as incredible as it is undeniable."

"Not so incredible, perhaps, when your lordship knows what else is behind," said the Captain. "Sir John's consent to Pauncefort's marriage with Miss Hollinstone is necessary, as otherwise – "

"I know, I know," the minister interrupted. "Sir, you can add nothing that I do not know already; nothing that I cannot now perceive for myself."

It was the Captain's turn to be astonished. But he was careful to show nothing of it.

"Oddslife!" swore Lord Carteret. "I suspected yesterday that he required Sir John's pardon for purposes of coercion with the lady. I did not know that the betrothal stood annulled. But you have made all clear to me. My Lord Pauncefort shall be taught a lesson that will last him all his life. As for you, sir, it remains for you to see to't that the lady's credulity is not abused as mine has been. I could desire no better agent than yourself. That rascal Pauncefort is to marry her this evening."

The Captain's self-possession all deserted him on the instant. He changed colour; his eyes dilated.

"This – this evening!" he faltered.

"Do not be alarmed," his lordship smiled. "You will be in time to prevent it." He resumed his seat. Under an exterior now of habitual iciness, anger still raged fiercely in Lord Carteret's bosom at the thought that he should have been no more than a tool – as he was forced to infer – in the hands of that spy whom he despised. Thus Lord Pauncefort was overwhelmed by the peril that ever threatens a traitor. The very hand that hires such men to their work is the very first to turn against them at the suggestion that they betray their present as they betrayed a former trust.

"Even were I too late to prevent, I should not be too late to amend it," said the Captain through his teeth. But the statesman held up a hand in warning.

"Do not misapprehend me, Captain Gaynor. Do not assume that I am sanctioning any such step as you have in mind. All that I desire is that you intervene in time to save a lady from marrying a blackguard. The rest you can very safely leave to others." He paused, then added: "If this wedding does not take place tonight, the world will be little troubled by my Lord Pauncefort hereafter." Then, taking up a pen, and speaking in a brisk voice: "I will issue an order for Sir John Kynaston's instant release," he announced, "and yourself, sir, shall be the bearer of it. Possibly Sir John may see fit to accompany you to Woodlands. Possibly, also, he may show a proper gratitude for the very timely service you have rendered him in returning so opportunely from your wanderings."

He wrote rapidly, almost whilst speaking; then, having sanded the document, he rose, and handed it to Captain Gaynor.

"There is the order," he said. He turned to Mr Templeton and desired him to stay for a word in private, and then he escorted the other two as far as the hall.

"You were seeking an appointment in the Colonies sir, I understand," he said to the Captain at parting, "but no doubt you will be changing your mind on that score if you think of marrying. If not, pray command me."

Captain Gaynor thanked him, and took his leave. But as he went down the steps of the mansion, arm in arm with Sir Richard:

"Whatever betide me," said he, "I'll never abide in England. Ye did me an ill turn in sending me hither, Dick. 'Tis too unsettled a country; too full of plottings and schemings and intrigues to suit my simple nature."

"I think you're right," said Sir Richard. "You men of action are no match for schemers."

"Ay, ay!" said the Captain sadly, and he shook his head. Presently he sighed. "Heigho!" And Sir Richard was not to guess that this was regret for dissimulation and intrigue of a singularly subtle sort – a regret occasioned by the reflection that for his very life's sake – and for the sake of others – he dare not tell the truth to this good fellow and best of friends, who was so uplifted to know him alive and well.

"I am coming to Woodlands with you tonight," said Sir Richard presently, "to see the end of this affair."

Chapter 22

ISRAEL SUAREZ

Woodlands, my Lord Pauncefort's seat in Surrey, was a handsome, red-brown Tudor mansion, situated in a park of some two hundred acres, within a couple of miles to the north of the town of Guildford.

His lordship had dined late on that July evening, for he had been late in arriving from town, and even then, ere he would dine, he must perform an elaborate toilet as befitted the bridegroom he hoped to be ere the night was out. He went below at length, an elegant, resplendent figure in a suit of grey satin with silver lace and dark purple linings; his pearl-grey silk stockings were decorated with ramifications of silver thread; diamonds hung like prismatic drops of water in the fine Mechlin lace of his cravat, and his long, graceful hands were almost hidden in his ruffles; buckles of French paste flashed on his shoes, and he wore a powdered tie-wig of the very newest mode, which emphasized the swarthy, male beauty of his face.

When he stepped at last into the long panelled dining-room, where the Reverend Thomas Pugh – the seedy hedge parson he had brought from London – waited impatiently with his hunger, the clergyman had gasped his admiration of so very dazzling an apparition, and had all but forgotten his inner gnawings in the feasting of his eyes. And had my Lord Pauncefort been at pains to find a foil that should throw his own splendour into greater relief, no selection could have been more happy than that of this squat fellow, black as a crow in his rusty parson's livery, his lantern jaws blue from the razor.

His lordship ate but little, and spoke still less during the repast. He was in a state of obvious nervousness vexed by the incompleteness of his preparations and anxiety lest he should fail to ruffle through and conquer Damaris in spite of this.

The dinner came to an end; the cloth was raised and the candles were lighted; still the two men sat on, over their wine now, with but little talk passing between them. Pauncefort reclined in his chair, frowning gloomily at the globular decanter of port, from which the candles struck fire, so that it glowed like a gigantic carbuncle. The long windows stood open to the stifling air, and the twilight sky was of a velvet blackness streaked with a fading but ominous purple. Not a breath stirred. The candles in their gilt sconces on the wainscoting burned steadily, throwing long shafts of reflection upon the polished timbers of the dark brown floor.

At last, from the distance, faintly, came the sound of hoofs. It approached rapidly, and with it now came the grind of wheels advancing up the avenue. His lordship listened, and he seemed to have ceased to breathe. His eyes glowed feverishly. She came at last!

"I think 'twill be the bride," ventured the parson timidly – for these long spells of silence and the moodiness of his host were fretting his ill-conditioned nerves.

My lord paid no heed to him; so the reverend gentleman sipped his wine and uneasily eyed his companion from under shaggy brows.

The carriage halted. Unable longer to remain still, his lordship rose, thrusting back his tall chair. He glanced at the timepiece on the overmantel. It wanted a few minutes to nine; and nine was the hour appointed. This trifling earliness augured well, he thought.

The door opened quietly behind him. He swung round in sudden, trembling eagerness to face the liveried servant who entered, and to receive an announcement which was as a shower of cold water upon his feverish impatience.

"Mr Suarez is here, my lord, asking to see you."

"Suarez?" His lordship's voice rasped harshly with sudden anger. Yet his dilating eyes and loosened mouth were evidences of still another emotion. "Suarez?" he repeated.

"I told him, my lord, that your lordship could see no one tonight. But he insists that his business is of the greatest urgency."

"And so it is, my lord," came a deep voice from behind the servant, and immediately the heavy figure and ovine face of the usurer made its appearance in the doorway.

He had followed the lackey, determined to force himself into his lordship's presence and fearing that did he wait for permission he might wait in vain.

The servant attempted now to detain him: but it was too late. The Jew thrust the fellow contemptuously aside, and rolled into the room.

"What do you want?" his lordship challenged him. His face was white with anger and his eyes were murderously set upon the intruder.

"Vat do I vant?" echoed Mr. Suarez, his manner excited and his speech thick with passion. "Vat do I vant? I vant a deal, my lord, I promise you. To begin vit', I vant an explanation."

"By God!" swore his lordship. "Ye're a daring rogue to thrust yourself in here in this fashion."

The other waved a fat, powerful hand. "Bah! I don't vant vords, and I don't vant ugly names. I charge for ugly names, my lord, and the rate of interesht on t'em is heavy. Shall I speak before t'ese?" And he waved his hand again, to indicate servant and parson. "Or vill you see me alone? 'Tis all one to me," he added contemptuously.

His lordship considered the man an instant, mastering his rage. Then he turned to the servant.

'Leave us," he said shortly, "and you too, Pugh. Go wait in the library."

The parson finished his wine, and departed with the servant.

Suarez looked on, a sneer on his heavy face. "Ha!" he commented. "Very 'igh and mighty! Ve-ry lordly for a damned pauper!"

Israel Suarez was none of your gabardined, bewhiskered, cringing Jews, over-conscious of belonging to a despised race. Himself proud of his Jewish blood, he had naught but contempt for those who despised it. Being enormously wealthy and knowing the power of wealth, he used that power remorselessly, and upon none so remorselessly as upon those who dared to show their scorn of him on the score of race. To these he repaid contempt with contempt, insult with insult; and since he had the power on his side, his contempt and his insult usually proved the more hurtful and crushing in the end.

In appearance he had almost the air of a man of fashion, saving perhaps that with his natural taste for Oriental splendour he rather overdressed the part. His claret-coloured coat was stiff with gold lace, as was the crimson waistcoat under it, every button of which was a ruby of price. Brilliants flashed in his lace neckwear and on two fingers of each hand. A gold-hilted sword hung at his side.

Massive and powerful of frame, with large liquid eyes, a pendulous nose and a shaven olive-tinted skin, this Spanish Jew was a somewhat extraordinary and compelling personality. The consciousness of power he derived from his vast wealth lent him a forceful air. Obviously he was not a man with whom it would be safe to trifle. Save for a trouble with the aspirate, the "w" and the "th," his English was fluent and good.

My Lord Pauncefort had made the mistake of undervaluing him. He had trifled with him; he was trifling with him now, running a scornful, critical eye over the man's person and apparel, and expressing his contempt for one and the other by the deliberate curl of his lip.

The Jew's watchful eyes observed all this. His answer to it was not long delayed. He strode to the table and poured himself a glass of port without hesitation or "by your leave." He tasted it, smacked his lips and paused appraisingly.

" 'Tis a good vine," he said, with marked satisfaction. "I 'ope I 'ave a good stock of it in my cellar 'ere."

"What the devil do you mean – damn you!" said Pauncefort.

Mr Suarez coolly drained the glass, and sat down unbidden, leaving his lordship standing.

"I suppose I can drink my own vine in my own 'ouse vit'out explanations to you – damn you!" he answered in the same tone. He had his anger under control by now. Indeed, although by nature of a hot and fiery temper, he was your deadly fellow who knows how to be cold in the expression of it.

And then, before Pauncefort had recovered from that blow, Suarez crisply added enough to show his business there that night.

"Ye see, I've 'ad vord from my Lord Carteret t'at 'is varranty for you is vit'drawn. So my man Cohen is in possession of your 'ouse in town and I am 'ere. I 'ave a varrant in my pocket and t'ree men vit' me – in t'e 'all now. An agent of mine is on 'is vay to your place in Yorkshire. Ye see, I vaste no time." He smiled up at his lordship, who was too stricken to answer him. Presently he resumed. "You owe me t'irty t'ousand pounds, my lord. Voodlands 'ere vihl bring four t'ousand; your 'ouse in town perhaps t'ree, and your Yorkshire estate seven or eight t'ousand vhen I sell it. For t'e rest I must take your body until you or your friends see a vay to ransom it. Now you know vat I vant," he leered. "Now you know vat a damned impudent rogue I am, t'rusting myself into my own 'ouse, eh!"

Pauncefort leaned heavily against the overmantel to steady his trembling body. He was limp. His blood had turned to water. Of all that the money-lender had said, but one sentence remained with his lordship. This sentence he echoed now in a husky voice.

"Lord Carteret has withdrawn his warranty!"

"Just so," said Mr Suarez. "Myself I marvel t'at he ever gave it."

"But –" faltered Pauncefort, ceasing to wonder or to seek a cause for this, and coming straight to the urgent effect of it, "but even so! What does it matter?"

"It matters just t'irty t'ousand pounds," said Mr Suarez. "You know t'at not'ing but his lordship's varranty has kept me from claiming my own t'is mont' past."

"But my marriage is to take place tonight," cried his lordship. He was white and drops of perspiration stood upon his shallow brow – that one deplorable feature of his handsome face.

And now Mr Suarez returned the other's late silent sneer of his apparel.

"Ah!" said he, sneering in his turn. "Ye look very festive, codso! A very pretty fellow in your bridegroom finery!"

His lordship attempted to stiffen, but failed. The other was too much the master of this situation.

"You know – it is your business to know – the wealth of Miss Hollinstone. Is not that varranty enough for you?"

"T'at? Pish! No marriage prospects are varranty enough for me, as you vell know. Not only vould I not advance you a shilling on such prospects, but t'ey vould never have kept me from foreclosing on you if you 'adn't obtained me Lord Carteret's varranty that you vould be in a position to pay – failing which, your estates and your person – "

"But my God! you'll give me until tomorrow?"

"Not an 'our," said Suarez. "Vhy should I?"

"Because you'll be a fool if you don't."

Suarez laughed shortly. "I was never a fool yet in business, my lord. Never!"

His lordship advanced to the table and flung himself into a chair. He faced Mr Suarez with the board between them. He leaned across, and his white, clammy face glistened in the golden candlelight.

"Suarez," he said, "consider, pray, that all I have had from you in actual cash does not amount to over fifteen thousand pounds. You hold Woodlands, my town house and my place in Yorkshire, and you know – in spite of what you have said – that they will yield more than that sum."

"Ye don't suppose I should 'ave advanced the money unless I vas satisfied of t'at? Or do you imagine money lending to be a philant'ropy, my friend? It is a risky business, and in risky businesses the profits must be heavy to compensate. And ye leave out of all account the interesht my money vould 'ave yielded me elsewhere."

" 'Tis you leave that out of account when you come here with a warrant to seize my person. If you seize me you'll never see your filthy interest."

Mr Suarez closed one eye. "T'ere's t'e interesht from the entailed property," he reminded his lordship. "It is close upon fifteen 'undred pounds a year. Now, nicely lodged in the Fleet, my lord – and ve'll make you as comfortable as you can expect – you can live luxuriously on fifty pounds a year."

"D'ye mean I'm to spend ten years in a spunging-house?" roared his lordship, turning savage.

"Rather more," said Mr Suarez, with pursed lips. "Interesht will be running on the unpaid balances, ye see. But your lordship is very 'ealthy, and should easily last the time."

"Suarez," raged his lordship, "ye're a dirty Jew."

"Pauncefort," answered Mr Suarez imperturbably, "ye're a dirtier Christian to incur debts ye cannot meet."

His lordship leapt to his feet as if he had been struck. To be insulted thus by this scum of Israel! It was past endurance, past belief!

He was unarmed at the moment, or assuredly he would have drawn upon the fellow. As it was, his hand flew to his side where his sword should have hung. The Jew watched the movement with a cold smile. With a steady hand he poured himself another glass of wine.

"I vonder," he said, smiling reflectively, "vhen your lordship vill learn t'at unprofitable insult is t'e sport of fools? I am endeavouring to teach you." He drained his glass, and rose. "Shall ye be going now?" he asked, and his question had all the ring of a command.

Pauncefort steadied himself, his hands upon the table, leaning so heavily that his knuckles showed white as marble.

"Going?" he echoed.

"Did I not say t'at I 'ave a varrant for you in my pocket and t'ree men to execute it for me? Ye'ld never be so mad as to try resistance!"

"D'ye mean – " His lordship moistened his lips. "D'ye mean ye'll take me now – now? That ye'll not wait until tomorrow; until I am married and can repay you?"

"Married?" sneered the Jew. "D'ye still seek to bubble me vit' t'at?"

"Bubble you? It's the truth, man."

Mr Suarez considered him with brooding eye. "If it vere the trut', vy did Lord Carteret vit'draw his varranty for you? Pshaw!"

"It is the truth, nevertheless," the viscount insisted vehemently. "I await the lady now."

But Suarez was still incredulous. "To be sure you do," said he. "But I t'ink a bird in t'e 'and is vort' – "

"Listen, Suarez," cried the other desperately. "Leave me free to make this marriage, and you shall be paid in full by Monday next if not before. More, from now until the debt is liquidated I'll pay you further interest at the rate of a thousand pounds a day."

Now this was business, and to business Mr Suarez could listen. Also the earnestness of the proposal seemed to argue that, indeed, his lordship counted upon being married. But, on the other hand, he might be counting upon something very different. It might be a ruse to elude the moneylender and flee the country. He did not trust this gentleman who had manifested slipperiness already in the past. So he sighed over the offer, and shook his head.

"I'll make it two thousand – two thousand a day!" his lordship clamoured.

But now the moneylender's every doubt was dispelled. He laughed.

"Ye're over-reckless to be 'onest," he said. "Ye're lying about t'is marriage."

A sound in the stillness of the night caught his lordship's ears. His face flushed suddenly.

"Am I lying?" he cried. "Am I?" He was almost exultant. "Listen!" And he flung an arm towards the open window and the night beyond.

Mr Suarez heard the sounds of a carriage coming up the avenue.

"That will be Miss Hollinstone," his lordship announced with confidence.

The usurer stared at him for a long moment in silence.

"D'ye still doubt me?" cried Pauncefort. "D'ye still think that no marriage will take place. Why, man, did ye not see the parson here? Why else should I have sat at table with that crow?"

It was, indeed, something whose significance the Jew had overlooked. Quietly he resumed his seat at the table.

"I'll stay to see," he announced. His lordship heaved a sigh of relief, and fell to mopping his brow. A pause followed, ended at last by Mr Suarez. "Two thousand pounds a day further interesht you proposed, I think," he said.

"Yes, yes," was the eager assent.

"I'll consider the proposal," said Mr Suarez coolly.

"Will you, by God!" cried Pauncefort, who was rapidly recovering from his terror. "Ye'll accept it now, or ye'hl refuse it."

"T'en I'll refuse it," said Mr Suarez.

"No, no! I meant not that. Consider it, sir, by all means. But decide quickly – for heaven's sake!"

Mr Suarez laughed. "Ye're all 'ot and cold in a moment," he sneered. "If I consider it at all, 'tis purely to oblige you. Vell, vell – "

The servant entered, and his lordship turned to him a white, excited face.

"Miss Hollinstone has arrived, my lord."

Pauncefort flashed a glance of triumph upon the usurer. "Well?" he demanded. "You accept?"

"Ye-es – when I am sure of t'e business vich brings t'e lady."

Lord Pauncefort stared at him. Then, in disgust: "Ye're a reckless fellow, Suarez!" he said.

"I 'ave to deal vit' so many rogues," said Suarez in explanation. Then he looked towards the servant. "Ah?" said he significantly.

"Wait without," barked his lordship, and the man vanished, closing the door.

"You tell me t'at the lady comes to marry you now?" Suarez questioned.

"Yes," answered his lordship. "You saw the parson."

"Ah! Vell t'en, my lord, you shall 'ave t'is chance. I vill accept your proposal if t'e marriage takes place tonight, and I, myself, am one of t'e vitnesses."

Pauncefort glared at him between impatience and anger. But he mastered his feelings. "Be it so," he consented. "Meanwhile, will you join the parson in the library, and wait there until the ceremony is to be performed?" And catching a fresh look of doubt in the moneylender's eye: "You can place one of your men outside that door, another under the window, and another," he added, sneering, "on the roof, if you please, to see that I don't go up the chimney. Arm them, and thus you should be sure that I shall not escape you."

Mr Suarez bowed. "Very good," was all that he answered.

Chapter 23

THE LAST THROW

My Lord Pauncefort, alone in the dining-room, with pulses throbbing, partly from anticipation and partly from the stress of the recent interview, awaited the coming of Damaris.

Mr Suarez had left him shaken and rather dazed. He realised the imminence of his danger, the possibility that after all he might be unable to constrain Damaris into the wedding, seeing that he could not produce the pardon, which was the price agreed upon.

He beat down his fears almost angrily. He crossed to the massive sideboard and poured himself a glass of brandy to quiet his tremors. Scarce had he drained it when the door opened and, in wimple and hood, Damaris stood before him.

He sprang to meet her, at once the eager lover with no thought in the world that was not of herself.

"My dearest Damaris!" was his greeting, and he would have caught her to him but that something in her face and bearing held him off as if a harrier stood between them.

She was very pale, and under her eyes there were dark lines that told of the anguish in her soul. She stood erect and with a calm that was something like the calm of the martyr in the hour of doom. Her long, black cloak had fallen open, disclosing a deep purple gown below. He observed it, and almost shuddered at the omen of such colours on a bride.

"You have obtained Sir John's pardon, my lord?" she asked him.

"I have," he answered promptly.

She drew a deep breath, and for a moment closed her eyes. It was almost as if his answer occasioned her a shock – as if she had hoped that he would fail. Though, had he answered her in the negative, it is possible that she would have experienced a stab no less acute. Before her had lain a choice of evils so terrible that the abiding one must ever seem the worse because the more imminent. In either case must she have steeled herself to resignation.

She held out a hand. "Let me see it," she begged, her voice expressionless.

He showed no slightest hesitation, such as might convey to her that all was not as he would have her believe.

"It is not here," he replied, quite at his ease – as if what he had to say was what under the circumstances should be expected. "It has gone to his Majesty for signature, and will be delivered to me tomorrow."

She looked at him stonily a moment. Then she gathered her cloak about her again.

"You are sure?" she asked. "There is no doubt of this?"

"No shadow of doubt," he answered firmly. "My Lord Carteret has pledged me his word that I shall have it tomorrow." And so, indeed, Lord Carteret had all but done – subject to the marriage taking place tonight in proof that the pardon was no part of any bargain between Pauncefort and the lady.

"In that case, my lord, I will come again tomorrow."

"You will come again tomorrow?" he cried, the blank look in his face advertising the sudden dashing of his rising hopes. "But, Damaris – consider! You are here now – in the house of which you are to be the mistress. Need a few hours matter, then?"

"No," she answered, "they will not matter. Will you ring for someone to reconduct me to my chaise?"

He held himself very hard, to play the considerate, to show naught but solicitude for her. He smiled ingratiatingly, and heaven alone knew what that smile cost him in such an hour.

"In a moment, if you will," said he. "Though I still hope that you will not."

"'Tis a very unreasonable hope, my lord," said she.

"Will you not sit?" He advanced a chair. "A glass of wine?"

She declined one and the other by a gesture. "There is no reason why I should linger. I should not have come at all but for your positive assurance that the pardon would be in your hands tonight. I – I would I had not trusted to your word," she ended, displaying the first sign of weakness.

"You have no cause to say that," he reproached her very gently. "I have fulfilled my part. I have done all that I promised, and tomorrow when his Majesty's signature shall have been appended to the document, Sir John will be released. You cannot, surely, doubt me?"

"If I doubted I should not have said that I shall return tomorrow. You understand, my lord – I have sought to make it plain to you – that this is a bargain between us; and when you perform your share, I – I shall be ready to perform mine."

He turned from her a moment, biting his lip in his vexation. He was nonplussed, hard-driven. A postponement was impossible. Outside, Mr Suarez and his bailiffs watched and waited. Unless this marriage took place tonight he was wrecked and ruined for all time, beyond all hope.

What, he wondered in a frenzy of stifled rage, could have induced Lord Carteret to play this scurvy trick upon him – to withdraw that shielding warranty thus, in the eleventh hour?

He whipped a handkerchief from the silver-laced pocket of his coat, and mopped his clammy brow. The heat seemed to increase; the air of that summer night had grown more stifling. Suddenly, outside, there was an ominous rustle of wind among the laurels and a moment later the candle-flames in the room were beaten over by the draught.

"Damaris," he said presently, "you use me very cruelly. Can nothing that I do win me back the place I held in your regard? the place from which a moment's folly made me outcast? I love you, Damaris!" His voice shook with emotion; he was very humble, entirely the suppliant lover; and he was a very handsome and gallant figure of a man. "There is naught in all this world I would not do to pleasure you, no sacrifice I would not make to win your regard – no sacrifice, I swear, whatever it may be."

But he failed to move her. Not by his humility, nor his protestations, nor yet his personal beauty could he achieve it. She was but the husk she had proclaimed herself. She stood silent for a little moment, so that her words might not seem a direct and offensive reply to his appeal. Then: "I will go now," she said, and again she begged him to ring for a servant to escort her to her waiting carriage.

His manner changed on that. He had tried humility, and since that had failed with her, she should see him in his real mood. He had been a suppliant; but since she had no ear for his entreaties, she should listen now to the proclamation of his will.

"Nay," he said quietly, coldly almost, and he smiled, but no longer ingratiatingly. "Nay, Damaris, you are here, and here you stay. Take off your cloak, child."

Alarm gleamed in her eyes. Faintly her bosom began to stir. It seemed, then, that she was not quite the insensible thing she accounted herself.

"What do you mean?" she asked him, her voice straining a little.

"You promised to come hither and wed me tonight if I obtained you Sir John's pardon. I have obtained it. Tomorrow it shall be in your hands, if you require it. For that, however, you must take my word."

"Your word?" she cried, a world of scorn in her tone.

"My word," he answered firmly. "You came hither to become Viscountess Pauncefort, and Viscountess Pauncefort shall you be within the hour. All is ready and the parson is waiting. So take off your cloak."

251

She felt herself turn a little dizzy. The room seemed to sway about her, and one word boomed and reverberated through her mind. "Fool! Fool! Fool!" was that word. "Fool" – to have trusted herself alone into the house and power of such a man.

He strode over to the bell-rope and pulled it sharply. In the distance a tinkling note was heard.

"I will not!" she cried. "Let me depart!" And she turned to the door.

He sprang after her, and seized her wrist. Through the open windows came a sound of heavy raindrops pattering on the leaves.

"Listen, Damaris," he implored her, his face now within a foot of hers, awakening horror and sickly dread in her. "There!" he cried suddenly. "You hear the rain. There is a storm coming. You cannot go on such a night as this is like to be." Even as he spoke a vivid flash of lightning illumined the terrace and the gardens beyond it. "The very elements conspire to make you mine at once."

"I will not marry you until the pardon is in my hand," she answered, with a brave attempt to steady her voice. "Not even then, if you attempt further to detain me now."

"You will not?" he said, and gently seemed to mock her. "Very well! But depart you cannot. You see, there is a storm." And his mockery increased. "Be it as you will. Do not marry me until you have the pardon. But for your own sake I suggest – no more – that it were better you married me tonight than in the morning."

"Do you threaten me?" she cried, and wrenched herself free of his clutch.

"Threaten you? Nay, sweeting, I do not threaten. I warn. I admonish. Assume that by morning, wearied by your cruelty, I change my mind. Assume that I then no longer desire to marry you. What then, eh?"

She looked at him, and there was utter loathing now in her glance. He saw it; perceived that in his desperate haste he was playing his game clumsily; wherefore, being rendered still more desperate, he plunged recklessly on to issue his ultimatum.

"Nay, now," said he, "I swear to heaven that unless you marry me this night, Sir John's pardon shall be cancelled. I'll not be toyed with in this fashion. You shall not blow hot and cold upon me at your pleasure, mistress."

She put her hands to her face an instant; then looked at him again.

"You are a dastard, my Lord Pauncefort," she told him.

"I am a lover, madam," was his answer. "Choose now, and advise me of your choice. Shall Sir John go the way of Captain Gaynor?"

Overhead at that moment came a terrific crash of thunder, and instantly the pattering rain was changed to a torrential downpour.

"Here is the storm," said he. "Perhaps it will help you to a wise decision."

The door opened and the servant summoned by the bell stood to receive his lordship's orders.

"Bid them," he ordered, "put up Miss Hollinstone's chaise."

There was terror now in her face, the terror of the trapped creature.

"Very good, my lord."

"And – wait." He turned to her again. "Shall we have the parson in or not?" he asked her. " 'Tis as you please."

But she swung round to the servant. "No, no!" she panted. "I am departing now. Take me to my chaise."

Bewildered, the lackey looked at his master. Behind Damaris, Pauncefort was signalling the fellow to depart. He did so instantly, closing the door after him.

At bay now, she turned once more upon her captor. "My lord," she said, "you dare not do this thing. I will not marry you now or ever. You do well to show me from what I have escaped. Let me depart! Let me depart at once, or you shall suffer for it as there is a law in England."

"You'll be none so eager to depart in the morning," said he. "As for the marriage, I use no coercion. If you will not, you will not. Yet tomorrow you may sing in a different key, my sweeting." The mask was off him now. He was frankly brutal and menacing.

She fronted him intrepidly. "You shall rue it, my lord," she promised him with conviction. "Terribly shall you rue it."

"Rue what?" he mocked her, with false pleasantness. "Rue it that I could not commit the inhospitality of suffering a lady to ride forth in so wild a night? Come now," he added, with an attempt at rough good-humour, "think better of it, Damaris. See, here comes the parson. Do not send him empty-handed away."

She heard the door open behind her, supposing, as did his lordship, that it was the parson who now entered. She did not turn, but using his lordship's countenance as a mirror, she realised that in the doorway at her back stood not the parson but some unexpected and terrific apparition.

She saw Pauncefort's whole body twitch convulsively, his flushed face turn livid, his mouth fall loosely open, whilst his eyes bulged and bulged as he stared past her at that something in the doorway. Some of his unutterable horror communicated itself to her, so that she dared not turn to look behind her, but stood there with aching head and throbbing pulses, waiting for this thing to reveal itself to her senses.

And then, after a long pause, that revelation came. It was borne to her by a voice – a pleasant voice that rang now with sinister crispness, a voice at whose sound her heart leapt wildly and seemed to stand still, whilst a great fear took possession of her; for surely it was the voice of one who was dead.

"For a man engaged in villainy, Pauncefort," said that voice, "you are singularly careless of your doors. I had not hoped to find so easy an admittance."

Pauncefort answered nothing. He continued to stare, wide-eyed, at the ghost of the man who, by his agency, had been hanged at Tyburn a fortnight since. But Damaris staggered as the voice ceased; she uttered a little moaning sob, and swayed there until a strong arm came suddenly about her waist to steady her. The voice spoke again, in her very ear now and scarce louder than a whisper.

"Be not afraid, Damaris. 'Tis I."

She looked up at last, fearfully, to meet the gleaming eyes of Captain Gaynor. Although she had known what vision to expect, yet the sight of it almost drew a scream from her. But she controlled herself. All this was a dream, she knew now, the bitterly ironical conclusion of a nightmare.

Then Pauncefort found his tongue at last. "In God's name, who are you?" he cried, in a quavering voice.

"Captain Henry Gaynor – at your service," said the apparition. "I think I am as opportune as unwelcome," he added, smiling.

At last my Lord Pauncefort awoke to the realisation that here was no apparition from beyond the tomb, but a living man; formidable, perhaps, and damnably inopportune, yet to be dealt with in human fashion and at once.

By what miracle the Captain had been preserved to present himself at such a season was a matter whose explanation could wait. Meanwhile, for the second time that night his lordship's hand stole to his side, where his sword should have hung, and for the second time he cursed its absence.

Captain Gaynor observed the gesture, and smiled his understanding.

"That shall be amended presently," he said, with meaning. "There was a foul game we played one night a month ago at your house in town, my lord. We played it with cards, and fortune favoured you – a cheat. We will resume that game in a moment, my lord, and it shall not be played out with cards this time."

He felt Damaris tremble as she lay against him, supported by his arm. She, too, was beginning to realise that this was not the dream she had supposed it, but an amazing reality; that the heart that beat just where her shoulder rested was the heart – the living, throbbing heart – of one who was believed to be dead.

"Besides," Captain Gaynor was continuing, "I have another score to settle with you. It seems that you have been giving my honourable name to a Jacobite rascal known as Captain Jenkyn, who was hanged at Tyburn, and on the strength of that spurious identity you foisted upon me, you procured the arrest of Sir John Kynaston for having harboured me."

Pauncefort leaned heavily against the table. He understood nothing. His amazement effaced for the moment every other consideration.

"But that," Gaynor resumed, "is a matter upon which Sir John himself is here to question you."

"Sir John?" Pauncefort muttered, despite himself.

"Sir John is here?" exclaimed Damaris, too.

"Why, yes. When I presented myself to Lord Carteret today, my presence was in itself sufficient to reveal the absurdity of the charge against your uncle. He was instantly released, and since I was informed by my Lord Carteret that you were to be coerced into a marriage here tonight, upon certain false pretences of this trickster, we came straight hither from town, bringing with us an old friend of mine, in case we should require support. I left them in talk with a parson. But I think they are here now."

And as he spoke they entered, Sir John first and Sir Richard Templeton close upon his heels.

And now Pauncefort understood at last the thing that ever since the admission of Mr Suarez had been plaguing him: the reasons that had led my Lord Carteret to withdraw his warranty. Plainly, seeing Captain Gaynor alive and hearing him disclaim all connection with that Captain Jenkyn who had been hanged, the Secretary of State had concluded that he, himself, was being imposed upon. Whatever else remained impenetrable to Pauncefort, at least he realised to his dismay that not all the protesting in the world could now induce Lord Carteret to think otherwise; that not all the proof that he, himself, might produce, could stand against the overwhelming, self-evident fact that whoever Captain Jenkyn might have been, he was not Harry Gaynor.

Sir John took in the situation at a glance. "Ha!" said he. "I gather from the parson that we arrive in good time. Damaris, my dear child, this was – a little wild in you – I mean, to trust this villain." Then he turned to the viscount. "Pauncefort – " he began, and there he ended.

Abruptly he turned his shoulder upon the fellow. "Pshaw!" said he. "To what end recriminations? Let us begone, Harry."

"If you will take Damaris," said the Captain, "and Dick will remain, I have yet something to say to his lordship, a – a little game to conclude."

But Damaris suddenly swung round and clutched his arm, looking up fearfully into his face.

"No, no, Harry!" she pleaded. "Leave him! Let us go! Come with us."

Upon that my Lord Pauncefort spoke at last. "If he is the coward I deem him," he said, in a voice that choked with rage, "he will give heed to you."

"You hear him, sweet," said Captain Gaynor, with his wry smile.

"And is your courage a thing that can be blown upon by the breath of such a man as that?" she asked him. "Oh, Harry, I have suffered for you – you can never know what I have suffered. You are restored to me, I know not how. I understand nothing. My senses are all confused. But I understand that you are here and alive. Presently I shall thank God for it, and seek to understand the nature of this miracle. Meanwhile, my dear, I ask this of you. 'Tis the first thing I have ever asked of you. If you love me, Harry, you will come with us now."

"Not a doubt," sneered Pauncefort, "but he'll shield himself behind a woman's plea."

"It seems to me," said a fresh voice, a rich, oily voice, "t'at my Lord Pauncefort is so ill-advised as to seek to pick a quarrel."

They swung round, startled. In the doorway now stood Mr Israel Suarez. Behind him loomed the shadows of his three bailiffs. He bowed to the company.

"Forgive my intrusion, madam and gentlemen. But it is timely. My lord's life is vort' fifteen t'ousand pounds to me – to be obtained t'rough veary years of vaitin'. I cannot permit 'im to jeopardise it."

"And who the devil may you be?" quoth Sir John.

"My name, sir, is Israel Suarez. Ye may 'ave 'eard of me. I 'old a varrant for t'is 'andsome young nobleman, who is my debtor and cannot meet 'is debt. I am sorry, gentlemen, to interfere, sorry to baulk you of a very vorthy object, sir" (this to Captain Gaynor), "but my lord belongs to me; 'e belongs to t'e law; 'is life is sacred; and if knowing t'at, 'e persists in insulting you, vhy – codso! – 'tis to 'is greater shame. In fifteen years or so, it is possible t'at I may 'ave done vit' 'im. Your little affair must vait until t'en. T'e first satisfaction must alvays belong to t'e law."

"Ha!" said Sir John. His blue eyes twinkled. He turned to Captain Gaynor. "I think his lordship will be quite safe with Mr Suarez."

"Quite," said the Captain, who understood now to the full what Lord Carteret had said. "Though I think he would have found me more merciful. Shall we be going, Damaris?"

"In God's name, yes!" she sobbed.

With a dull roar of anger Pauncefort sprang after them. The towering bulk of Mr Suarez rose suddenly before him, an insuperable barrier.

"Be calm, my lord; be calm," said the moneylender affably. " 'Tis but a lost trick in t'e game of life. Patience, t'en! T'e gods love a good loser."

Pauncefort fronted him a moment, cursing foully; then, exhausted and sobbing, he collapsed into a chair.

Over him stood the benign Suarez, like a protecting but very proprietary deity.

It was Sir John who proposed that as the night was wild and the roads becoming difficult the party had best divide itself, since they had two carriages – the one which had brought Damaris and the other in which Captain Gaynor and his friends had come to town. That proposal was well enough, but when in his further proposal for the division of the party he sent Damaris and the Captain ahead in one carriage and himself followed with Sir Richard in another, he showed a very culpable and reckless disregard of the proprieties.

Said Damaris to her Captain: "You are regretting the intervention of that man," by which she meant the intervention of Mr Suarez to avert the meeting between the Captain and his lordship.

"Nay, sweet," he answered her, "I am glad on't. It made it easier for me to follow my heart, and do your bidding."

"You confess, then, that you hesitated?"

"If I did 'twas because his life was a menace to me and to others. But gaoled and discredited as he is, his fangs are drawn and we may now be easy on that score. I think we are the more sweetly avenged, and – and my hands are not soiled."

"There is much I don't understand! so much!" she said.

Thereafter he explained.

Rafael Sabatini

Bellarion

Bellarion, a young man set on joining the priesthood, is diverted from his calling to serve the Princess Valeria. He remains with her for five years, serving her faithfully despite her cold response. Yet when the time comes for him to leave, they both find that the passion and romance of Italy has left its mark…

Captain Blood

Captain Blood is the much-loved story of a physician and gentleman turned pirate.

Peter Blood, wrongfully accused and sentenced to death, narrowly escapes his fate and finds himself in the company of buccaneers. Embarking on his new life with remarkable skill and bravery, Blood becomes the 'Robin Hood' of the Spanish seas. This is swashbuckling adventure at its best.

Rafael Sabatini

The Lost King

The Lost King tells the story of Louis XVII – the French royal who officially died at the age of ten but, as legend has it, escaped to foreign lands where he lived to an old age. Sabatini breathes life into these age-old myths, creating a story of passion, revenge and betrayal. He tells of how the young child escaped to Switzerland from where he plotted his triumphant return to claim the throne of France.

'...the hypnotic spell of a novel which for sheer suspense, deserves to be ranked with Sabatini's best' – *New York Times*

Scaramouche

When a young cleric is wrongfully killed, his friend, André-Louis, vows to avenge his death. André's mission takes him to the very heart of the French Revolution where he finds the only way to survive is to assume a new identity. And so is born Scaramouche – a brave and remarkable hero of the finest order and a classic and much-loved tale in the greatest swashbuckling tradition.

'Mr Sabatini's novel of the French Revolution has all the colour and lively incident which we expect in his work' – *Observer*

Rafael Sabatini

The Sea Hawk

Sir Oliver, a typical English gentleman, is accused of murder, kidnapped off the Cornish coast, and dragged into life as a Barbary corsair. However Sir Oliver rises to the challenge and proves a worthy hero for this much-admired novel. Religious conflict, melodrama, romance and intrigue combine to create a masterly and highly successful story, perhaps best-known for its many film adaptations.

The Shame of Motley

The Court of Pesaro has a certain fool – one Lazzaro Biancomonte of Biancomonte. *The Shame of Motley* is Lazzaro's story, presented with all the vivid colour and dramatic characterisation that has become Sabatini's hallmark.

'Mr Sabatini could not be conventional or commonplace if he tried'
– *Standard*

10483117R10152

Made in the USA
San Bernardino, CA
16 April 2014